Steaming ahead

Pat Cadigan's short fiction has appeared in various publications, including *Omni* and *Isaac Asimov's Science Fiction Magazine* and in many anthologies. Her first novel, *Mindplayers* (Gollancz), was nominated for the Philip K Dick Memorial Award; *Patterns* (Grafton, 1991), her short fiction collection, has been nominated for the Bram Stoker and the Thorpe Menn Awards, and her second novel, *Synners*, has just been published in the USA (Grafton, 1991). She has been nominated for the Nebula, the Hugo and the World Fantasy Awards, and her work has been translated into French, German, Polish, Japanese and Czech. She lives in Kansas with her husband Arnold Fenner, a designer and artist, and their son Bobby.

Karen Joy Fowler's publications include a collection of short stories, *Artificial Things* (Bantam Books, USA, 1985), another collection, *Peripheral Vision* (Pulphouse, USA, 1990), and *Sarah Canary*, a novel (Henry Holt, 1991). She was the winner of the John W Campbell Award for most promising new science fiction writer in 1987. She lives in Davis, California.

Pat Murphy edits the *Exploratorium Quarterly*, the magazine of the Exploratorium, a museum of science, art and human perception, founded by Dr Frank Oppenheimer (brother to Robert Oppenheimer). Her fiction has received a number of awards, including the Nebulas for Best Novel (*The Falling Woman*, St Martin's Press, 1986) and for Best Novelette ('Rachel in Love', *Isaac Asimov's Science Fiction Magazine*, April 1987). 'Dead Men on TV', one of the stories in this collection, was included in the final ballot

for the 1988 Nebula Award for Best Short
Story. Her short fiction has been published by
Interzone and Pan Books has published her most
recent novel *The City, Not Long After*. She travels
as often as she can – to Mexico, Thailand, Nepal
and Europe – but always comes home to San
Francisco, where she lives.

Letters from Home

Stories by

Pat Cadigan

Karen Joy Fowler

Pat Murphy

The Women's Press

The following stories have been published previously:

Pat Cadigan:
'After the Days of Dead-Eye' Dee', *Isaac Asimov's Science
Fiction Magazine*, May 1985;
'The Pond', *Fears*, ed. Charles L Grant, Berkeley 1983;
'In the Shop', *Omni*, October 1983;
'*Johnny Come Home*', forthcoming in *Omni*;
'The Coming of the Doll', *The Magazine of Fantasy and Science
Fiction*, June 1981;
'In the Dark', *When the Music's Over*, ed. Lewis Shiner,
Doubleday 1991.

Karen Joy Fowler:
'Letters from Home', *In the Field of Fire*, ed. Jeanne van Buren
Dann and Jack Dann, TOR 1987;
'Lily Red', *IASFM*, July 1988;
'Contention', in *Artificial Things*, Bantam Books 1986;
'The Faithful Companion at Forty', *IASFM*, July 1987;
'The Duplicity Principle', *IASFM*, December 1989;
'Lieserl', in *Author's Choice*, Pulphouse, 1990.

Pat Murphy:
'His Vegetable Wife', *Interzone*, Summer 1986;
'On a Hot Summer Night in a Place Far Away', *IASFM*,
May 1985;
'Dead Men on TV', *Full Spectrum*, ed. Lou Aronica and
Shawna McCarthy, Bantam Books 1988;
'Prescience', *IASFM*, January 1989;
'Clay Devils', *Twilight Zone*, April 1987;
'In the Abode of the Snows', *IASFM*, December 1986.

British Library Cataloguing in Publication Data
Cadigan Pat,
  Letters from home.
  I. Fowler, Karen Joy II. Murphy, Pat.
  813.0108

  ISBN 0–7043–4280–4

Sarah Lefanu would like to give special thanks to Uwe
Luserke for his enthusiastic help in initiating this project.

Phototypeset by Intype, London
Printed and bound in Great Britain by
Cox & Wyman, Reading, Berks

This book is dedicated to the memory
of James Tiptree Jr

Contents

Introduction

The title story of this collection, Karen Joy Fowler's 'Letters From Home', focuses on a war as it is experienced by those who stay at home. The narrator, writing to her lover who went to Vietnam and whom she never saw again, suffers from a sense of loss and from a deep uncertainty. The present, her present of marriage, children and respectability, is called into question by the uncertainties of the past. Can history be trusted? What proof is there, one of her friends asks her, that the Vietnam war wasn't a TV movie of the decade? A miniseries? A maxiseries?'

Like all Karen Joy Fowler's stories, 'Letters From Home' raises questions about fiction and reality. It is not that nothing is what it seems. But it becomes increasingly difficult to choose between the multiplicity of semblances, particularly as the self, the seeing I, is unsure of its own authenticity. In the television, video and computer age, the nowadays in which most of these stories are set, the position of the observer is neither simple nor innocent. In another of Karen Joy Fowler's stories, 'Lily Red', Lily is flagged down by a policeman for speeding. ' "Lady," he said and she wondered if policemen on television always called women *lady* because that was what real policemen did, or if he had learned this watching television just as she had.'

The writers in this anthology are all American, and are known as writers of science fiction – a genre that was transformed by the work of feminist writers in the 1970s and 1980s. They have been published in science fiction magazines and are active in the debates about writing, politics and gender that make the science fiction field, more than any other area of genre writing, so lively. Pat Cadigan, Karen Joy Fowler and Pat Murphy also write stories that are *not* science fiction. This collection will show, I hope, the range of their writing and will introduce them to a new audience.

As many of the stories collected here engage with the idea of home, and in particular the relationship between women and home, it seemed appropriate to entitle the whole collection *Letters From Home*. The reader will find that it is not just the traditional image of home as a place of safety and warmth, but also its obverse, home as a site of oppression for women, that is questioned. Home in science fiction has been earth and hearth, the planet left behind; it has also been the place in which new forms of social and sexual organisation struggle to be born and survive. In the stories in this collection women send out messages from home not knowing who will read them or how they will be read. More than that, their own sense of home is fraught with uncertainty.

Home is more than just a physical place. It is a metaphor for memories, dreams and hopes, a land of the imagination that can be viewed nostalgically. It is also a present locus of lost dreams and desires, an entrapping matrix filled with other people's needs and demands. In Pat Cadigan's 'After the Days of Dead Eye 'Dee' the middle-aged 'Dee remembers her childhood when she earned the soubriquet 'Dead Eye' and meditates on the life she has led between then and now. As she looks back on the aeons of her life as a housewife, hope blossoms that the monster that lurks threateningly outside the house will offer her an escape from her endless present, an escape back into the adventurous potential of her girlhood. But it doesn't: the hope of escape is as illusory as the offer of a dream home that she has just received in a glossy package of junk mail. This story is reminiscent of James Tiptree Jr's 'The Women Men Don't See', in which the escape of mother and daughter with aliens from elsewhere was seen by many readers at the time as offering a strongly pessimistic view of relations between women and men. Tiptree (an elusive and mysterious writer who overturned gender expectations when she finally revealed herself as a woman) seemed to be suggesting that it was better to go off into the unknown with a boatload of aliens from another planet than to stay with men, the aliens at home. But here, in Pat Cadigan's story, 'Dee realises, with disappointment, that the alien does not offer her escape. It wants her where her husband has kept her all their long married life: at home.

Concepts that are familiar to science fiction readers appear in these pages: a startling acceleration of time in Karen Joy Fowler's moving story about Einstein and his daughter, 'Lieserl', reading the future in Pat Murphy's fateful 'Prescience', creatures from elsewhere in her elegiac 'On a Hot Summer's Night in a Place Far Away', in 'After the Days of Dead Eye 'Dee', and in Karen Joy Fowler's 'Duplicity'. But, with these last, the stories are not *about* alien creatures: they are stories about time, subjectivity, shifting relationships. They are about women, a variety of women, lost, exiled or peripheralised, attempting to grasp meanings from slippery, puzzling circumstances.

This may make the stories sound deeply pessimistic, gloomy about the possibilities for women in the contemporary world and any future ones. But they are not. There may be no grand schemes, nor visions of utopia, but by constantly questioning the world around them the characters display a sturdy, and encouraging, pragmatism. Dead Eye 'Dee finally acts, in rage, against the colonisation of her life. In another of Pat Cadigan's stories, 'Johnny Come Home', the narrator sees all too clearly how the hunger for belief and meaning makes people vulnerable to messianic promises. Lily, in Karen Joy Fowler's 'Lily Red', refuses to be the plaything of other people's gods.

It has been argued that science fiction is fiction that embraces most easily – or persuasively – many of the tenets of modern philosophy. These include a deep uncertainty about the universality of any belief system, and a corresponding uncertainty about the status of self, and of self and other.

Karen Joy Fowler's delicate handling of fictions piled upon fictions leaves her characters in 'position doubtful' as the cartographer Alice says in 'Duplicity'. And Karen Joy Fowler enjoys, too, playing around with the relative positions of power between writer and reader. She has, she says, suffered for years 'from an excessive concern over the fate of extremely peripheral characters'. Her sad and funny story 'The Faithful Companion at Forty' centralises a sidekick and performs a feat of marvellously reductive transformation on the hero.

Many of these stories are concerned with doubt. Characters find themselves at odds with the reality around them and question the constructed nature of that reality. There is an edginess here that comes from the tension between uncertainty and the characters' determination, in the face of that uncertainty, to invent their own solutions, to make their own plots. They have to escape, in particular, from family mythology. The young woman in Pat Murphy's 'Dead Men on TV' finally defies the authority of her dead father, Xavier Clark in 'In the Abode of the Snows' achieves a different kind of satisfaction far from home, and even the vegetable wife rebels against her creator and takes her revenge.

Science fiction offers endless possibilities for the exploration of abstract ideas through metaphor. A living, breathing, sexy god; darkness that speaks and lays out moral choices to be made; a woman who can be planted and tended and made to grow like a tree: these are not realistic images, but they are part of realistic narratives, in which all that happens is minutely observed and psychologically believable, that explore our deepest doubts and hopes and fears. These stories are not fantasies, although they may use the fantastic. They explore the possibilities of extended metaphor, of the contradictory language of dreams and the unconscious.

The same close observation of the workings of mind and imagination is apparent in the horror and ghost stories included here: Pat Cadigan's 'The Pond', 'The Coming of the Doll' and 'In the Dark' and Pat Murphy's 'Clay Devils'.

What makes these stories resonate is the way the horror is built out of an authenticity of detail that makes the women's lives totally credible: the traditional culture that makes Dolores submissive to her ambitious husband in 'Clay Devils', the cruel madness of what is clinically known as 'post-natal depression' in 'The Coming of the Doll', a mother's tragic entrapment in her own childhood in 'The Pond' and the terrible burden of shame, guilt and anger inflicted on a young girl by a violent father in 'In the Dark'.

The stories collected here are iconoclastic, quirky, and wonderfully eclectic, using all the paraphernalia of an end of the century consciousness with its mass consumerism and the growth of information technology. The ideas that are explored by these three writers are informed by contemporary feminist thought. This is not to say that this is a collection of utopias (for some reason 'feminist' and 'utopian' seem to have become conflated over the last decade, although there are probably as good arguments for conflating 'feminist' and 'dystopian'), nor that the stories are united by a common political agenda. There is a sense of complexity confronted, the complexity not just of relations between women and men, but the complexity of individual lives.

While home may be a site of contradiction for women, the letters that come from it seem to be optimistically defiant. Here we are shown women and men who refuse to be contained by expectation and who reject the panacea of mass-produced dreams. There is a tension in these stories between the profound uncertainty of the nature of external reality and a laconic, ironic, or even simply survivalist, acceptance of that uncertainty. It may be that such acceptance, and the willingness to explore it, comes from women's long familiarity with that recent discovery of postmodernist men, the fragmentation of the self. Whatever the reasons, it is heartening to read such questioning, troubling and compassionate stories in these premillenarial times of growing evangelism and fundamentalism.

Sarah Lefanu
Bristol, April 1991

Pat Cadigan

After the Days of Dead-Eye 'Dee

The third night Brett was gone, Merridee put out all the downstairs lights and waited at the window by the kitchen table, the shotgun loaded and ready. She'd left all the upstairs lights burning; the glow they threw down let her see the backyard pretty well, considering. At fifty-eight her eyesight wasn't as dependable as it had once been – thus, the shotgun and not the rifle. You didn't have to be a crackshot with a shotgun, though at one time she'd been handy with either weapon. Dead-Eye 'Dee, her brothers had called her back in her target shooting days. They should have seen old Dead-Eye 'Dee now, she thought, crouched on a chair in a dark kitchen with a shotgun, waiting for God-knew-what.

A hundred yards beyond the house, she could just make out the silhouette of the stand of trees near the well Brett had sunk twenty years ago, only to have it dry up a year later. That was where it came out of, those trees. Maybe it was actually holed up in the old well. If it were, she couldn't imagine how it was getting out. She shifted position on the chair and carefully set the shotgun on the table. A moth hurled itself against the screen and fluttered away, up toward the light. Awfully late in the year for moths, Merridee thought idly; maybe it wouldn't come tonight. Maybe it had wandered off or died or something.

There was a rustle of leaves; a small puff of chill October air came through the window. Merridee blinked, adjusting her glasses. Uh-huh, she thought. Dead leaves danced across the yard as the shadow detached itself from the stand of trees and approached the house. Would it think she was upstairs (if it thought at all)? Or could it sense her waiting in the dark?

The thing moved awkwardly, as though it were used to much different terrain. She could see it a lot better from the kitchen window than from upstairs, where she'd watched it the previous two nights. She hadn't been able to tell much about it at all, not even whether it was worth creeping down-stairs to phone the sheriff about. But tonight she'd get a good look at it, see if it were man or beast, and then she'd know what to do. Maybe.

Just out of the range of light, it stopped and she thought she saw it hunker over, as though examining the ground. It was man-sized but she could tell the limbs were all wrong, the one arm she could make out was too long even for an ape. Maybe it was some poor freak, simple-minded as well as deformed, looking for shelter and food.

It made a strange sound and she jumped slightly, putting one hand on the shotgun. It wasn't a very fierce noise, some-thing between a sigh and a growl, or maybe a sigh and a snore. Not very animal-sounding, but not human, either.

She peered through the screen, wanting to call to it just to make it step into the light. It sigh-growled again and shuffled along the grass and dead leaves, stopping when it was opposite the window.

It knew she was there. The thought gave her a sudden flash of panic. An image of Brett popped into her head. He knew she was here, too, here in the house alone while he was days away, fishing and hunting in Oklahoma with his friends. His friends knew where she was, too, and his friends' wives, and her son and daughter-in-law; they all knew. But none of them knew the way this thing knew. The thoughts chased each other around in spirals in her mind as panic passed, leaving behind a rationally cold fear.

She picked up the shotgun. Weeks ago, she had hinted to Brett she'd have enjoyed a camping trip. It had been a long time since they'd taken one together. He'd only reminded her of the rheumatism in her shoulders and knees, that she'd just be in pain the whole time. So he was gone with his friends now and she was safely at home, no rheumatism acting up, watching this shadow. She wished she were anywhere else. Then this thing, whatever it was, could have had the run of the whole place and she wouldn't have had to know about it, she wouldn't have been trapped in the kitchen, wondering if she should shoot it.

It didn't move again for a long time. Because it could see in the dark, she thought, and it was looking her over. She imagined how she must look to it, wide-eyed behind her glasses, her loose, broad face homely with old-lady worry, a shotgun in her thick hands like a rolling-pin. Not much of a damsel in distress. Somewhere in the back of her mind was the irrational idea that every bit of her life had been pointing toward this moment and whatever happened afterwards would be mere time-keeping till the grave.

She untensed the tiniest bit, her fear smoothing into puzzlement. All right, now what did the thing want? Was it going to attack or not? Should she phone the sheriff and let him come take care of it? Puzzlement mixed with impatience. Suppose she just walked out there, walked right out there and said *What do you want?* as bold as you please? With the shotgun, of course. Would that goad it into doing something? Anything was better than this cowering in the dark.

The notion of going out to it blossomed suddenly into a powerful urge. Yes, she would go out to it, get a good look, confront it. It certainly wasn't going to come in for examination. She thought of Brett sound asleep in the camper. He might think to call her and he might not. It wouldn't enter his head that anything could possibly happen to dull old dependable Merridee securely at home. She was always securely at home as far as he was concerned, him and everyone else. Except that thing, waiting for her in the dark.

Maybe, she thought as she slid quietly off the chair, it just wanted some food and she should throw it some stale bread.

Hunger. That idea took her as strongly as the notion to go outside. She paused with her hand on the deadbolt. *Hunger.*

One-handed, she fumbled a loaf of that tasteless white stuff Brett was so partial to out of the breadbox on the counter, the shotgun seesawing in the crook of her other arm. Maybe it wouldn't like the stuff. No; rubbish, she thought. If it were hungry enough, it would eat anything.

She opened the door slowly and poked the screen door with the shotgun. Well, she couldn't fool it into thinking she was upstairs any more, she thought. But deep down, she knew she hadn't fooled it at all. *Go out. Hunger.* She wavered a little before she stepped over the threshold and let the screen door flap shut behind her.

The thing shuffled along in the grass and leaves again. Her coming out hadn't stampeded it; the knowledge made her feel satisfied and bold. She stood up a little straighter as she hurled the bread in the thing's general direction. The package landed just inside the lighted area where it lay like litter thrown from some out-of-towner's car.

Go on; take it, you blamed thing, it's for you. She wanted to say it out loud but the words stuck in her throat. She heard the hesitant rustling of grass and leaves; the trees on the north side of the house seemed to echo it. Leaves swirled down between herself and the thing. Its shadow stood out a little more clearly to her now and yes, it was all wrong for any man or beast.

It approached the bread with excruciating slowness, like an old fox coming upon a baited trap. Maybe she should have taken the bread out of the bag, Merridee thought. There was a sound like a grunt and she heard something slither along the ground. A lump appeared in the dead leaves beside the bread. Then fingers, big and thick, much thicker than her own or Brett's or anyone else's, broke through and clutched the package. Big, thick fingers, the color of a thunderhead about to let go, and only three of them, only three big, thick, blue-grey fingers. Merridee stared owlishly, unable to holler or run, the shotgun a meaningless weight in her hands. In some part of her mind, she was screaming her head off but it was so far removed it might as well have been someone else.

One of the all-wrong fingers pierced the plastic and tore into the bread, shredding it. And then . . . she blinked, her eyes watering madly. Something else strange, as though the arm belonging to those fingers had telescoped as the body came closer. Then the arm showed in the light and she saw it was exactly that way, not jointed but extendable, exactly like a telescope.

Without warning, it thrust its face into the light. Merridee stepped back, bringing one hand up defensively, the shotgun forgotten. At last she found voice enough to gasp; screaming was way beyond her. The face hung over the package of bread, refusing to go away. *Come out. Hunger.*

She hadn't had it quite right. It had wanted her to come out and it was hungry, but not for bread.

Merridee fled into the house.

She woke just after dawn, lying on top of the bed fully clothed with the shotgun beside her, the stock resting on Brett's pillow. For a moment she stared at it, not remembering. Then she sat up quickly, looking around the bedroom. *The thing* – well, it wasn't here with her unless it was hiding in the closet. The closet door was wide open, exposing thirty-four years' accumulation of clothes and personal belongings. No room for a *thing* in there. She flashed back to her childhood, a million years ago it felt like, the days of monsters in closets. Not her, but her brothers, Charlie and David. Her mother had always been soothing their nighttime terrors, turning on the lights, showing them there was nothing in the closet but the most mundane items of clothing and shoes, while she lay in her own room listening, not a bit afraid. There had never been monsters in the dark for Merridee Dunham. Nor for Merridee Percy, married to Brett and living in this house for 500,000 years, nor for their one child, who was more of Brett than of herself.

She rubbed her hands over her face, feeling as unwashed

and weary as a hobo. It was hard to believe in the thing in the daylight, the same way it had been hard to believe in her brothers' closet monsters. Now she could only vaguely remember the face it had shown her; she remembered her fear and she remembered running from it. But she remembered nothing after that.

Well, obviously, she'd been so tired from staying up that late she'd gone right to bed without even bothering to undress, just like some old man (*Brett*; who else) who'd spent all day and half the night in a duck blind.

She looked at the shotgun lying on Brett's side of the bed. If that wasn't the silliest thing in the world and dangerous besides, sleeping with a shotgun. She left it there while she went to wash.

Later, sitting at the kitchen table with a cup of coffee and two pieces of sourdough toast, she looked out the window at the stand of trees. All the leaves had blown off them now; the bare branches clawed at the sky in the wind. She tried to imagine how it would look, that creature coming through the trees and shuffling towards the house. It was like trying to picture the shirts and coats in her brothers' closet congealing into a monster. She couldn't do it. Shaking her head, she smiled to herself. Like two different worlds people lived in, one filled with strange, inexplicable shadows, one utterly prosaic, and she had never doubted once in her million-years-long life that she existed in the latter.

As she was getting up to refill her coffee cup, she caught sight of the spot where she had thrown the bread. It was gone; not even a shred of the plastic wrapper remained. Squirrels, she thought. And birds, the tough little sparrows who hopped through the bitter snows. And the wind had blown away whatever had been left behind.

In the early afternoon, she bundled herself up in two sweaters and one of Brett's old hunting jackets and went for a walk. The phone had not rung all day and she was tired of waiting for a call that probably wouldn't come. The house was clean

– the house was always clean – and there was nothing that needed doing urgently. Brett could recaulk the windows and put up plastic himself after he came back. He was expecting her to do it while he was gone, she knew, but she didn't feel like it. Let him grumble over it. She would just tell him: *I didn't feel like doing it.* What would he make of that? She didn't know and didn't care. *I'm apathetic but who cares*, she thought, and giggled, still tickled at the old joke.

She walked the quarter mile down the dirt drive to the mailbox. The October wind tore at her hair and made her eyes water behind her glasses. She took the glasses off and tucked them into her jacket pocket. There wasn't much to look at. It was very pretty country but she'd seen it and seen it. Seen it for a million years.

The mailbox leaned forward over the paved road as though it might have been watching for oncoming traffic, of which there was very little on any given day. The mailman had left only one envelope, a brown and green announcement that she, Mrs Merridee Percy, had another chance to enter the biggest sweepstakes of the year. A quarter-mile hike for a piece of junk mail. But she didn't begrudge the time or effort. She put her glasses back on and examined the brightly colored enclosures on the walk back. A $100,000 dream house, a yacht, a brand-new Lincoln-Continental (she could just picture it destroying its suspension on the dirt drive), a full-length mink, a home entertainment system with a big screen TV and a record player that took funny-looking little records – compact discs, the brochure called them – a video-recorder and lots of other things. Any of them might be hers already. There was also a sheet of little stamps offering cut-rate subscriptions to magazines. No purchase was necessary to enter this wonderful sweepstakes but she examined the stamps anyway. Maybe she might order a magazine or two, something that had articles on foreign places or one of those science magazines if they had one that wasn't too technical to understand. Brett had given her the *Ladies' Home Journal* once, years before, but she'd found little in it to pique her curiosity. She'd already been living in the *Ladies' Home Journal* for a quarter of a million years by then.

She reached the house, paused, and then walked around the back. The trip to the mailbox had not been sufficient to relieve her cooped-up feeling. The sweepstakes announcement was crammed into a pocket. She kept her hand on it while she approached the stand of trees. She wasn't looking for the creature, she told herself, absolutely not. It was getting harder and harder to believe in it as the day wore on. But if anything unlikely did pop out at her from somewhere, she'd pull the sweepstakes announcement out and throw the brochures right in its face. *All right*, she'd say, *you tell me how you can be real in a world that has sweepstakes and cut-rate magazine subscriptions!* Well, it wouldn't be able to, that was all there was to it, and the thing would just melt away into thin air, and that would be the end of the matter. A $100,000 dream house didn't come with monsters in the closets. Reality would take care of any old thing better than a shotgun would.

She found the package of bread lying torn up on the boards Brett had nailed down over the dried-up well. Some of it had been nibbled at. *Squirrels*, she thought firmly. And birds. Squirrels and birds for certain and apparently they didn't like that bland white stuff any better than she did. And monsters didn't eat Wonder Bread, whether they lived in closets or dried-up wells.

She left the enclosure describing the $100,000 dream house crumpled up next to the bread and walked back to her own house.

When evening came, she went upstairs to the bedroom and looked at the shotgun still lying on the bed.

'Slept all day, did you?' she said aloud and laughed at the absurdity of the statement and the sound of her own voice. She'd hardly ever spoken out loud in an empty house; unlike some people, she wasn't in the habit of talking to herself, never had been. Oh, when that Brett called – *if* he called –

she'd give him what her grandfather had called Billy Blue Hill. *You go off shooting up half of Oklahoma and what happens to your stay-at-home wife but she becomes a babbling idiot, talking to shotguns and sundry. And seeing shadows in the back yard.*

She cradled the shotgun in her arms. Not thinking, not feeling anything at all, she took it downstairs to the kitchen and stood it against the wall next to the table while she made supper.

She ate staring at the barrel. *No*, she imagined herself saying to someone who didn't know anything about how people lived (and she couldn't think who that might be), *no, we generally don't eat supper with our shotguns handy, or sleep with them either. It's just a funny kind of thing I'm doing here and I don't know what for.*

A funny kind of thing. Come to think of it, there was lots of room in her life for funny kinds of things. She could set down her spoon, get up, walk around to the shotgun, pick it up and blow a hole right through any one of the four walls, or all of them. She could shoot up the whole house and dance naked in the ruins until Brett came home, if she wanted to. Or she could run upstairs, pack a bag and take off to see the world. She could fling her plate of pork and beans on the floor and roll around in the mess singing; she could phone the fire department and say there was a brush fire raging out of control behind the house; she could start the fire herself and not phone anyone. She could have done anything that came into her head no matter how foolish or malign, and there were plenty of people whose lives were so crowded up with such things that there was barely room for the things they hadn't done yet. But her life was spacious enough to accommodate a Sears-sized catalogue of antics. Even in the days of Dead-Eye 'Dee, there'd been plenty of latitude and a look down the coming longitude would have shown nothing but the traditional, famed, proverbial and inescapable straight-and-narrow.

I see, said the imaginary person she had been relating all this to. She froze, bent over her plate. A tingle crept along her scalp from neck to crown. She had forgotten this imaginary person, the one who didn't know anything about how people lived. She had done with that stray notion but here it was hanging on in her head as though she didn't know her own mind.

She turned her head to the window; it was closed and she saw only her own reflection against the night. Her reflection nodded at her slowly, with great certainty.

She didn't hurry. She scraped the rest of the pork and beans into the garbage pail and washed the bowl thoroughly, leaving it to drain in the dishrack. Then she slipped on the two sweaters and the jacket, taking time to adjust the rumples and pull the sleeves down. The shotgun – well, of course, she would take it. She found extra shells in the utility drawer and put them in the empty pocket in the jacket.

Light? She went upstairs and put all the lights on again but she didn't turn off the kitchen light. There was no more bread to offer it except her own sourdough and she wasn't going to give it that – that was the good stuff. Tonight she'd fling the rest of the contest brochures at it if it got too active. Maybe then it would get the hint. And if it didn't, there was the shotgun.

Prepared, she stood in the middle of the kitchen and counted to thirty before she picked up the shotgun and went outside.

There was the smell of coming rain or snow in the chill air and the wind had picked up. Merridee walked forward a few steps, her feet crunching on the newest layer of dead leaves. She'd just keep going until there was some sign that she should stop.

The sign came as a feeling of pressure high on her chest, as if the wind pushing against her had suddenly become deep water. All right, she'd stop. She hefted the shotgun impatiently, wanting to get this whatever it was going to be over with, just as if she didn't have what amounted to all the time in the world.

She could practically feel all that time all around her,

stretching away from her in every direction, past, present and future. Far, far away, almost too far to see was Dead-Eye 'Dee, still shooting and hitting nearly every bull's eye. You could only see her from behind; maybe she'd known even then there were no targets to shoot at ahead of her. After Dead-Eye 'Dee there was a big patch of present, forty years of Now, one day almost interchangeable with any before or behind it. And then an area that rose up unseeable into the dark, into the night sky for all she knew, but if it had been steps, she would have liked to climb them.

And if she did climb them, what might she find? Nothing so prosaic as, say, a $100,000 castle in the air or heaven. No, something else, something *really* else, that couldn't be weighed or measured by the standards of white bread or shotguns or sweepstakes. There would be closet monsters and strange, inexplicable moving shadows and ideas you'd have liked to have in your head to do if you could even have conceived of them, and things –

and things that moved in an atmosphere neither air nor water but something in between. They didn't eat anything like pork and beans or sourdough; they didn't eat. They were consumed themselves by something that might have been food in the real world of shotguns and somehow they emerged not just whole but more than they had been before, and they didn't take notions to do this or that, notions took them and they found themselves in this notion or that one. It was a world where they did not dream; the world dreamed them and lived through them as instruments. And as instruments, their limbs bent in odd angles and directions, and their joints telescoped –

And their faces. She looked at its face now without fear, without anything. Their faces were an asymmetrical arrangement on an oval of puckered openings, none of which were eyes and at the top a large irregular dark pad crisscrossed with tiny lines, like a picture in a science book of human skin enlarged a hundred times to show detail. It would be sensitive, that pad, like sight and smell and taste and touch and hearing all run together and enlarged a hundred times as well, and the size and shape of the patch would determine what the creature it belonged to was like –

'I see,' Merridee said, even though there was no need to speak out loud. But she wanted to tell it the same thing it had told her. She lowered the shotgun, resting the stock on the ground.

The thing bowed its head, aiming the dark pad at her and its arm telescoped out, sliding through the grass and leaves until the three-fingered hand lay within six feet of her. The thing crouched and its arm telescoped inward, dragging the creature's body closer to her. The pressure against her chest increased.

Poor thing, she thought. It was hungry for its home. And where it touched her mind, it let her know that she was right. Yes, hungry to be home and it was going home soon.

Going home with her help . . .

Merridee's nerves gave a jump and she wasn't sure she had understood it that time. But it prodded her gently in her mind again (she still didn't think to wonder how it could do that) and she knew she had understood. Going home with her help. She would take it home.

'Me?' she whispered. 'I can do that?'

Yes. She could.

She put a hand to her mouth. It was too – All her life – Nothing ever – The thoughts came and went in flashes. She looked back at the house (half a million years of nothing and he couldn't even find heart enough to take you on a camping trip, leave you behind with the rest of the furniture) and back at her life (Dead-Eye 'Dee shooting bull's-eyes with her back to the future because she knew nothing would come to a girl who didn't even get monsters in her closets) and back at her world (where sweepstakes announcements came solely to show her what other people would be having, at her correct address) and then she turned back to the creature with her eyes tearing in the cold October wind, a million years of life with all that room in it falling away from her old lady body like a worn-out skin. Yes, yes, she would take it home and gladly, if she had to carry it on her back, she would take it home if the effort tore her into a million bloody pieces. She would take it home. Yes.

No.

The negation in her mind was strong and deep enough to make her reel. She caught herself, leaning on the shotgun until the dizziness passed. The thing shimmered in her watery vision. Panting a little, she wiped her eyes and leaned toward the creature with pained confusion. 'No?' she whispered. 'But I thought – I thought you – ' She remembered the thickened medium it lived in, the way its nourishment consumed it (what a bad time it would have had trying to get bread to eat it rather than vice versa); she remembered all the wonderful strangeness it had showed her and thought a question mark at the end. *I thought you wanted me to take you home?*

Its home receded in her mind and was replaced by the house behind her.

'What?' she asked and even as she spoke, the answer was forming. The dark pad, touched to her open mouth. She tasted something thick. The all-wrong limbs collapsed, the body shrank in on itself, the head going down like a deflating balloon. Gone home, at home in her and in her house and her world, where they would stay together, its own world only in their joint memory. She would remember what it remembered, know the things it knew. But she would remain in the house, waiting for Brett, and it would be home.

'Going home . . . to me? In me?' she said, incredulous.

The image of her open mouth pressed to the pad flashed in her brain again. No pain. No fear. No difference.

'You son of a bitch.' She raised the shotgun and pulled the trigger.

The explosion seemed to echo for hours. She wasn't used to the noise of a shotgun; it had been years. The shotgun had bucked in her hands but Dead-Eye 'Dee had always been able to stand up to any kind of recoil. She waited until the ringing in her ears began to fade before she walked over to examine the thing.

She had literally blown it to pieces. There was hardly a fragment larger than the palm of her hand, except for its arm, which had still been extended. It lay like a forgotten pole in the leaves, the fingers limp and boneless. There wasn't blood, just a kind of syrupy jelly glistening on the dead leaves. She had a crazy urge to swoop the jelly up and touch it to her mouth, but the urge died quickly.

Even as she watched, the pieces of the thing were melting. Like snow. She poked one of the fragments with the barrel of the shotgun and made a face at the slime it left on the metal.

Here it had come creeping around the house, peering into her mind, showing her things, showing her all those wonderful things, touching her, making her feel different and letting her believe it would take her away, take her out of the house of white bread and Brett and sweepstakes – and all it wanted was for her to stay right where she was, knowing what was out there and not being allowed to go to any of it. Just like Brett and everybody else.

'You son of a bitch,' she said again. 'To hell with you.' She kicked some leaves over the remains and turned back toward the house. The sight of the hand, melting like all the rest of it, stopped her for a moment. Then she walked on, hoping it had known at the end just what it was like to have a last chance snatched away from it.

It melted away completely during the night in spite of the cold temperatures. There was no trace of it at all in the morning, not even in the frost.

The Pond

The pond was evil.

That was a sad, silly thought to have on such a beautiful May afternoon with the trees whispering in the fresh wind and the distant sounds of insects buzzing and birds singing coming to her dreamily from the small woods that cupped the pond like protective hands. The pond itself was lovely, smooth and untroubled today, reflecting the surrounding trees like dark glass. Occasionally ripples appeared here and there on its surface, spreading out from tiny points where something had pricked the water. It should have been an idyllic spot.

Paula Stromsted leaned back on her palms and looked at her five-year-old daughter Richie, who was trying unsuccessfully to weave a garland of the flowers and leaves wilting in a pile between her folded legs. She had seen a picture of fairies dancing with wreaths of flowers around their heads in a storybook and the idea had captivated her. The girl worked meticulously with the tremendous concentration only the very young seemed capable of. After a few moments, she felt her mother's gaze on her and looked up.

'Mommy, I just can't get them to go in a circle like in the book. They won't stay.' She wrapped two daisy stems around each other and grimaced when they fell apart. 'See?'

Paula sat up, brushing her hands on her jeans. 'Well, what do you say we head back to Grandma's house for something cold to drink? We've been down here for almost an hour and I'm getting thirsty.'

'Do we *have*ta?' Richie looked longingly at the pond. 'It's so nice here. This is my favoritest spot in the whole world.'

'I thought Funland was your favoritest spot in the whole world.'

'It's a different favoritest,' Richie said seriously. 'Can we stay one more mimit?'

'Minute.'

'Minute. Please, Mommy?'

She sighed. 'Just one. Then we go back to the house and no arguments. OK?'

'Well, OK.' The girl got up and went looking for more flowers, bending over with her hands on her knees in a perfect imitation of her grandmother inspecting the vegetable garden. Paula felt a little guilty. How was a little girl to understand the way she felt about the pond? To Richie, it was what it was – a pretty lake, a place to play and daydream, a welcome change from their cramped apartment in the city and the tiresomely cheerful daycare center where she spent the hours Paula was at work. For Paula, it was something else.

Dare you. Double dare you.

Darers go first.

She closed her eyes. That day twenty-five years ago had been warm and beautiful, too, when she and her cousin Jeffrey had come down to the pond to play Robin Hood. She and Jeff didn't always get along very well – there was something cold and mean in the bright blue eyes that grown-ups were always exclaiming over, much to her Aunt Kitty's proud delight. *Hasn't he got the most beautiful blue eyes*? people would say. For some reason, they never saw the meanness that was waiting to come out later as a painful twisting pinch on Paula's arm or a foot stuck out to trip her when she was running or the slow, thorough dissection of a grasshopper while the tormented creature scrabbled its remaining limbs helplessly in the air. But she had seen it. Her mother had seen it, too, and wasn't happy about it. But Jeff was her only sister's boy, she'd told Paula, and they had to try to be nice to him. Maybe if he saw how people were supposed to behave, he'd try harder to be good and the meanness inside of him would shrink away to nothing. Paula had tried, but privately she felt that Jeffrey would always be a nasty little boy even after he'd grown up. And people would still be oohing and aahing over his beautiful blue eyes.

She hadn't wanted to come down to the pond with Jeffrey that day. But he was just there for the weekend with Aunt Kitty and Uncle Rob and there wasn't anyone else around to play with. Jeffrey had seemed a little nicer than usual but as soon as they'd gotten to the pond, he'd started making fun of her. She was a girl; girls were stupid and weak and scared of everything; he was going to catch a snake and scare her with it.

She wasn't scared of anything, she'd insisted, and there weren't any snakes anyway.

Are so, fraidy-cat. She could almost hear his voice, just as plain as anything, his childish, mocking treble, the way she had heard it twenty-five years before when they'd been eight years old. *Are so. There's snakes in the pond. If you're not scared of 'em, I dare you to swim in it.*

Steadfastly, she had shaken her head. He knew as well as she did that they weren't even supposed to go wading. Her father had warned them they could get sick from the water, which was murky and muddy. As well, the bottom was treacherous, parts of it suddenly dropping down ten feet or more without warning. But Jeff had kept after her. *I dare you. Double dare you.*

Darers go first, she'd said primly.

And then he had spotted her new watch that her father had bought her as a No Special Reason surprise. Jeff's parents never gave him No Special Reason surprises and he was very jealous. She'd taunted him a little about it; she couldn't help it. At last she had something she could lord over him. She should have known better, her mother had told her later. She should have realized she couldn't get the better of Jeffrey's meanness.

He had demanded that she hand the watch over. When she wouldn't, he chased her, tackled her, and tore the watch from her wrist. Paula still remembered her enraged frustration as, still sitting on her chest, he began to put it on his own wrist. Then he saw the picture of Cinderella on the dial.

A stupid girl's watch! Shoulda known it would be a stupid girl's watch! But he wouldn't give it back to her, no matter how much she demanded and pleaded. He got up off her and went down to the edge of the pond. *Let's see if it's waterproof.* Before she could stop him, he had lobbed it almost halfway across the pond. There was only a tiny splash when it hit the water and the ripples it made were soon gone.

Now you'll have to swim in the pond if you want to get your stupid watch back. Dare you do. Double dare you.

Paula had run home crying, knowing with bitter satisfaction as she sobbed and hiccupped out her story that Jeffrey was really going to get it for this one. He must have known it, too, she'd realized later, and it hadn't made the slightest difference to him. The pleasure of the act outweighed the consequences for him and that had frightened her. She could still see him as he had been, standing at the water's edge grinning nastily at her, enormously pleased with himself. The mental image chilled her. It was almost as if he was there still, standing in that exact spot and if she opened her eyes she would see him, still eight years old and every bit as nasty, daring her to jump in and get her watch.

The wind rustling the trees died down and a quiet settled over everything. Paula opened her eyes. A small figure *was* standing at the water's edge, leaning forward and peering curiously into the pond.

'Richie!' Paula jumped up. 'Richie, get away from there!' She hurried over and jerked the little girl back from the water.

'What? I didn't do anything!' Richie stared up at her with round, startled eyes.

Paula pressed her lips together, suddenly embarrassed. 'I know, honey,' she said after a moment, stroking the child's soft fair hair. 'I just don't want you to go near the water. I've told you that before, remember?'

Richie nodded. 'I just thought I saw something in there. Something shiny.'

'You were wrong,' Paula said firmly. 'Come on now, let's go back to the house.' She didn't look over her shoulder at the pond as she and Richie walked up to the road.

'Did you and Richie have a nice walk?' Paula's mother asked as they sat in the kitchen drinking lemonade at the round wooden table.

'We ended up down at the pond. As usual,' Paula said. 'She likes that place so much.'

Her mother pursed her lips. 'It's a pretty spot.'

'Yes. She seems quite drawn to it. She's made me take her down there every day.' Paula half-rose from her chair to look out the window over the sink. Richie was in the back yard picking dandelions, presumably to try her luck at making a garland of them.

'You don't sound very happy about that.'

'Why should I be?'

'Paula, that was such a very long time ago.' Her mother's voice was gentle but Paula could detect a small hint of exasperation.

'I know, Ma, but I can't go there without thinking of that little bastard. That little sadist.' Paula rested her head on her hand, digging her fingers into her dark, shaggy hair. 'I know it's an awful thing to say. But I'm not sorry. I never was. There was something terribly wrong with Jeff. Aunt Kitty and Uncle Rob refused to see it. Not Rob so much as Kitty, really. She thought the sun just rose and set on her darling Jeffrey.'

Her mother sighed, folding her wrinkled hands around her glass. 'Kitty had a lot of trouble delivering Jeffrey. It almost killed her and she never could have any more children. That was the saddest part, I thought.' She sighed again and gave Paula a pained smile. 'That was all Kitty had, being Jeffrey's mother. It wasn't like it is today for women. All Kitty ever really thought of doing was raising a family. When she could only have Jeff, she put a tremendous load on him. He had to be the best of every child she couldn't have. I think that may have helped make him the way he was.'

'Maybe. *I* think he was born that way like some people are born deformed. Only his deformity was up here.' Paula tapped the side of her head. 'Things turned out for the best, Ma. I thought so then and I'll always think so.'

Her mother raised her eyebrows, dipping her salt-and-pepper head slightly to the left. 'I find it a bit disconcerting that after twenty-five years, you're still so bitter about the boy.'

'It's the pond.' Paula rubbed the back of her neck tiredly. 'It's tainted now. Jeffrey polluted the place so that it'll never be the same. Whenever I go there, it seems like he's still around. I can almost feel him there. Hell, I *can* feel him there. His poison's seeped into everything, the water, the trees, the wind – ' She made a face. 'I sound crazy, don't I?'

'Obsessed. Perhaps you shouldn't go to the pond any more.'

'Perhaps I shouldn't.' Paula sipped her lemonade. It had gone warm and the taste was sourly cloying. 'But Richie would be so disappointed. And I certainly don't want her going down there alone. If something happened, I'd never forgive myself.'

'Sometimes I don't think you *have* ever forgiven yourself.'

Paula blinked. 'Say again?'

'I don't think you're really glad about what happened. You're not that kind of person. At least I hope you're not. I think maybe the little girl inside you still takes Kitty's awful words to heart and keeps them there.'

'Oh, for God's sake.' Paula got up and dashed her lemonade into the kitchen sink with a flip of her wrist. She glanced out at Richie, who was squatting on the grass with her back to the house. 'Ma, I *don't* blame myself for what happened. I never did. If you want to know the truth' – she turned away from the window – 'I don't even feel guilty about not feeling guilty. It might have been me instead.'

Her mother shook her head. 'If you ask me, that's what's poisoning the pond for you. You were talking a little while ago about Jeffrey being abnormal, not quite right. What about the way you keep harping on this? You insist on working yourself up about it. If you could stop living in the past, you'd be a lot better off.'

'I don't live in the past.'

'When it comes to Jeffrey, you do. He hasn't been around to make you unhappy for a quarter of a century but you've managed to keep him closer to you than ever. You use him to make yourself miserable.' Her mother pushed away from the table. 'If you continue this way, you'd better think about getting some help because it's going to turn you into a sad case.'

She left the room, her footsteps loud on the hardwood floor. Paula turned back to the window. Her mother had never known what it was like to be at Jeff's mercy. That was the sort of thing that could really leave a mark on a person. She fixed herself a glass of ice water to get the taste of the lemonade out of her mouth. If only she could rid herself of the taste of Jeffrey as easily. She leaned against the counter, sipping her water thoughtfully.

She had found the grown-ups sitting at the kitchen table playing whist when she had come home wailing from the pond. Through her tears she had seen each of their reactions, Kitty putting her hand to her mouth, Rob throwing his cards down, her mother looking to her father, who got up to wipe her tears away with his handkerchief. *That boy*, Rob had said angrily, *that boy is going to have to learn a few things.*

Now, Rob, don't hit him. Kitty, sounding syrupy about Jeff as usual. *Striking a child doesn't teach him anything.*

Her parents had kept quiet except to try to comfort her. Not long after, Jeff had come in and there'd been a scene, mostly Kitty shouting at her husband while shielding a smirking Jeff with her body. In the end he'd gotten a mild spanking, after which Kitty brought him to Paula so he could deliver an apology and promises to pay for the watch out of his allowance and never to do such an awful thing again, all of it dictated to him by Kitty and played back with occasional prompting.

Paula had stared at him through the whole thing until he got to the end. He smirked all the way through it. She knew all the adults were looking at her, waiting for her to be very grown-up and ladylike about everything and accept the artificial apology. But a devil had gotten into her and instead of pronouncing her forgiveness, she had reared back and exploded.

I'll never forgive you! she had screamed into his face, startling him so much that his smirk had actually disappeared for a few seconds. *I hate you and I wish you were dead!*

Kitty had clutched her son to her side in horror while Paula's father – a bit reluctantly, it seemed to her at the time – marched her upstairs to her room and told her to stay there until after supper. Paula had known her outburst would strain relations between the two families even further, but she hadn't cared. Or had tried not to. Later, her mother had had a quiet talk with her on the virtue of being civilized and not sinking to a certain other person's level. Her father had been more understanding; he tucked her in with a promise to teach her how to defend herself.

The next morning the situation had escalated into frenzy when Kitty discovered the front door open and Jeffrey missing. Sometime during the night or early morning, he'd gotten dressed and run away. Because of what Paula had screamed at him, Kitty said. He had run away because his feelings were hurt. Paula had doubted it.

Rob and her father had driven all over the county looking for him while Kitty sobbed and she hid in her room. It was just after lunchtime when the phone rang. Paula's mother had answered it.

She couldn't quite remember the exact sequence of events after that, or exactly when she had found out what had happened and from whom. Her father had stopped at the pond on the way back to the house and found Jeffrey's shoes and socks near the water. He and Rob had called the police from the grocery store down the road. The police had come out with a diver and several men to comb the woods, but the diver found him after all, lying at the bottom of a seven-foot drop-off.

Kitty had had to be sedated but Paula heard her screams through the whole house before the medication took effect. Paula had done it to Jeffrey. Paula had said she would never forgive him so Jeff had gone out to the pond to try to get her watch, just so they could be friends again. And it was Paula's curse that had done it. She had wished him dead and now he was.

Paula had found herself strangely numbed by the whole experience. She felt a little regret and a certain amount of horror for how the boy had died. But through it all she couldn't shake the thought that if Jeff had really been trying to retrieve her watch, it was only because he hadn't wanted to give up part of his allowance to pay for it.

But that hadn't been why he'd gone out to the pond.

Dare you. Double dare you, he'd said.

Darers go first, she'd replied.

And so he had. So that the next time they were away from the grown-ups, he could say he'd gone into the pond and then try to force her into the water. And when he'd gotten her there . . .

Paula came slowly back to the present and shoved the memory aside. Her mother was right. She was rubbing salt in wounds that should have healed over at least two decades before. Even Kitty had apologized to her, months after the funeral Paula hadn't attended, telling her she hadn't meant all the awful things she'd said. But the apology had had a curious flat sound to it, as though it had been fed to her the way she had fed Jeffrey's to him. But it didn't seem right, when Paula thought about it, that her feelings about Jeffrey should still be so strong. The image of the pond appeared in her mind and she felt herself tense. Jeffrey was the pond to her now and always would be. Well, she could help herself by refusing to dwell on it, starting right at that moment. She looked out the window again. Richie was still crouched down on the grass, studying something. Paula smiled. At least one good thing had come out of the experience. The memory of Jeff's death had persuaded her to take Richie for toddler swimming lessons at the Y before she was even three years old. She had decided there wasn't going to be another accidental drowning. The girl could swim like a little fish. Still smiling, she went out to see what her daughter was so involved in.

'What's up, buttercup?' she asked, ruffling Richie's hair.

Richie looked up at her guiltily. There was a pile of dandelions beside her and grass smears on her knees. Something small and brown wriggled between her fingers.

'Richie!' Horrified, Paula slapped the grasshopper out of her daughter's grasp and stamped on it. Then she yanked the girl to her feet and shook her. 'What were you doing?'

Richie tried to shrink away. 'Nothing, Mommy, I – '

'That's a terrible thing to do, a terrible, evil thing! How would *you* like it if a giant tore *you* apart bit by bit! How could you? How *could* you?'

Richie flopped back and forth in her hands. 'Mommy, you're hurting!'

'See? See what it's like?'

'I only caught him, I was only looking at him – '

Paula's grip tightened on the child's arm. 'Don't ever let me see you doing anything like that again!'

Richie burst into tears. 'I didn't do anything! I was just looking at him and you killed him! You killed him!'

Paula released her and the girl fled into the house, wailing for her grandmother. Uncertainly, Paula watched her go and then looked down at the crushed insect in the grass. With her shoe, she mashed the remains into unrecognizability and kicked the dying dandelions over them.

'You know,' Paula's mother said, looking up from the magazine on her lap, 'little kids don't really know that kind of thing is wrong. If, indeed, that's what she was doing. She may have been just looking at the grasshopper like she said.'

Paula looked away from the television program she hadn't really been able to concentrate on and shifted her position in the overstuffed chair. 'Maybe she was. But I recognized that position, the way she was holding her fingers. It was the way Jeffrey looked when he was pulling those poor things apart.'

'Paula, really. Jeffrey again. And all over a *bug*.'

'Really yourself, Ma. Suppose it were a puppy or a kitten?'

Her mother leaned against the arm of the couch and put her feet up on the cushions. 'Richie would never do anything like *that*.'

'Not anymore, that's for sure.'

Her mother made a disgusted noise and set her magazine aside. It was this week's *Rolling Stone*, Paula noted with detached amusement. 'You scared that poor kid almost into hysterics. And over nothing! *All* little children are fascinated by insects. Pulling them apart is just a way for them to try to figure out how they work. Like an experiment. It's curiosity, Paula, not sadism.'

'It's sadistic, whether they realize it or not. I'm not going to stand for that. Richie is going to realize that other living things are entitled to exist unmolested.'

'I suppose *you* never did anything of the sort,' her mother said sarcastically.

'Did you ever catch me at it?'

'It's occurred to me that there was probably a good deal that I didn't catch you at.'

'Well, I never did anything like that.'

'Never? Not even once? Never picked the wings off a fly? Or a ladybug?'

'*No.*' Paula suppressed the memory of watching Jeffrey with horrified fascination when she had first seen him removing the hind legs of a grasshopper. What he had done after that had made her feel sick.

Her mother shrugged. 'All right. You were good and kind and merciful, a sensitive little soul who never harmed a fly. If you insist.' She picked up the magazine again and leafed through it to find her place. 'But I still think your reaction was entirely inappropriate, no matter what Richie was doing or not doing.'

'I am *not* going to have her turn out like Jeffrey.'

'Jesus Christ!' Her mother slammed the magazine down on her knees. 'Jeffrey, Jeffrey, Jeffrey! I had less of him when he was alive! Once and for all, Paula, lose this hang-up you've got about him. He's dead. Twenty-five years dead. Lay him to rest!'

Paula said nothing, turning her gaze back to the television set. The images on the screen made no sense at all to her.

'You only have a few more days of vacation left,' her mother went on quietly. 'Try to make them pleasant. For Richie's sake. And you ought to go up to her room right now and apologize to her.' She looked at Paula sharply from under her eyebrows. 'Believe me, it's far more important for grown-ups to apologize to children than vice-versa. That is, if you really want a kid to grow up with the kind of integrity you want her to have.'

'All right,' Paula said resignedly. 'I'll go up and talk to her.'

Her mother was smiling as Paula walked out of the living room and into the front hall. At the foot of the stairs she paused, frowning at the open front door. The dying sunlight made a red-gold block on the floor. The screen door wasn't even latched. Paula shook her head. An authority on children and a subscriber to *Rolling Stone* and her mother still couldn't remember to lock the front door at night. Anyone could get in . . .

She froze in the act of closing the heavy wooden door. Anyone could get in – *or out*.

'Richie!' she yelled, pounding up the staircase. 'Richie!'

She tore down the hallway on the second floor and burst into her daughter's room. 'Richie!' She didn't have to turn on the light to see the empty bed, still neatly made. '*Richie!*'

She pounded back down the stairs, colliding with her mother at the bottom.

'What's wrong? What did she do?'

Paula pushed her mother's groping hands away from herself. 'She ran away, she's not in her room!'

'Have you looked in the back y-'

'*You* look! I *know* where she is!' Paula ran out the front door, feeling her pocket for her car keys.

'Where are you going?' her mother called after her.

'The pond!' Paula jumped into the car and fumbled the key into the ignition, ignoring her mother's plea to wait.

It took her just a little over a minute to drive to the pond. She knew that was the only place Richie could have run to. To her favoritest spot, because she was angry and she knew she wasn't supposed to go there by herself. Paula forced herself to press lightly on the accelerator, in case the girl suddenly appeared walking in the middle of the road. 'Richie,' she moaned, her hands trembling on the steering wheel. 'Richie, if I catch up to you – ' Her heart thudded when she realized what she'd said.

When she reached the pond, she pulled on to the dirt shoulder and put on the emergency flashers. 'Richie!' she yelled, running the fifty yards down to the spot where they'd been sitting earlier. '*Richie!*' Her voice echoed, shattering the quiet. A few feet from the water she stopped, listening for the sound of an answer. The trees rustled, patchy silhouettes against the darkening sky.

'Richie, please answer me! I'm not mad at you, I'm not going to hurt you, Richie – '

She spotted the shoes sitting side by side on the ground with the little white socks stuffed neatly inside them at the same time as she heard the splashing.

'*Mommy!*'

Far out in the pond, two little arms waved, scrabbling at the air before they dipped below the surface.

Then she felt it, like the terrible oppressiveness before the onset of a storm. She had been right after all. Jeffrey had poisoned the pond, but in a hideous, evil way she'd never dreamed of. He'd been there, waiting to get her for twenty-five years and when he knew he never would, he'd gone to work on Richie, drawing her to the pond, luring her into the water. If Jeffrey couldn't have Paula, he'd take Richie and, in a way, that was better for him. Jeffrey had always known exactly what would hurt her most.

All this passed through her mind in less than a second. Then she was tearing into the water, pushing with all her strength toward the little arms that had bobbed to the surface again and the choking voice that cried *Mommy!* with hopeless terror.

The filthy water splashed into her eyes and mouth as she struggled against it. It seemed as though she were moving with terrible slowness, as though the water were becoming as thick as hardening molasses. Every time she looked up, Richie seemed further away than ever, her voice becoming weaker. Paula strained against the water, feeling it resist her almost like a live thing. *You can't have her, Jeffrey!* her mind screamed. *You can't take her from me, I won't let you!*

The water suddenly churned around her, bubbling madly, sucking at her arms and legs, pulling her down. Panic exploded inside her like an electric shock. She fought to keep herself at the surface, to stay in sight of her daughter. The drag became more powerful, the water lifting when her arms lifted, swirling around her body like liquid ropes. She felt her head forced under and her hands lost the air; her legs kicked uselessly but she kept struggling, all the way to the muddy bottom.

The little girl sat at the water's edge, soaked, chilled, and panting. Several times she swallowed, making a face at the muddy taste in her mouth. The sun had set and there was only a little bit of a red glow left in the sky. She should start back before it was really dark. Mommy had always said it was dangerous to walk on a road after night had fallen, even if you were wearing light-colored clothing.

She stood up and looked out over the pond for a long moment. The surface was smooth again. 'You got her,' she said quietly. Then, a little louder: 'You got her. OK? That means you don't need to get me, right? You said. You did.'

She seemed to listen to something, but there was nothing to hear except the nighttime noise of crickets chirping. 'You better not try to get me now, OK?' Her face puckered a little. 'Well, you better not! You *said*!'

The pond lay impassive, not even a ripple disturbing it, promising nothing.

Richie turned and ran up to the road.

In the Shop

Mrs Tedescho thought that hell must look exactly like the waiting room for Motorama Auto Service – same drab concrete walls, uncomfortable plastic chairs, and old magazines. There was no piped-in music; it would have been inaudible over the grinding yammer of drills and other tools. She sighed grumpily and looked at her watch. Over an hour now.

From the garage came the sound of an engine gunning ferociously.

She looked down at the article she'd been trying to get interested in. 'Rebore: Yes or No? The Answer Will Surprise You!' Mrs Tedescho doubted it. She flipped the pages of the magazine dispiritedly, tossed it on the battered coffee table in front of her, and picked up another. Something that sounded like a power saw arguing with a steel beam squawked and then cut off, leaving her nerves jangling.

'How Dependable Is *Your* Car?' asked serious black type on the page she'd absently opened to in the magazine. She made a face. That was like a bad comedy routine. *My car is so dependable. How dependable is it? It's so dependable that the moment I think I'm going to be able to spend a weekend accomplishing all the things I've been putting off for a month or more, it comes down with automobile flu.*

The edges of the magazine crumpled in her hands. She'd been driving home from work making a mental list of things to do when the damned thing had suddenly started running rough, chugging on hills, stalling on lights, and worst of all, dieseling abominably after she'd coaxed it into her driveway.

To Mrs Tedescho, dieseling was the height of automotive insolence.

Well, it had just better run after this, she thought grimly, or she'd take a tire iron to it. She wasn't prone to violence, but a car that ate fan belts the way this one did and developed mysterious leaks that cleared up as soon as a mechanic even glanced at it could bring out the beast in her.

She became aware of the thin, tinny sound of a radio playing rock music. *Wonderful*, she thought; *first metal tools, now metal music*. But no yammering drills rose to drown it out, and gradually she realized she hadn't heard anything but the radio for the last minute or so. *Now* what was going on in there?

A sign on the grease-stained door to the garage warned that only employees were allowed past that point; Mrs Tedescho ignored it and pushed through. The huge garage was completely still. Cars sat in repair bays with their hoods yawning open like forsaken dental patients.

'Hello?' she called, her voice echoing. 'What is this, lunchtime already?' No one answered. In the middle of the garage, a man's cap lay on the floor. She picked it up between two fingers. Mixed in with the old and new grease stains were spatters of dark red. There was some on the floor too. Near a gaping Toyota, a tall chest of tools had tipped over, scattering sockets all over the place. Whatever had happened had been covered by the sound of drills and other things.

A sudden sharp banging sound from the last repair bay made her jump.

She hurried to it, stepping over rags and tools and other caps strewn around the floor. Now she could hear the mutter of an engine perfectly tuned, the idle set low and throaty.

Hello?' she called again as she reached the bay. The car idling there revved, rolled forward a few inches, and stopped short.

'*There* you are, you bastard!' she shouted. 'What the *hell* are you doing? Do you *know* how long I've been waiting, reading goddamn *Motoring Monthly*? Thanks to you, the whole day is shot!' She slammed her purse down on the hood; the car backed up until its rear bumper thumped the wall.

'*Stop* that, you son of a bitch, and get this hood open!'

The hood popped up. Mrs Tedescho took one look and slammed it shut again.

'I *thought* so! You greedy, stinking piece of junk, you had to have all of them, didn't you. One wasn't enough, was it? Do you know what it's like trying to find a place that will take a foreign car? *You* ought to have to do it – then you wouldn't go around gobbling mechanics like fan belts!'

The hood popped open again, and a black cable came snaking out. Mrs Tedescho swatted it with her purse. 'Spoiled little shit today, aren't you?' She grabbed a nearby crowbar. 'Try that stuff with me and I'll turn your crankcase into a collander.' A tremor ran through the car from bumper to bumper as it squeaked mournfully. Mrs Tedescho dropped the crowbar, stood to one side, and crooked her finger. The car rolled forward, and the driver's side door swung open. 'Let's go,' she said, getting in. 'I'd like to get the grocery shopping done at least.'

She pounded the horn with her fist. 'I mean now, dammit!'

Whimpering, the car rolled through the empty garage.

Johnny Come Home

There was nothing for me to do in Moscow but drink.

Well, that and look for Johnny, and I no longer really had to do that. The Sense told me he was in the city, eventually our paths would cross and I would reel him in. But until that happened, I had to do something and drinking was it. Bars as Westerners know them were still relatively new in Moscow. Most of them little more than empty storefronts with the bare essentials; if you wanted atmosphere, you brought it with you. Or, if you were an especially wealthy tourist, you could go to one of the headjob parlors, where they gave you a happy-hood and a couple of gloves so you could enjoy your Stoli in whatever virtual environment they were running that night – provided, of course, you'd made your reservation the required six to eight months in advance.

I figured it was artificial reality either way and, not being an especially wealthy tourist, I opted for the austerity plan. Besides, in Moscow, it was the booze that carried importance, not the place where you drank it, and Stoli seemed to have a deeper understanding of the drinking organism. It certainly understood *me* – besides being mellow and friendly, it had the salutary effect of enhancing the Sense. The bad news was that sobering up dulled me, but that was easy enough to take care of.

So there I was, boozing and cruising in Moscow. They all envied me back home – my turn to fetch Johnny and I got to go to Russia to do it. First time I'd ever been off the North American continent, too. But here's a little Home Truth for you (and why not Home Truth, seeing as how we've had the Awful Truth, Nothing But the Truth, and Cheap Truth, God help us each and every one): one place is pretty much like another, and once I understood what I could do in Moscow, I might have been anywhere, the language difference notwithstanding. Even now – or maybe especially now, in the last weeks before the millennium turned. Well, not a full turn – next year would be the real first year of the new millennium, but everyone in the world seemed to be stuck on the idea that 2000 was the Big Year. Certain ideas died hard, and others wouldn't die at all. Like Johnny's ideas.

He could live a thousand years himself and never give up on those sweet, mad ideas. Master of my fate, captain of my soul, world full of miracles, tomorrow's another day (or another millennium), anything can happen and it probably will.

Yah. Dream about it, Johnny. He'd be doing that right now, somewhere in Moscow, living in his own brand of artificial reality, dreaming hard enough to kill someone while I held my place at a bar that had once been some kind of counter – kitchen? grocery? – it was hard to tell in this light – in another dingy ex-storefront.

As usual, there were lots of foreigners. Some were tourists and business travellers, but a good many of them were what the government was calling 'temporary long-term'. No doubt plenty of those were skating along on forged papers, hoping to find some way to establish residency later. Russia had been through a lot of changes in the 1990s right along with the rest of the world, but people themselves never really change, no matter where they are. Nor do situations. That's some more Home Truth, and you could figure that one out even without the Sense.

So I maintained, anyway. The Sense is not one hundred per cent infallible but the group back home believed it was a constant, all-over advantage. I was of two minds, you should pardon the expression, about that, myself, and it sometimes caused more friction among us than Johnny's periodic coop-flying. 'Loyal opposition' is not an easy concept to put over to organisms like us, but we all understood disloyal opposition. We had Johnny. Or we would when I brought him home again, tired, disillusioned, and hung-over from his freedom bender, to play docile prodigal and rejoin. Until all those sweet, mad ideas built up enough to set him off again.

I was on my third Stoli, watching the bartender sort out orders and make change, when the front door opened wide with a blast of frigid winter air. Over the multi-lingual gabble, someone started calling for papers in six different languages, and the person on my left dropped like a stone.

I looked down. A pretty, heart-shaped face framed by dark blond hair looked back up at me, eyes wide.

'Pamageeteh menye,' she whispered. *Help me.*

I was on the verge of telling her I wasn't Russian. Then I moved so that I was standing directly in front of her, my ankle-length coat spread to hide her. She had been at the end of the bar next to the wall, so perhaps no one had seen her duck. Even if someone had, this wasn't the type of crowd that would alert the immigration officers now moving through the place and shining flashlights on documents held up for inspection.

Chatter became hushed and most movement ceased, except for the sweep of the flashlight beams standing out hard in the smoky air, like light-swords in some old science fiction movie. The bartender moved slowly down the counter, picking up empty glasses, running a rag over the chipped formica, until he came to where I was standing. Folding his arms, he leaned against the wall and looked around in an aimless, bored way before letting his gaze rest pointedly to my left.

I showed him my passport and shrugged. He made a fist, wincing. His thoughts were like a bellow in my skull, a mostly incoherent expression of anger, at me with my coat so obviously spread, at the woman hiding behind it, at the immigration officers, at the world in general for interfering with him. He was very young, one of the post-*glasnost* generation, with no memory of a different time, when this empty storefront would have been equally empty even with a store in it, when he might have begged the blonde's jeans from her to sell on the black market and ended up crouching in the dark with her, hiding from the KGB, not immigration.

Or perhaps he was a member of a hate-group. I could get no clear indication from him. Even with plenty of warm, Sense-enhancing Stoli in me, his tension was an occluder.

The bartender's gaze shifted and I turned to look at the immigration officer now standing on my right. Without moving my elbows from the bar, I showed her my open passport. In the peripheral glow from the flashlight, her face was calm, unworried; she might have been an acquaintance looking at pictures of my family.

She moved the flashlight beam to my face. I stared past it to the two pinpoints of reflected light, all I could see of her eyes now. Everything stopped.

After a while, she said, 'Thank you, Maria Tell,' her accent making the words musical. She held her head high as she turned around. I could feel the bartender staring hard at me as the woman made her way to the door, where the other officers were waiting. They filed out in another blast of Moscow winter wind that cleared a little of the smoke and briefly over-rode the ancient space-heaters. I could still Sense her aching feet, her fatigue, her discomfort in the cold, her wish that they could just give this foreigner watering-hole a fast once-over and leave empty-handed, through for the night; and if by chance there were *refuseniks* with forged papers among the crowd, then please don't let her have to find them, let it be one of the others who would have to stay up the rest of the night inputting and contacting embassy officials and whatnot. All she wanted was to go home and see what had been downloaded from the International Net.

That made me the genie who had granted her wish. No wonder she'd thanked me so politely.

The blonde emerged from under my coat, swiping at her mussed hair and looking dazed, as if she had just awakened with no idea how she'd come to be here. 'God, I had no hope that would work, I was just desperate and crazy–' She saw the bartender and her expression became wary. But instead of throwing her out, he leaned on the bar and looked directly into my face.

'Do you have a brother?' he asked in heavily accented English.

And then, of course, I knew exactly what Johnny had been doing all this time in Moscow.

'I'm in it for the same reason as anybody else,' said the blonde, puffing along beside me in the cold. 'Artistic freedom.'

I made a polite noise, or tried to. My lungs felt frozen. The blonde's name was Evie Gray, and she was now my friend for life.

'The Russians *understand*,' she went on. 'They know what repression really *is*. They make movies here where people drink and use drugs, they can make fun of religion. They've got *Huckleberry Finn* in the libraries – it's pretty weird in Russian, but they've got it in the original English, too. And God, rock music! All kinds of stuff you can't hear in the States any more, old rap, new rap, heavy-fucking-metal that tells you to kill yourself, for chrissakes. And in the happy-hood parlors, it's anything goes, hardcore, softcore, violence, whatever you want, and no goddamn Council for the Prevention of Mind-Control to come in and pull the plug on you – hell, you can even get abortions on demand here, did you know that? On *demand*. All you have to do is walk into a clinic and you don't even have to give them a reason–'

'Still can't burn the Russian flag on the steps of the Kremlin,' I said. 'But I guess nobody's perfect, eh?'

She didn't hear me. She ran on and on about the Constitution being fucked like the air and water and land had been fucked and how it was just going to get worse and worse. Whether she was saying all this for my benefit or her own wasn't clear even to her. Not that it mattered any more. Her visa had run out three weeks before and she was now officially *refusenik*, subject to arrest and deportation.

I wondered if she was aware of the original meaning of *refusenik*, but I wasn't curious enough to use the Sense to find out. There were scads of these new *refuseniks* running around Moscow and elsewhere in the Soviet Union. I couldn't decide whether they were yet another pre-millennial nut-group, the start of a real movement, or just more people living in their own brand of artificial reality. But then, I predated the Berlin Wall and, at my age, sometimes everybody looked like just another nut. Even when the Sense told me they were all quite sane, if not especially wise.

What Evie Gray was more than anything else was especially wealthy. I didn't point out to her that this was the only way she could have managed this dramatic flight to freedom. It's yet another Home Truth that only the richest and the poorest ever attain freedom, the richest because they can afford it, the poorest because nobody's ever looking for them.

'You don't share a brother–sister resemblance,' said the woman with the long, straight hair. 'More like mother and son. If you'll pardon my saying so.'

I smiled at her; she didn't smile back. Russians were sparing with their smiles. Whoever had taught her English had been from Boston. 'He's adopted.'

'Excuse me?' She looked puzzled.

'Nothing. Yuri at the Kropotkin hard currency bar gave me this address.'

Her gaze slid to Evie Gray. 'Did something happen at the Kropotkin?'

'No. Almost, but it was averted,' I said.

'Good answer,' Evie murmured.

'I understand,' said the woman, stepping to the dark velvet curtain behind her. She sounded friendlier but she still didn't smile. 'You realize that this is a very exclusive *mesto;* foreign visitors who come here must reserve many months in advance and the waiting list is already a year long.'

The bundle in Evie's outthrust hand was obscenely thick. 'I can pay.'

The woman made it disappear almost before my new American friend realized she had taken it. 'Next time, you should be more discreet. Put it in a little sack and pass it. If others saw, you could be marked as worth robbing.'

'I wouldn't let that happen,' I said, 'but we promise we'll be more careful in the future.'

'*Harashow*. This way.' She pulled the curtain aside and stepped into the headjob parlor.

I liked the simple descriptiveness of their name for it: *mesto* – literally, *place*. *Some place else* might have been more like it. The Russians had embraced virtual reality with a religious fervor. Having been through only a few days of a Russian winter and hearing it called unseasonably warm, I could understand. But virtual reality was just as major in the States and any other country developed enough to maintain the technology. I could understand that, too. It was merely the next logical step after television and video games, really.

The *mesto* wasn't much like an American arcade. Instead of little single or double booths, there were rows of what looked like old barber chairs, about fifty altogether, all of them occupied by people wearing headpieces and action-gloves. Lots of weird hand-motions going on, some I could guess at and some I wouldn't have wanted to. They were no individual units – all the cables from the equipment disappeared into the floor. Centralized transmission; no variety, but it would make the *mesto*'s operating costs a lot cheaper, increasing the profit margin to something that even an old 1980s greed-is-good throwback would call more than respectable.

'How long have you been operating?' I asked the woman as I followed her to the end of the last row of chairs.

'Almost a year,' she said.

At the end of the row was a vacant chair, the only one in

the room, with a headpiece sitting on it like an abandoned crown. 'Your companion bought you an hour's worth,' the woman said, gesturing at it. 'Take your pleasure.'

I blew out an irritated breath. 'That's not what I'm here for.'

'If you want to see your *brother*, you'll take the hour.' She picked up the headpiece and held it out to me.

It didn't make any sense, and I was having a hard time with the Sense as well. The long, cold walk from the Kropotkin had sobered me up and I was dull. But the little flicker that I managed to get from her indicated that somehow, she was telling the truth. Maybe Johnny wanted me all tangled up with wires and distracted with fancy pictures before he'd talk to me, figuring that would keep me from sussing him out. As if this artificial reality could come between us any better than the one he'd made for himself. Dream on, and on, and on, Johnny.

The woman helped me with the gloves and then started to put the headpiece on me. 'I'd like some Stoli, please,' I said.

'This is not a voluta bar,' she said. 'We don't serve anything. If you wanted drinks, you should have brought your own.'

'Get her some vodka.' Evie slipped a hand into her pocket. 'You can get me some, too.'

The woman hesitated.

'And bring a straw. You know, one of those hollow tube things you can suck liquids through?' I added, in response to her blank look. 'Unless you're hiding some dispensers for the headpieces?'

'Yeah, it's the same fuck-the-tourists crap all over,' said Evie.

'Shut up,' I told her.

'Sometimes there's a bottle back in the office. A straw–' the woman shrugged. 'I'll see what I can find.' She took something from Evie – discreetly enough, I supposed – and slipped out a nearby door. Evie moved to help me with the headpiece.

'Hold it,' I said.

She drew back a little, looking stung.

'I can't go on helping you indefinitely, you know.'

'Can't?' She gave me a fast, pained grin. 'You mean *won't*, right?'

'Look, I can fix it so tired cops don't see what they don't want to see. But I don't forge residency papers. And I'm not staying in Russia any longer than I have to.'

'But you could make someone forge papers for me, couldn't you?'

I wanted to shake her. 'Is this place really so much better than the US? You think Russia is heaven just because they've got *Huckleberry Finn* on the shelves and rap music on the radio and abortion on demand? Does the name "Stalin" mean anything to you? How about "Pamyat"? They were just another anti-Semitic hate group in the early 1990s, but now even their staunchest sympathizers are afraid of them. And they're not the only haters running around loose, all of them with their own agendas, but two things they all agree on: they hate Jews and they hate *refuseniks*. You think all of the missing ones are just blending in with their forged papers? Plenty of them are lying on slabs in a Moscow morgue, gutted like cattle, courtesy of Pamyat.'

'Pamyat is a bad word around here. Don't use it.' The woman reappeared and thrust a bottle that was a little over half-full at me. 'Scares away our business. Sorry, no straw. And I have no idea what you'll do with it when you're inside.'

I took a couple of healthy swigs and stuck the bottle between my thighs. She shrugged and looked at Evie.

'I'll wait right here,' Evie said.

'Hurry up and take your hour. There's a long line behind you.' She pushed the headpiece all the way down so that my face was covered and the eye-screen lit up immediately.

I joined a standard dolphin's-eye sequence. As soon as artificial reality had become feasible for the mass-market, everyone had gone for the dolphin and whale stuff. Out of guilt, maybe: sorry we killed so many of you, so we'll be you, or pretend we are. I would have been bored except the quality was way beyond anything I'd ever seen before. The Russians must have been cranking away on hardware R&D, boosting definition and whatever else. But the headpiece hadn't looked like it was anything so extraordinary.

The perspective cruised past a formation of opalescent, eye-shaped bodies that turned right and then left as one, lifting themselves out of my path like a curtain. Near a boulder, a fleshy squid ignored me, its tentacles rippling. Seaweed drifted, sank away into the shadows. Nothing new here, nothing in the least, but the quality – my inner ear kept flashing swimming messages to my stomach, where the disloyal Stoli had turned on me with a threat. Disloyal opposition. I hung on to the arms of the chair and tried to keep part of my awareness tuned to where I knew my body was, waiting for Johnny's presence to press in on the Sense.

I might have been cruising the ocean for ten minutes, or almost the whole hour; my sense of time had slipped away like one more darting ocean creature. But the novelty was wearing off and I felt bored, impatient, and slightly dizzy.

The perspective made a sudden wide arc to the left and passed through a multi-colored rock formation. Something with nasty looking jaws peered out of a dark hole but never moved as I passed.

Just beyond the rocks was a giant clam, the ridges of the shell perfectly formed. It began to open as I approached – more standard stuff – displaying the giant pearl in the giant clam was usually the climax and indicated a change to the next sequence. So much for my hour and finding Johnny, I thought, watching the clamshell rise. When I got out of the chair, I was going to chug the rest of the Stoli and use the Sense to make the *mesto* hostess do cartwheels until she dropped.

Sadistic idea. Not like you, Maria.

The clamshell was gaping wide and it wasn't a pearl displayed there but a man, curled up in the fetal position. He unfolded slowly and gracefully, the way everything moves underwater, and turned to look at me.

Same old sweet, mad Johnny. His shoulder-length brown hair was floating around his head, his hazel eyes were like stars in his lovely, open face.

The Sense couldn't get a good fix on you until you jerked the cop in the voluta bar. I used the Sense on the cops just that same way myself, till I found something better. He smiled at me. *Come for to carry me home, sweet Maria? Sorry, not this time. This time, I beat you. I beat you all.*

You always say that, Johnny. What is it now, a woman, or another man again? Even without the Sense you could make them fall in love with you. Lots of people can do that. But you can't make them love you. That's something very different from falling in love, Johnny, and after the last three times, I'd have thought you'd have known that. You'll end up killing this one with your needs, too. Just like the others. The group forgives your sin because we understand. But nobody else will. At the very least, they'll put you in jail and there you'll be, far from us and us far from you, all of us feeling the Lack. That's bad, Johnny. Remember how bad it is to feel the Lack? After your lover isn't falling in love with you any more and you're without us?

I was working the Sense on him, of course, and he was pushing back just as hard, maintaining the balance of pressure as only those endowed with the Sense could. It was a balance he couldn't have with someone outside the group, the give and take of the Sense that we all needed, whether Johnny wanted to admit his own need or not.

It's different this time, Maria. I let my lover go right after I found this.

Found what — artificial reality? You can get that anywhere. Come home and we'll buy you your own booth.

But they don't have centralized transmission back in the States. A multitude all looking at once, invisible to each other but all visible

to me. And I can have them all, not just one at a time but together.
He spread his arms. *I found this lonely technician, got her to scan
my likeness into the simulation. The scanning equipment here is so
much better than ours, they've been working so much harder on it.
And between me and my likeness—*

He didn't have to explain. Even without the Sense, I could
have felt how it was, I think. Johnny's likeness might as well
have been him. It had its own power within the artificial
universe, blocking our little exchange from the rest of the
clientele. A hundred people looking and none of them saw.
I would have said a connection between a living being with
the Sense and a likeness was impossible, except obviously
none of us had tried it until now.

*Of course, I have to stay in . . . keep the headpiece on, and the
gloves. They're making a whole suit for me, it's almost finished.
What I've done for business here – it was great before but now it's
taken a real jump. We're going to expand. More of them for me,
more and more, wanting to be in some beautiful, otherworldly place,
one that I create. They give me their wanting and needing and I
feel no Lack, none at all. I don't have to stay locked into the group
any more, Maria. I'm free now.* Free.

*Why, Johnny? Who do you have to have them? Why don't you
just come home and get the same thing from the ones who really
know you and understand you?*

He looked away from me, dreamily reaching up to run a
finger along the belly of a passing shark.

Because it is always the same. I want different. *I want to wake
up in the morning knowing that I might see anybody, be with
anybody, go anywhere. This way, I can. I don't want to be chained
to the group, the way so many of them are chained to lives they
never wanted. This way, anything really is possible. It really is a
world full of miracles.*

*Dream about it, Johnny. I worked the Sense harder on him.
It's still only a dream, and when you wake up, you'll still be what
you've always been.*

The push came so forcefully that I would have sworn he'd
found someone else with the Sense and the two of them

were ganging up on me. The likeness, I realized; Johnny had invested a great deal in it as the would-be escape hatch from the prison of his life, and wherever Johnny went, the Sense went with him. I had Stoli, but Johnny had this, and it was bigger.

Still, I strained for him, trying to make him – him and his likeness? – acknowledge the connection between us and fortify its existence.

I almost had him. Perhaps I had had him – his miracle world was more wonderful, but I was more familiar.

And then rough hands tore the headpiece away and I heard the *mesto* hostess say, 'Time's up.'

The cold was what really brought me to, though I was already staggering along Gorky Street. Famous Gorky Street, I remembered; every few years the Russians would change the name to something else, but for some reason they'd always end up changing it back again. Evie Gray had her shoulder wedged under my armpit and my arm slung across her shoulders. She was chattering away but my head was too bad to make sense (or Sense) of what she was saying and the traitor Stoli in my gut was like a washing machine on the heavy soil setting.

Somehow, little old Evie knew – I say it's a Home Truth that in times of stress, everybody's got a tiny spot of the Sense – and got me to an alley where I could throw up in peace. Goodbye Stoli, and goodnight, Gracie. Or Evie. I was dulled out.

After a while, Evie got me moving again. She was still chattering – Christ, this woman never ran out of breath, I guess – and I caught the word *problem*.

'The real problem, Evie, old girl,' I said, talking loudly over her, 'the real problem here – and I think the Russians really do understand this–' I swing my free arm out to gesture at an empty storefront and almost sent us both down on the cold pavement ' – the real problem is, people think life is a ladder, and it's really a wheel. That's a real Home Truth and we ignore it. It's there for us to see, everything is there for us to see, we've got Home Truth coming out of our ears, we know everything there is to know to get us through the day in one piece, and we ignore it like it doesn't exist. Hell, the *earth* is round, it *turns*, you'd think anyone could take a hint that blatant, but even someone with the Sense, who's supposed to know a little more than the average pilgrim, can still look Home Truth right in the kisser and say, 'No, thanks, artificial reality for me, please.' I don't know what to do about that, Evie. Even with the Sense, I just don't know what to do about it.'

I heard her clear her throat. 'Why don't you just shut up?'

She took a real chance dumping me at Intourist. She could have just left me on the street for the authorities to pick up – probably nothing would have happened, I wasn't *refusenik*, after all – and the fact that she got me indoors before she disappeared indicated a sweet generosity of spirit within that foolish chatterbox exterior. I liked her retroactively, for all the good that would do her.

I got a plane out the next morning – all I had to do was find an Aeroflot ticket agent with a xenophobic bent and give a little push. The genie of the bottle grants your wish and leaves your country.

The layover in London was supposed to be just a few hours, but Gatwick shut down indefinitely with a bomb scare – bomb scares were coming more frequently as 31 December approached – so I took the train into London, figuring I might as well be comfortable. Besides, I'd never seen London.

Forgot my own Home Truth: one place is pretty much like another. There was nothing for me to do in London either but drink. But London *really* understands the drinking organism the way Moscow was trying to. The pubs were warm and mellow. Guinness was even better on the Sense than Stoli had been, and I almost didn't care when Gatwick stayed shut another day and another, and Heathrow with it.

I didn't call home. They'd all know by now, anyway. I would only be telling them the details, and those could wait.

Those could wait and I could drink, and like anyone in artificial reality, I lost track of the time, which was how I came to be in London on Christmas Eve, looking down a week to the (artificial) dawn of the (artificial) new millennium. Feeling the Lack and filling it with Guinness. Travel was impossible now. There were riots every day, and not just in London. The Messiah was coming, they said; the Messiah was coming.

Then the transmissions from Russia began. But I didn't bother trying to tell anyone that it wasn't really the Messiah. Just Johnny.

Happy-hood parlors all over London filled up, left the pubs empty (more for me, I thought, wavering at times between bitter and Guinness). Centralized transmission. No variety, but the quality . . . oh, the quality. Lost nothing bouncing off a satellite, not with Johnny on the job. Johnny on the spot, all the spots. The (artificial) dawn of the (artificial) new millennium. What everyone wanted all along, I guess.

And as to what Johnny wanted . . . not to be chained, to be free. He got both, thanks to the Sense, in any reality he chooses.

The Sense is a funny thing, and it can even be a good thing. I worked it pretty hard on him, but as I told Evie Gray, nobody's perfect. We'll get what we wanted, too, me and the rest of the group back in the States, when the transmissions to America begin, when poor, sweet, mad Johnny finally comes home.

The Coming of the Doll

I'm not a screamer, but I scream anyway. Once, loud and long, and when nothing happens at the end of it, I scream again, much louder and a good deal longer. And, still, nothing happens, nothing changes. There is still a charming little baby doll lying on its back in Rowena's crib with its butter-soft plastic limbs sticking up in the air and its Cupid's-bow mouth permanently puckered around a small hole meant for a baby-doll bottle. I do not touch the doll; the fingerprints of whoever took Rowena and left it in her place could be on it. I have enough presence of mind to think of that even if I am screaming.

I look at the window. It's open but I opened it myself this morning. If the kidnapper came in that way, he was careful to close the screen behind him when he left. I back out of the room slowly – nice room, decorated bit by bit all the months I was pregnant, pleasant without being icky-sweet – and run down the hall to the stairs.

Someone is banging on the front door, hard, and the door-bell is going mad, bonging so fast it can barely keep up with itself. I hesitate, clutching the rail until I hear Betty Thornton's voice calling over and over, 'Sharon, are you all right? Sharon? Sharon?'

She's heard me, I realize. I screamed and she heard me. I run down the stairs, thumping, almost slipping on the carpeting and fetch up against the door. Clumsily, I paw the chain lock off and flip the deadbolt, thinking he could not have come in this way, not through the chain lock and the dead-bolt. Then the door is open and Betty's mouth is moving and her eyes are blinking and she shakes me hard, even though I'm not screaming any more.

'Rowena's gone,' I tell her. 'Someone took her. Someone climbed through her bedroom window and took her.'

Betty is all in-charge and calm authority. She has three children, and she knows when to get the Band-Aids and when to call the hospital. 'Are you sure?' she says, giving me a final shake to settle everything inside me back where it should be. 'Are you sure she didn't just crawl off somewhere?'

'She was having her nap in her crib,' I tell her. 'She can't crawl well enough, and even if she could, she couldn't get out of her crib without falling, I would have *heard* her!'

This convinces Betty. She pushes me down on the sofa and goes for the telephone. She dials the police from memory – *memory*, she's that kind of mother – and speaks quickly but clearly. When she finishes, she looks toward the stairs and then at me, and decides to stay down here.

'They'll be here right away,' she says, sitting down and folding one arm around my shoulder. 'You calm down so you can tell them what happened. I'll be right here by you.' I ask her what about her own kids, out playing with a child-snatcher loose, and she tells me not to worry, they aren't babies and they won't go with strangers. I worry anyway, thinking the kidnapper must be collecting children, picturing him – yes, *him*, kidnappers have always been *hims* to me – with a large black sack full of dolls. He is exchanging them for children, and now Rowena is at the bottom of the sack, suffocating under a load of squirming arms and legs, all children he has taken and replaced with dolls. Why am I thinking that? Betty dabs at my face with a tissue, and I realize I'm crying tears of fear. Tears of fear, tears of fear, my mind says over and over until the police come in the still-open front door.

I jump up. Betty restrains me from flinging myself at the uniforms. All I really see are the uniforms, deep dark blue with shiny, no-fooling badges. And guns. God bless the guns, they look so beautifully huge. They'll shoot the man with the sack dead, and all the children will come home again. Rowena, too.

It takes both me and Betty to tell them what's wrong. They look from one of us to the other, following the volley of our words back and forth. Then one says, 'Bert, you have a look upstairs. Try to stay calm, Mrs Petersen. Where is your husband?' I tell him I'm divorced as Bert goes up the stairs. I can see by the position of his arm that he has his hand on his gun, even though I've said there is no one up there. 'Could her father have taken her?' the policeman asks me. I shake my head. Am I sure? I'm sure. Was there a custody fight? No, no custody fight. I am explaining that I am between jobs and living on savings with Betty interpreting the garbled spots, when Bert comes to the head of the stairs and says, 'Dave, you'd better have a look at this.'

Dave looks up at his partner and sees something very, very bad, something I have not seen, and I grab at Betty until she has to press my hands between hers. Then he looks at me and sees something even worse, and I think that the man with the sack must have dropped Rowena, dropped her out the window and killed her, and they think I did it.

We all go up the stairs, Betty and I following Dave slowly because I can't let go of her. He leads us down the hall to the cheerful-awful room. If Betty were not holding me, I would not be able to go in. But she is being brave for me, and we do go in. Bert is already back in the room, looking not out the window but down into the crib. Dave goes across the room and looks, too. Then they both turn to me and Bert says, 'Mrs Petersen, do you take drugs?'

Betty disengages herself from me and walks to the crib as though the floor were made of eggs. I stand just inside the doorway all alone now, unable to think why they are asking me if I take drugs? Drugs? *Drugs?* What have they found in Rowena's crib that I did not see? All three of them are staring at me and their eyes say they cannot believe themselves. So I go, too, across the room and look down into the crib.

The doll is still there. It hasn't moved, of course. It can't move unless I move it, and I haven't moved it because of the fingerprints.

Betty touches my shoulder the way I have seen her touch her best crystal. 'See, Sharon?' she says. 'Rowena must have, ah, crawled under the blanket and hid from you.' Her eyes are not right, the way they're on me.

Bert – or Dave, suddenly I can no longer tell them apart – lifts the doll's little shirt with a careful finger. The afternoon sun is harsh on the plastic navel-less stomach. 'About three months, is that right? She seems well-treated.' He sounds dubious, but then he smiles. 'Don't want to wake the little beauty. Maybe we'd better go back to the living room and, ah, thrash this out.'

The other policeman – marked *Shelton*, I see for the first time, but I still don't know if it's Bert or Dave – is having trouble with his face. His mouth is sliding around and he can't decide whether he should look at me or Betty. Betty's arm slips around my shoulders and grips me firmly. 'I think we should call someone first, officer,' she says. 'Someone to look after the baby while I stay with Sharon.'

The baby? *'The baby?'* I say, looking into Betty's face. I can't believe I heard her right, but there is something she finds equally incredible of me. I can tell. Our eyes are mirrors.

Then I jump forward and yank the light summer blanket out of the crib. It's yellow, soft, with little green horses galloping all over it. 'Do you see a baby hiding in this blanket?' I demand, shaking it to show there's nothing in it, nothing at all. I throw it on the floor and pick up a rattle. 'Can a baby hide behind this? Or this?' I am plucking Rowena's toys out of the crib like vermin, a spongy ball, a soft plastic train, a teddy bear, and hurling them to the floor until there is nothing on the mattress but that hideous sweet doll. I grab it up by one leg and hold it out over the floor. 'Do you see a baby here?' I shout. 'Do you? This is just a doll! It's nothing but a *doll!*'

The silence in the room is horrified. Then the Shelton policeman has his hands under the doll as though it were alive. He looks into my eyes and he says, so quietly, so gently, 'Mrs Petersen, please let go.'

I do and now I am the horrified one, because he is holding that thing like a baby, exactly the way you should hold a baby, and its eyes are open. It's an expensive doll with eyes that fall open and closed, and brown curly hair, not just painted on, the kind you can really comb. But it could never be mistaken for a real child and it looks nothing like Rowena. Her hair is dark, yes, but not so curly and her mouth is not a frozen Cupid's-bow. But the Shelton policeman is murmuring to it, and Betty's hands are fluttering around me like pesky birds, and the other policeman is saying, 'Mrs Thornton, do you know Mrs Petersen well enough to tell if this is her daughter?'

And Betty says—

Oh, God, Betty says – she says—

'Yes, that's Rowena. I've babysat her and I have three of my own. I *know* one child from another and that's Rowena.'

I slap her traitorous paws away from me. How can she? How can she? Anyone can see it isn't a child! Anyone but Betty and these two awful policemen.

And then Betty is telling them all kinds of things about me, about how Rowena broke up my marriage because Jeff couldn't stand her getting all my attention and how I lost my job and blamed Rowena and Rowena got sick and I slept through her screaming and I would have gone on sleeping if Betty hadn't come by and Rowena began choking and I didn't know what to do and I use sleeping pills because I can't adjust to the divorce.

'You sneak!' I shout in her face. 'You snooped in my medicine cabinet, *how dare you!*'

Betty looks hurt, like I slapped her, but she's the one who slapped me, going through my things, telling the police gossip about me, insisting this plastic thing is Rowena. They all look to each other, and I see they have decided on a common expression to use because their faces are identical when they turn to me again. The Shelton policeman gently transfers the doll they think is Rowena to Betty's arms, and I run out of the room.

I only mean to run into the hall where I won't have to watch this travesty, but the policemen holler in rough voices. They scare me so much I run down the stairs faster than before when Betty was pounding and ringing to get in. The Police are thundering down the steps after me, and that scares me even more because they are obviously deranged, mistaking a doll for my Rowena. I'm out the screen door with them still chasing me when I realize they are not deranged at all, they are in league with the man with the sack.

And then I really run, pumping my legs for all I'm worth, across the street without looking and between two houses. My chest is burning already, I'm no jogger, but I keep going because if I stop I won't stand a chance of getting Rowena back. They'll force me to accept the doll and treat it like a baby, and I'll never see my daughter again.

Behind the houses is an alleyway where the garbage trucks go to pick up trash. I cut across the unfenced yard on the right, surprising the man standing at the barbecue with a steak speared on a long fork. I see in passing that his little boy is playing in a sandbox, moving trucks and cars around. The man with the sack wouldn't dare try to take that little boy, his father would stab him like a steak with that fork, I just know it. I don't wonder what the father thinks about the policemen chasing me across his yard. I can't think about anything except getting away and the burning that has become a squeezing wildfire in my chest. The alley is cracked and pitted with ice heaves and potholes, but I'm leaping over them and skirting around them. I'm not going to trip and fall. I'd let Rowena down if I tripped, and I'm not going to let her down this time.

At the end of the alley I see the police car pull up and stop. I veer away to the left, and almost before I know it, I leap a fence, hit the grass on my feet and keep running, glad for once all I ever wear are jeans and sneakers, nothing nicer. I pound through the yard, around the house and burst through the front gate. Then across another street, into another yard and down another alley. My knees are beginning to weaken, my thighs are shaky, and there is no oxygen in the great whoops of air I take. But I run, for Rowena I run between the houses and down the sidewalks until the houses aren't even vaguely familiar and the penned dogs in the fenced yards snarl in deadly earnest, smelling the total stranger of me, just the way they would snarl at the man with the sack if he came here. When I finally pound to a stop, my whole body jarred with each slowing step and my chest rising and collapsing like crazy bellows, when I bend over coughing with my trembling hands on my watery knees, no one comes up behind me to say I'm under arrest. I am alone. I have outrun the police. All for Rowena. I see now that it's true that maternal instinct enables a woman to perform super-human feats. By outrunning the police I have just performed one. Because I am a good mother and have the maternal instinct. I could chew through solid steel to get to my child. I could lift ten thousand pounds if my child were under them. I could sprout wings and fly to the moon if my child were stranded there. I would never let her lie for hours in dirty diapers while I slept knocked-out on sleeping pills. A doll perhaps, but not Rowena.

I look around as my breath comes back, but there are still no police in sight. It is a miracle that they don't know where I am. I'm standing on the sidewalk of a street not very unlike my own. I wonder if the babies on this street will grow up to go to school with Rowena after I get her back. Across from me is the edge of the park, where older children go to play on the swings and the seesaws and hang upside-down on the jungle gym, or just run around on the grass or climb on the picnic tables. The man with the sack would love to come here and carry off unattended children, leaving dolls lying on the ground for their grieving mothers to find later.

It occurs to me he is there now, wandering through the park with his sack. I will find him and grab that sack away from him and wrestle Rowena out of it. Then I'll run home and show them, all of them, the policemen and that gossipy Betty Thornton and the man with the fork, that my Rowena couldn't possibly be that doll.

I go quickly across the street and into the park, down a grassy slope to the picnic table area. The swings and seesaws and jungle gym are further on. I can hear the children playing on them. I'm heading straight for the voices when I see the woman sitting reading at the picnic table with the doll standing nearby.

I can't help it. I have to stop when I see the doll. It's three feet high and its skin is too pink to be real, its cheeks too plump, the golden banana curls too perfect. Yes. I recognize it now, from when I was a little girl. It's a Shirley Temple doll, left there by the man with the sack. He has exchanged it for the real little girl while her mother was reading, and the real little girl is now in the sack with Rowena and the other children. And then I realize that this doll he has left is *my* doll, *mine*.

I take a step toward it. The woman closes her book with a snap and stands up. 'Time to go home, Denice. Daddy'll be home any time now and he wants his supper when he wants it.'

The doll just stands. Of course it doesn't answer. It just smiles and holds its arms out as though it were a real little girl who wanted a hug. But it isn't. The woman doesn't seem to know this.

'Don't one-more-minute me, we've been out here for hours, let's go!' She grabs the doll's arm and begins dragging it away across the grass. The doll bumps along clumsily and after a few steps the woman stops. 'Pick up your feet, can't you? You're wearing down your shoes and they cost a god-damn fortune!' She gives the doll an angry yank. I put my hands over my face and turn away. This is too horrible. The woman doesn't know her little girl is gone. She has no maternal instinct, not like me.

I force myself to walk in the other direction. It's too late for her. If I find her little girl when I get Rowena back from that awful man with the sack, I will keep her myself. I'll tell the police she's my niece or my cousin. I won't let them take her; they don't know the difference between a real girl and a doll, either.

Almost to the swings, I stop again. There is a little girl, a *real* little girl sitting on the grass, playing with a doll. I have to rub my eyes because the afternoon light makes the doll almost – *almost*, not quite – look like a baby. But it's stiff, with straight blonde hair that is obviously fake, like a bad wig. The little girl is holding it and talking to it as though it were a baby, the way little girls play. I think, how sweet, and then, no, *no*. Little girls shouldn't play just with dolls. They should have other toys so they won't be stereotyped, so they won't be fooled into thinking they have the maternal instinct if they really don't have it. When I get Rowena back I'll let her have only one doll. Just one. So she won't get fooled, like–

The little girl suddenly holds the doll up and says, 'Alice Ann, you're a bad, bad girl!' And then for *no reason* she lays the doll across her lap and spanks her!

I rush over. 'Stop it! What has she done for you to punish her this way?'

The girl looks up at me. She is a solemn little thing of eight or nine. I hope Rowena will be much happier when she's that age and not spank the one doll I give her.

'Who're you?' the girl asks. Her hand still hovers over that poor, no, plastic bottom. I squat down and pick the doll out of her lap, straightening its clothes and stroking its hair. It's a very pretty doll, though nowhere near as pretty as Rowena. Not even as pretty as the doll that the man with the sack left in its, *her* place. This doll has only painted eyes that stay open even during naptime. Painted eyelashes, too, and raggedy hair. But it's pretty because it's a baby. A baby doll.

'I'm a mommy,' I tell the girl. 'A real mommy with a real baby.'

'Where is it?'

'*She*. She's–' I could almost choke this brutal little brat, but then I see she's not really unkind, just thoughtless. She lacks the maternal instinct. Her little face is innocent. 'She's not with me right now. I'm on my way to get her. You should treat your baby much gentler. She's only a little tiny girl and she can't take spankings yet.' When I get Rowena back, I'll never spank her unless she's really, *really* bad. That's not going to be till she's much older, naturally.

The girl takes the doll away from me and holds her possessively. Holds her all wrong, too. 'Not like that,' I say. 'You'll hurt her. Hold her like this, with your arm supporting her little head. There. That's right. Make a cradle of your arms.' The girl is watching me with suspicion, but I don't care. They're all suspicious at that age. Except I hope Rowena won't be. 'You know, a terrible thing can happen if you don't treat your baby right.'

'Like what?' she challenges. She doesn't believe me.

'Well,' I say, being patient as all good mothers are, 'my mother told me a long time ago that if I wasn't a good girl, a man with a great big black sack would come and he'd put me in the sack and in my place he'd leave a –' No. That isn't right. I know it isn't because I'm not in the sack. 'If you're not good to your little girl,' I begin again more confidently, 'a man with a great big black sack will come and take your baby away and he'll leave a doll in her place. You wouldn't want that to happen, would you?'

The girl looks down at the doll and up at me again. 'But Alice Ann *is* a doll. She's not a real baby.'

'In that case, you'd better be extra good to her,' I warn, 'or the man with the sack will come and he'll take the doll and leave a real baby behind. And real babies are an awful lot of trouble to take care of, much more trouble than dolls. Do you know any lullabies?'

She only knows 'Rockabye Baby.' We are halfway through

our third time singing it when the police finally catch up with me.

It has taken a lot of fast talking, but they haven't locked me up. I could tell they didn't really want to as we rode back to my house in the patrol car. The police are very busy and don't lock someone up just because she has the maternal instinct. That isn't a crime. I didn't tell them about the man with the sack, though, and I guess that is a crime, but they'd never find him anyway. Only mothers can find him, mothers who really have the maternal instinct, and babies.

When we came home, I went straight into the house and found Betty sitting in the living room in my rocking chair, rocking the doll. The sight of her with it in her arms made me so tired. I didn't argue with her. I just took the doll from her and held it exactly the way she did. Then *I* sat down in the rocking chair and *I* rocked the doll. Betty talked to the policemen for a long time, but I didn't pay any attention. I just stared at the doll, moving it up and down so its eyes opened and closed more like a real child's would. The policemen finally went away but Betty stayed. She called her husband and then she sat down on the couch and watched me. She's still sitting there and she's still watching me, but not as closely as she was. She keeps looking at the electric clock on the TV set, like she's waiting. Well, I'm waiting, too. The front door is still open and the daylight is fading through the screen. After Betty leaves, I'm going to let the front door stay open like that, with the screen door unlocked. I have an idea.

If I'm very, very good to this doll and demonstrate that I really do have the maternal instinct by changing her diapers right away and not sleeping through her crying, the man with the sack might come back and return Rowena. It's a chance. I could have been wrong, back there in the park. Maybe if you're good to your doll, the man with the sack comes and gives you a real baby. Maybe he'll come this evening. I'm going to expect him. Betty acts like she's expecting someone herself. Couldn't be him, though. Betty's always had the maternal instinct. It's inevitable after three kids, I bet.

But I've had only Rowena, and I didn't have her very long. Nonetheless, I know I have the maternal instinct, too. I'll prove it with the doll.

And yet, that could be a problem, I think to myself, moving the doll up and down. The eyes open and close. Open and close. Click-click. Click-click. Dolls never cry. How will I know when she's hungry? How will she tell me?

In the Dark

My mother had an IV going in one arm and a tube in her nose, and the stitches in her lip where her teeth had gone through looked like little black spiders. In my family, we're built to take it. If she'd been conscious, my mother probably would have made a Timex joke about it herself. Great sense of humor, my mother. Of course, she wouldn't have found it too funny if she'd known I'd taken the Timex off and flung it as hard as I could into the darkness of Comanche Park. With any luck, she'd be too distracted to think about it after she woke up. I hadn't wanted the Timex and I didn't need it to know that it was after midnight now, so it wasn't my birthday any more.

Actually, I was thinking mostly about Jonas as I sat in the dimly lit hospital room. I wished he'd change his mind and come in even just for a few minutes. Of course, I couldn't have said what that would have accomplished; Mom was asleep, sedated-asleep, and I wouldn't have been able to rouse her even if I'd wanted to. And it probably wouldn't have been so great for Jonas to see her like this, but considering what-all-else he'd seen tonight and other nights, I couldn't see where it would be especially harmful, either.

I knew what my mother would have said about it. She'd have told me to stop moping around in a hospital room and go see to my little brother – she was taken care of, whereas he was probably down in the solarium watching God-knew-what on TV. Get him out of there, Jan, she'd say, get him to bed and make sure he gets off to school all right, I'll be home by the time school lets out tomorrow afternoon.

Unh-unh, not this time, Mom, I said silently. I'm no expert but a tube up the nose doesn't suggest a simple overnight to recover from a few contusions.

I felt pretty grown-up, knowing a word like *contusions*. *Contusions. Abrasions. Lacerations. Subdural hematoma.* I've always had a big vocabulary.

The door whispered open slightly and the nurse who had assisted in the ER poked her head in. She didn't exactly smile at me but it was a friendly type of look. She knew us; she'd been on duty some of the other times. I knew what she wanted and I didn't want to discuss it around my mother's inert body, so I got up and went out into the hall with her.

'Does your mother still have the number for the shelter?' she asked me quietly.

I shrugged.

'I can give it to you, then. You and Jonas could go there now. I'm sure they have space for you at least for tonight.'

'Thanks,' I said, 'but I just don't get a good night's sleep unless I'm in my own bed.' My mother used that one whenever the hospital tried to keep her, when she could talk.

She took my chin between her fingers and made my look into her face. It was a very nice face; she was maybe twenty-three. That would put her in the second grade when I was born. I tried to picture it, her as a second-grader and me as a baby.

'Everything is *not* all right now,' she said. 'If your mother isn't going to think about what she's going to do, then *you* have to. For your sake, and for your brother's.'

I pulled away from her. 'Jeez, I better go find him. He'll never get up for school tomorrow.'

She caught my arm. 'You can't go on this way. I know you're a smart girl, Janet–'

'*Jan*. Just Jan.'

'–and if no one's going to think about you and your brother, then you have to. I know it's a hell of a burden to put on a fifteen-year-old girl–'

'Sixteen,' I said. 'Today's my birthday. I mean, yesterday. Yesterday was my birthday.'

She gave my arm a squeeze. 'All right, sixteen. You *know* you have options. Take them. It'll be hard, but can anything by worse than this?'

I prised her fingers off my upper arm. 'I don't know,' I said, 'but it looks to me like things can be rough no matter where you go or what you do.'

'Would it make any difference if I told you that I know what you're going through – that I *really do know?*'

I didn't say anything.

'I'm trying to *help* you,' she said, sounding a little desperate now. 'What can I say to you that will get through?'

I shrugged again. 'Say "Happy Birthday." '

Jonas had fallen asleep in front of the TV in the dark solarium. There was a war movie flickering on the screen but no sound. I shook him awake and herded him out of there. The nurse had gone back down to the ER, fortunately, but we had to pass through there to get out, and I had to stop and use the pay phone to call a cab. I always remember to get cabfare out of the stash I'm not supposed to know is in the old flour cannister. Things were mostly pretty quiet – people don't routinely come into suburban hospitals in the middle of the night with gunshot wounds or from car accidents – and I was glad, because there's always a wait for a cab.

I'd just hung up the phone when suddenly this kid was brought in, a toddler, really, screaming his lungs out. The sound went right through me – the kid was obviously in agony and I thought my hair must have been standing straight up. I could feel the tension level shoot skyhigh in the ER; suddenly there were half a dozen nurses and a doctor and a really young woman who must have been an intern or a resident or something clustered around this woman with this screaming, thrashing child in her arms. The woman looked pale and scared but still kind of cool, like she was just holding off on a nervous breakdown until she was in a safe place. Right behind her was a guy who had to be her husband; he'd thrown a pair of jeans on over his pyjamas. The shirt was half-untucked, and you could see the bottoms of the cuffs poking out from the jeans over his bedroom slippers. He looked dazed, like he was just now waking up.

I couldn't move. I stood there hanging on to the telephone, listening to the kid scream and scream. The doctor took them behind a curtain and the kid kept on screaming like they were killing him and everybody was talking at once, trying to calm the kid down and tell the doctor what was wrong.

Right about the time I thought I was going to lose it and start screaming myself, the doctor's voice cut through the din, sounding super-calm and super-competent, the way you want a doctor's voice to sound. 'That's a nasty ear infection, but they're all nasty at this age. I don't see a rupture.' His voice changed as he started talking to the kid. 'A lot of real hurty stuff, huh, big guy. Yeah. Don't you worry, we're gonna put in some medicine and you're gonna feel all better. Mommy, you hold his arms – like that – OK, big guy, I'll make this as fast as I can–'

The kid's screams began to sound more indignant than anything else. I looked for Jonas. He was standing a little ways away with his back up against the wall and his arms crossed over his chest with his hands stuck in his armpits, like if he let go he'd fall apart. He wasn't looking toward the kid but just staring off at nothing in another direction.

'Come on,' I said, 'let's wait for the cab outside. It's not cold.'

I put my hand on his shoulder to steer him out and he twisted away from me, still holding himself. The little kid stopped screaming as we got to the door and I turned around to look back. The nurse who had come up to see me was standing by the curtain, making notes on a clipboard. I moved us out before she could look up and see us. But the image of her standing there kind of hung in my mind all the way home and I began to get the idea she'd known we were there even though she hadn't looked.

The house was all lit up when we got home but my father was gone, which meant we were locked out. Or we would have been, except Jonas shimmied up the drainpipe and did a high-wire act without a net – without a wire, for that matter – to clamber into his open bedroom window. Every time he did it my heart just went into my mouth, because I could see the drainpipe suddenly ripping away from the house and crashing down, hitting the neighbors' fence and dumping him on his head in their shrubbery. This time, I heard the drainpipe bend a little as he was stretching over to the little ledge outside his window, to work the screen up with the toe of his sneaker. Eventually, he was going to be too big, too heavy for the drainpipe to hold him. Maybe in another few weeks or months, too; he was eleven.

He got the screen up a few inches and then it stuck. Working quietly in the light from the streetlamp, he changed position so he could reach over and pound the bottom of the screen up with his hand. It went up a little more, enough for him to get his legs in so he could sit precariously on the windowsill.

'Slide in,' I whispered up at him, looking around. We were a neighborhood watch area and I could picture a patrol car suddenly pulling up at the curb and the cops trying to arrest us for breaking and entering. But then I figured if no one had called the cops earlier, no one was going to call them now.

Jonas couldn't seem to get his little butt, skinny as it was, through the window, and he kept sitting there, balancing mostly on his thighs and hanging on with one hand while he pounded the stuck screen with the other. Then he stopped and I couldn't tell what he was doing. A moment later, I heard this sort of ripping, and the sound of metal bending and scraping against something, and I saw he'd torn out the screen and pulled the aluminium frame all out of shape. I didn't rag him for it; I knew just how he felt.

He got in and a moment later the ruined screen came down

into the yard. Jonas poked his head out. 'That didn't hit you, did it?'

'Nah, just let me in so we can get some sleep, ok?'

I'd have to get an extra set of keys made, I thought, as I locked the front door behind me. No, two sets – one to hide around the outside of the house somewhere in case I lost the extra set somehow. They told us not to do that at the neighborhood watch meeting, because experienced burglars know all the hiding places. But I decided I could be smarter than a burglar when it came to hiding keys. Dad didn't have to know. Mom, either.

I cleaned up the mess in the kitchen. The turkey really stunk after being left so long and the smell lingered. I'd have had to wash the floor thoroughly with the mop and the Mr Clean and the whole bit to get rid of it and I just wasn't up to anything more than sopping up the worst of the grease and blood and junk with paper towels.

The living room was a bigger problem; the coffee table looked like we'd started to chop it up for kindling and there was glass all over the rug, from the table and from my mother's favorite Klee print. The print was over in the corner by the brass floorlamp. The frame was done for but I thought the print might be salvageable. It was a little creased in spots but I could try ironing it, on the back.

There was still the problem of the glass all over. Thank God we didn't have pets or a toddler; thank God neither Jonas nor I brought friends home from school. The vacuum cleaner was broken again, so getting all the shards out of the fibre was going to be one hell of a job. 'One motherfucker of a job,' I said out loud, but very quietly, as if there might have been someone around to hear me talk like that. I never talked like that, and I wouldn't let Jonas get away with it, though mostly I couldn't see the harm in it if you needed to blow off some.

Anyway, I sure couldn't start combing through the carpet at – I squinted at the clock – one-fifteen in the morning, but Jonas might get up early and wander into the living room before he was completely awake. Then we'd be back in the emergency room maybe having to get stitches in his foot, or even both feet.

I took a roll of toilet paper from the bathroom and roped the living room off with it, sticking the ends of the long piece up on the woodwork of the entryway with masking tape. Then I took a piece of blank stationery from the little desk in the hall by the stairs and wrote DANGER: FALLING GLASS AREA and stuck that up on the toilet paper.

I was just about to go upstairs when I saw I'd left the light on in the kitchen. I went back in to shut it off and then I saw it on the counter by the sink, almost completely untouched, except for where a little turkey grease had splattered on it. The chocolate sheet cake my mother and Jonas had made and decorated together. Chocolate cake with strawberry-flavored pink icing. My mother had put on a few red blobs that were supposed to be flowers or something in the corners; the lettering was unmistakably Jonas's hand. RAD B-DAY TO U.

I put foil over the cake and tossed the unused candles in the junk drawer.

The sound of the front door roused me out of the light doze I'd fallen into and I rolled over and glanced at the clock. 2:12. Not a personal record, even for a weeknight. I had no idea where he went when he left, or what he did. Maybe he just drove around. He wasn't drunk, anyway. I could tell by his footsteps. They were sure and even and they cut off suddenly as he got to the living room entryway.

'What the hell is this?' I heard him mutter. I could hear him quite clearly, probably because the house was so quiet. His voice seemed to vibrate up through the floor to me. Then: 'Stupid shit. Looks like hell.' Silence, and then a rustle as he tore down the paper barrier and crumpled my sign. A few moments later, I heard the tinkle of broken glass and a grunt, and then footsteps going through the kitchen to the back door. Getting rid of the ruins of the coffee table. Right.

The cleaning lady was coming tomorrow – excuse me, today. Couldn't let her see *that*. Might give her the idea something bad happened. I wondered if he'd actually clean up the worst of the glass, too, or whether he'd leave it to me to tell her a story. Giselle had heard so many stories.

It sounded like he got rid of most of the glass before he shut himself up in his den at the bottom of the stairs. On the bad nights, he slept on the couch down there. At first, I'd thought it was because he was actually ashamed, at least temporarily, and it was his way of punishing himself or something, but as I got older, I stopped thinking that way.

I waited until I hadn't heard him move around for twenty minutes; than I got up, slipped into my clothes and tiptoed downstairs. He'd left all the lights on, like it hadn't occurred to him to shut them off. I didn't bother, either. I just left by the back door for the park.

Comanche Park was this weird little pocket of wild in the middle of hardcore suburbia. There was a covered picnic table area and a few barbecue grills, a small playground for the kids, and the storm drain where Jonas and his friends rode skateboards. Back behind the clearing was the woods, a remnant of what the area used to be like before the developers moved in and made things safe for people who kept boats in their driveways.

There were a few trails stomped out, and if you followed the main ones, you came out on the other side facing the Maple Creek development cul-de-sac and the tennis courts. But there were wilder, thicker, darker places where the police never patrolled and the kids never explored. Transients hid out in them, I guess; occasionally, I'd found an empty whisky bottle, or some discarded piece of clothing. It always made me picture some ragged old bum finishing off a bottle and saying to himself, well, what the hell, I guess I'll leave my shirt here.

I didn't go into any of those places at night, but I didn't have to. The sign said the park was closed after 10 p.m., but there was no gate to close, no chain to put up, nothing to stop me from going in and very little light to hold the darkness back in the thick of the trees where it stayed during the day.

There were three swings on the rough wooden frame in the playground area, one for infants and two sling-type things. I sat on the one nearest the woods and let myself drift back and forth, watching the darkness creep.

The fight had started early. This was the Birthday Fight. My parents fought any time, but there were certain occasions that called for something special. Birthdays were a must. I'd been up in my room not doing my homework when the shouting had begun. The sound went right through me; I sat there at my desk and it seemed like I could feel Jonas doing the same thing in his room, just frozen wherever he was, listening to it start.

I went downstairs and they were in the living room, yelling things at each other, as if they had to yell to make themselves heard over the aroma of the turkey roasting in the oven. I don't know what they were fighting over exactly, not the surface issue, so to speak. The actual issue was, of course, my birthday. Jonas appeared at the top of the stairs as I opened the front door. I didn't have to beckon to him. He just came down quickly and we went out to the park.

It was only starting to get dark then, but there wasn't anyone else around. Jonas and I sat at a picnic table, not saying anything. I used to take him on long, long walks when he'd been younger and didn't know what was going on. Now we went over to Comanche Park and sat it out. I threw my watch at the woods just before we left. There was no one and nothing else to take it out on.

Everything was quiet when we got back; my mother was in the kitchen, carving the turkey and sniffing, with her eyes all red. My father was sitting at the table with his chin on his fists, staring at the placemat. Jonas and I sat down and there was only the sound of my mother sniffing and the smell of turkey. Then my mother turned around.

My father's right hand had come up and smashed the

platter of turkey out of her grasp. She had screamed something at him, or maybe she'd just been startled, and as she'd moved toward the mess of white meat and drumsticks and gravy on the floor, he'd gotten up out of his chair and given her a hard shove between her shoulder blades, so she'd gone face-first into the lower kitchen cabinets. She'd started scrambling to get up and it had been like some kind of real mean slapstick movie clip the way her feet kept slipping on the turkey, pieces of it skidding all over the linoleum in every direction. Jonas and I started to get up, get away from the table and Dad had gone over to Mom and pulled her up by the back of her shirt, jerked her around to face him, and let fly backhanded. Like he was swatting her. That had been when her teeth had gone through her lip. She'd been on her way down to the floor again when his fist had caught her in the stomach. The punch had lifted her off her feet a few inches. He'd stepped back to let her fall then. She hit my chair going down and tipped it over. Jonas and I were backed up against the refrigerator. Dad stepped back and she pulled herself up, using the chair to get to the table. With one arm across her stomach, she half-stumbled, half-lunged around the other side of the table, going past me and Jonas. Dad watched until she got to the hall and then he walked out after her. She made a gagging noise and I heard the phone fall on the carpet. Jonas ran for the living room and I ran after him to pull him back; I got to the entryway just as Dad brought the Klee down on her back. He flipped it away like a frisbee and as she reached out for him, he grabbed the front of her shirt and shoved her down on the coffee table. He had to pull her up and shove her down again before it broke. Dad turned away unhurriedly and his gaze passed through us without stopping as he walked out of the room and out the front door. He hadn't looked crazy or dangerous or even particularly angry. More like he'd just broken something and was going in search of a dustpan.

I pretended that the darkness asked me what I was going to do and I said I didn't know, which I didn't. From where

I was sitting on the swing, I could look back the way I'd come, through the parking lot and across Fall Avenue to our street. Our house was the third from the corner of Fall, easy to pick out now since it was the only one showing any lights.

Tonight's episode must have been pretty audible; I could have probably sat right where I was now and heard the glass breaking. Every other house looked peaceful, unaffected in any way. Which they were, as far as I could tell, something that made me feel funny. Not because I thought anyone should have called the cops and sent them to our rescue – mine and Jonas', anyway – but because it felt like as long it was happening at our house, everyone else was safe from it happening at theirs. Like we were the designated house for this.

So, the darkness said, who would you wish this on, if you could?

Good question, I told the darkness. I thought about the DiMarias, on our left. The window of my room looked right down into their living room, and I could see their two little kids playing on the rug every night. It looked like a collision between a magazine stand and a toystore in there – the DiMarias were not real concerned with being neat, but then, both of them worked and their kids were in daycare. I guess they figured they had better things to do than housework and not enough left over for maid service. I tried to picture Carl DiMaria losing it in that cluttered house with their kids playing on the rug and Sheila trying to get away from him, and I turned that movie off quick, I can tell you.

The Changs, on the other side, were about as unimaginable, in a different way. They'd only been in the house six months or so; Mr Chang was some kind of engineer with a communications company and Mrs Chang didn't work. They were a little older than my parents, with one son in college somewhere in the east. I hardly knew them but they had nice smiles, and they moved around each other the way you see people moving around fragile vases. The Changs seemed about as likely to shout at each other as the sun was to rise in the west.

Directly across from us were the Shapiros. They were older people and Mrs Shapiro took care of her grandson two or three days a week for her daughter, who was divorced or something. I saw Mrs Shapiro in the park a lot with the kid. She was a pretty sturdy woman, strong enough to keep up with her grandson, who was always trying to climb to the top of the wooden blockhouse, but she didn't look like she was really built to take it.

The Foleys, on the corner; they had dogs instead of kids. Across from them, in the smallest house on the block, Lisa What's-Her-Name, the photographer who had a lot of boyfriends.

Maybe her, I thought, idly. She could break up with a boyfriend if there was trouble. Couldn't she?

The darkness said it wasn't that simple.

I ran through everyone else I knew and several I didn't know but had seen at one time or another. No, I told the darkness, there wasn't anybody who could be the fighting house instead of us.

It was just a weird game I played with myself. I guess you could call it *Who Would You Wish Your Life On?* or something like that. Or maybe, *Why Me?*

I got up and wandered around the playground area, just to be moving around. Trying to pick up some momentum I could use to make myself walk home. The way the air had cooled down, I could tell it was later than I'd ever been out. School was going to be impossible, might as well not even bother.

By the time I decided that, I'd wandered over to the covered picnic area where Jonas and I had sat earlier. Since then, someone had stopped for a beer and left the can half-crumpled on one of the long tables. High up, the trees whispered in the night breeze and the darkness flowed up from the woods in deeper, thicker waves. Your eyes play tricks like that on you when you're overtired, I thought, and waited for the dark patches to break up on the grass near the covered area and reassemble in the woods.

But they kept coming, and I started thinking that maybe I was seeing animals, but then they were too big to be any animals that could live in the park, too big even for people. I wanted to turn and run, but the darkness reached the edge of the covered area and stopped, as if it were waiting. I couldn't see a thing; I groped my way along one of the tables and the darkness flowed around the covered area like a curtain, shutting me in.

I sat down, hugging myself against a cold I didn't really feel. I didn't really feel scared, probably because I was so out of it from needing sleep, but I wasn't sleepy, either. I was just there, in the dark, totally in the dark, and then I heard Jonas say, 'Jan?'

'What are you doing out here in the park?' I whispered. Like someone was going to hear us, right?

'I'm not in the park,' he said. 'I'm in the dark, same as you. Where we've always been.'

I looked around but I still couldn't see anything. And then, unbidden, the sight of my mother in the hospital bed rose up in my mind. I could see her as clearly as if I were back there with her, the tube in her nose, the IV, the stitches, and, beneath her closed lids, her eyes moving back and forth, back and forth.

I'm dreaming, I thought. I'm dreaming that I got up and went to the park.

Not this time, said the darkness.

'Sometimes, you can do things,' Jonas said. He sounded real young and real old all at the same time. His voice would be changing soon, and the drainpipe wouldn't hold him much longer, I thought. 'Sometimes, when everything's right, you can – um, *do* things.'

'Where are you?'

'I told you, same place you are,' he said tiredly. 'Hurry up. This isn't gonna last forever, you know.'

He's eleven years old, I told the darkness. He's just eleven years old, it isn't fair—

There were no words – there never had been, really – but now I could feel what was being directed at me and how it had been there all along, flicking at the fringes of what I knew as real divided from unreal. That was a smaller issue than I'd thought; after all, what was real in our house wasn't real in any of the others on our block.

Which made me wonder, then: did someone else, sitting in the dark somewhere, wish this on me?

No, said the darkness, this was always yours. But sometimes, when the conditions are right . . . when an offering has been made . . .

I saw myself flinging my watch at the darkest part of the woods, and I could see how it was an action that had been part of this really convoluted arrangement of things that could have happened – like, there was another part of the same thing where I was a lot older and I hit somebody, and sometime else when I wasn't much older and somebody hit me, and some other things. But I'd thrown the watch, because there wasn't anyone or anything else to take it all out on. Just a little offering at the right moment.

And I was thinking then that there was something in my dad that had come out of the darkness, but right as soon as I thought it, I knew I was wrong, it was the other way around altogether.

So . . . what, then?

Fix it, said the darkness.

Picture of myself at school, just before final exams and suddenly all the test answers dropping into my lap out of nowhere. I should be so lucky, I thought, but it was like that. Putting in the fix. So few of us, you know, are smart enough or lucky enough to be able to resist something like that, to not need it. Especially if you know something bad'll happen to you unless you go for it.

'Mom won't do anything,' Jonas said hollowly. '*You* won't do anything. *I can't* do anything. What am I gonna do – go to a shelter all by myself and ask if maybe I could be an honorary battered woman? That'd be pretty cool, right?'

'What do you want me to do?' I said. I knew, though, and Jonas knew I did, but he said it anyway.

'Put it on somebody else. Let somebody else be in the line of fire, let somebody else take it. It's us as much as Mom. Someday you'll be where Mom is. And someday –' He cut off, but I heard him. *Someday, I'll be like Dad*. Shitty thing to have to know about yourself.

'That's an awful lot of return to get just for one watch,' I said, laughing a little. I'm not sure why I was laughing, nothing was funny. 'One little birthday watch.'

So, Rad B-day to U.

Here was the deal. Better anyone else than us, right? Or would I really let things go on, let Mom keep a tube in her nose so the DiMaria kids wouldn't have to grow up like we did, so Mrs Chang wouldn't have to have a tube in *her* nose? So Mrs Shapiro's daughter wouldn't have to ride in the ambulance with her to the hospital? I could see my father, not with that strange blank look but smiling or looking sad or being like just a regular person, and my mother not telling stories about how she was accident-prone, and Jonas and me not waiting for the storm to burst. I could see it all, and I wanted it more than anything. What the hell, if it's going to have to happen anyway, let it happen to someone else.

But the thing was, when it did, we weren't going to call the cops, either. Nobody ever would. Neighborhood watch area – we only call the cops on strangers, suspicious persons lurking about, not the people we live with. And if I thought I was going to do it, I was wrong, because that was part of the deal. I didn't have to do anything, and the person I would be after the deal was made wouldn't want to.

And I heard myself say, just as plain as anything, 'I can't live with that, either.'

I don't know what happened then, but I opened my eyes and it wasn't dark any more, and my father was coming across the park with a grim look on his face while behind him on Fall, the early morning traffic was just starting to pick up.

He jerked me up away from the table and said, 'What the hell is this? What do you think you're doing?'

I looked past him and saw Jonas standing on the corner across the street, like he'd been abandoned.

'Doesn't your mother make things bad enough?' my father asked. 'You wanna get raped and murdered in the park, too?'

I twisted away from him and walked away, back through the park and across the street to Jonas, who was glaring at me like I was a traitor. Dad was following after us as I marched Jonas toward the house.

'Take your schoolbooks like you're going to school as usual,' I said in a low voice. 'But we'll go up to the hospital, and we'll wait in Mom's room, until this nurse I know comes on duty.'

'What good'll that do?' Jonas asked bitterly, not looking up.

'She knows how to get us some help.'

Jonas glanced briefly back at Dad, who was gaining on us. 'Is it gonna be enough help? What if he finds us and kills Mom, kills us all?'

'We're not killed yet. You wanted me to do something, I'm doing it. It's not so late that we have to make deals with – with whatever that is.'

'You coulda,' he said, and it was an accusation. 'You coulda stopped it, it would be over.'

'No,' I told him. 'It can't be over until you say, "I won't", not "anyone else but me".'

'You coulda fixed *me*, though. So I'd never be–' He glanced back at Dad again, who had almost caught up with us now.

'Sorry,' I said, grabbing his hand. 'You'll have to do that one all on your own. Just like me. Just like everybody.'

We broke into a run.

Karen Joy Fowler

Letters from Home

I wish you could see me now. You would laugh. I have a husband. I have children. Yes. I drive a station wagon. I would laugh, too. Our turn to be the big kids, the grown-ups. Our turn to be over thirty. It astonishes me whenever I stop and think about it. It has to be a joke.

I miss you. I've always missed you. I want us to understand each other. I want to tell you what I did after you left. I want to tell you what I did during the war. Most of all, I want to tell you the truth. This is what makes it so difficult. I have learned to distrust words, even my own. Words can be made to say anything. I know this. Do you?

Much of what I will tell you actually happened. You will be able to identify these parts, or you can ask me. This does not mean, of course, that any of it is true. Even among the people who were there with me are some who remember it differently. Gretchen said something once that echoed my own feelings. 'We were happy, weren't we?' she said. 'In spite of everything. We made each other happy. Ill-advised, really, this putting your happiness into other people's hands. I've tried it several times since and it's never worked again.'

But when I repeated this to Julie she was amazed. 'Happy?' she asked. 'How can you say that? I was so fat. I was being screwed by that teaching assistant. And "screwed" is the only word that applies. There was a *war*. Don't you remember?'

Can I tell you what I remember about the war? I remember the words. Vietnam was the language we spoke – secret bombing, the lottery, Vietnamization, self-immolation, Ho-Ho-Ho Chi Minh, peace with honor, peace at any price, peace, peace, peace. Somewhere, I imagine, on the other side of the world, these words meant something. Somewhere they had physical counterparts. Except for the last set, of course. If peace has ever had a physical value anywhere, none of us has been able to find it. But the other words corresponded to something. There was a *real* war going on and in many ways we were untouched by it. This is what I'm trying to say: if the words alone were powerful enough to shape us and our lives as they did, what kind of an impact must the real war have had on *its* people?

I remember sitting on our sofa watching television. Julie is on the floor at my feet. She's the red-haired Jewish one. She's studying set design and is busy gluing together a tiny throne, part of a mock-up for the set of *Saint Joan*. 'Women have fought in wars before,' she reminds us. 'But only when God tells them to.'

Lauren is next to me. She's black, though rather light-skinned and freckled. Her dog is on her lap, giving the television the same studied attention the rest of us are. Gretchen is standing in the doorway to the kitchen drinking a diet soda. She has short brown hair and heavy bangs, a white Catholic though not a practising one. She clings to Catholicism because it protects her from being a WASP. This unpleasant designation is applicable only to me. You know me. I'm the plain white one on the end there with my legs drawn up to my chest and my arms around them. And that ten-inch figure on the screen with his hands in motion before him and the map of Cambodia behind him – that's President Nixon. The Quaker. He is busy redrawing the Cambodian border and explaining to us that we are not really invading Cambodia, because the border is not where we have always thought it was. Gretchen swallows the last of her soda. 'My God,' she says. 'The man may be right. Just now, just out of the corner of my eye, I saw the border jump.'

Nixon is impervious to our criticism. He is content; he feels it is enough merely to have found something to say.

I am twenty years old. I believe nothing I hear.

I was not always like that. Here is an earlier memory. We are standing on my parents' front porch and you have your arms around me. You have driven all the way down from San Francisco to tell me you have been drafted. I find this incomprehensible. I know you could have avoided it. Isn't Allen in Manhattan Beach getting braces put on his teeth? Hasn't Greg moved three times in three months, burying his induction notice in the US mails? Hasn't Jim joined VISTA, taking advantage of the unspoken agreement that if you are reluctant to burn villages and bomb children, your country will accept two years of urban volunteerism instead?

You are so thin I feel your bones inside your arms. If you fasted, you could fall below the required weight. Why will you do none of these things? I can't help feeling betrayed.

You try to explain and I try to listen. You tell me that the draft is unfair because you *could* evade it. You say if you don't go, they will just send someone else. (Yes, I say. Yes.) You say that perhaps you can have some impact from within. That an evasion won't realistically affect the war effort at all, but maybe if you were actually there . . . 'Hey.' You are holding your arms about me so tightly, helping me to hold myself so tightly inside. 'Don't cry. I'm going to subvert every soldier I meet. The war will be over by Christmas.' And I don't cry. Remember? I don't cry.

You disappeared into the real war and you never got one word back out to me. I never heard from you or of you again. So that is what I remember about the war. The words over here. The war over there. And increasingly little connection between the two.

You are put on a bus and sent to basic training. You take the last possible seat, left rear corner. The bus fills with young men, their white necks exposed by new haircuts, their ears open and vulnerable.

It reminds you of going to camp. You suggest a game of telephone. You whisper into the ear closest to you. You whisper, 'The Geneva Accords.' The man next to you leans across the aisle. The message travels over the backs of the seats and crisscrosses the bus. When it comes out at the front, it is 'the domino theory.'

You try again. 'Buddhist bar-b-cues,' you whisper. You think the man next to you has it right, repeats it just the way you said it. You can hear the 'b's' and the 's's' even over the bus motor. But the large man at the front of the bus, the one whose pink scalp is so vivid you can't even guess what color the fuzz of his hair might be, claims to have heard 'strategic hamlets.' Someone is changing the words.

'Body bags!' You have shouted it accidentally. Everyone turns to look at you. Fifty faces. Fifty selected faces. Already these men are different from the men they were yesterday, a difference of appearance, perhaps, and nothing else. It may stay this way. It may be the first hint of the evolution of an entirely new person. You turn to the tinted window, surprised by your own face staring at you.

The other men think you have said, 'Operation Rolling Thunder.' Even so, nobody smiles.

When you leave the bus, you leave the face in the window. You go and it stays. So it cannot have been *your* face after all.

After you left I went to Berkeley. I lived in the student dorms for a year, where I met Gretchen and Julie. When we moved out, we moved together, into a fairly typical student apartment. It had a long shag carpet – even the rugs were hairy then – of a particularly putrid green and the appliances were avocado. The furniture had been stapled together. There were four beds and the rent clearly had been selected with four in mind. We advertised for a roommate in the *Daily Cal*. Although taking a stranger into our home entailed a definite risk, it seemed preferable to inviting someone we actually knew.

I remember that we flipped a coin to see which of us would have to share the bedroom with the newcomer and Julie lost. She had some procedural objection she felt was sufficiently serious to require a second toss, but Gretchen and I refused. The new roommate hadn't even appeared and was already making things sticky.

Lauren was the first respondent to our ad – a beautiful, thin, curly-haired girl with an elegant white curly-haired dog. They made a striking pair. Julie showed Lauren the apartment; the conversation was brisk and businesslike. Gretchen and I petted the dog. When Lauren left, Julie had said we would take her.

I was unsettled by the speed of the decision and said so. I had no objections to Lauren, but I'd envisioned interviewing several candidates before making a selection.

'I'm the one who has to room with her. I should get to choose.' Julie held out one long strand of her own red hair and began methodically to split the end. Julie was artistic and found the drab apartment painful. Initially, I believe she wanted Lauren mostly for decor. Lauren moved in the next day.

Immediately objectionable characteristics began to surface. If I'd had your address, I would have written long complaints. 'She dresses with such taste,' I would have said. 'Who would have guessed she'd be such a slob?' Lauren's messiness was epic in its proportions. Her bed could hardly be seen under the pile of books, shoes, combs, and dirty dishes she left on it. She had to enter it gingerly at night, finding small empty spaces where she might fit an arm or a leg. She would sleep without moving, an entire night spent in the only position possible.

'She's late wherever she goes,' I would have written, 'not by minutes or quarter hours, but by afternoons. On her night to cook, we eat in front of Johnny Carson.'

Then I would have divulged the worst complaint of all. 'She talks baby talk, to the dog, which is tolerable, to her boyfriend, which is not.' Lauren's boyfriend was a law student at Boalt. He was older than us, big, and wore his hair slicked back along his head. Of course, *no one* wore their hair like that then. There was a sort of Mafioso cut to his clothes, an intensity in his eyes. I never liked being alone with him, but Lauren called him Owlie and he called her his Sugarbear. 'It is absolutely sickening the way you two go on,' I told her and she was completely unabashed. She suggested that, although we didn't have the guts to be as up front about it as she was, we probably all talked baby talk to our boyfriends, an accusation we strenuously denied. We had no boyfriends, so the point was academic. Owlie studied judo as well as the law, and there was always a risk, opening some door, that you might find him demonstrating some hold to Lauren. Sickening, like I said.

I would have finished my letter by telling you, if you could only meet her, you would love her. Well, we all did. She was vivacious, imaginative, courageous. She removed some previously unnoticed tensions from our relationships – somehow with four the balance was better. By the spring of 1970, when the war of the words achieved its most intense pitch ever, this balance had become intricate and effortless.

I had gone out to protest the Cambodian invasion and come home in a cast. The police had removed their badges, donned their gas masks and chased us down, catching me just outside Computer Sciences. They had broken my ankle. Owlie was gone. His birthday had been drawn seventeenth in the lottery and he'd relocated to a small town in Oregon rumored to have a lenient draft board. Gretchen had acquired a boyfriend whose back had been injured in a high school wrestling match, rendering him 4-F with no tricks. He went off to Europe and was, consequently, very little trouble. Julie had switched her major from set design to Chicano studies. We heard that the National Guard was killing people on the campus of Kent State. I heard nothing from you.

You are in a small room, a cell. It is cold and the walls are damp stone. You sit cross-legged like a monk on the thin mattress and face the wall. There is so much moisture you can imprint your hand in it. By 10 a.m. the prints disappear. The sun has reached the wall, but it still is not warm. If you were sure no one would come to look, you would levitate yourself into the sunshine. You are thinking of me.

How much I expected of you. How stupid I am. I probably believed you could end the war by Christmas. You can imagine me believing that. Even now I am probably working out long chain-letter calculations – if you subvert four soldiers every day and they subvert four soldiers and *they* subvert four soldiers, how many days will the war last? When will you come home?

Do I expect miracles from a prison cell? Why should you provide them? You make a decision. You decide to be warm. You exhale your warmth into the air. It rises to the ceiling, it seems to disappear, but as you repeat this, over and over, the layers eventually drop to where they surround you. When you leave the cell, you will leave it filled with your heat.

It is a small room. Any man can accomplish a small task.

In response to the invasion of Cambodia and the deaths at Kent State (Can I say murders? Will you object? Will you compare those four deaths to the body count in Vietnam on any single day or on 4 May itself and believe you have made some point?) UC Berkeley suspended classes. When they recommenced, they had been reconstituted; they were now supposed to be directly relevant to the single task of ending the war in Southeast Asia. I will not pretend to you that there was no opposition within the university to this. But a large segment of the campus made this commitment together – we would not continue with our lives until the war was over.

At the same time Nixon made his own pledge to the American people. He promised them that nothing, *nothing* we could do would affect policy in any way.

The war of the words took on a character which was at once desperate and futile, a soul-dampening combination we never shook free of. We did the work because it seemed right to us. We had no illusions of its potency. It began to feel like a game.

Julie and I had volunteered for a large committee whose purpose was to compile a list of war profiteers so that their products could be boycotted. We researched mergers and parent companies; this list grew like a chain letter. It would have been quicker to list those companies not turning a profit in Vietnam. I remember Lauren perusing our list one day with great dissatisfaction. 'The counterculture makes roach clips,' she said. 'It makes liquid sculptures you can plug in and they change shape.'

'Lava lamps,' I told her.

'Whatever. It makes hash pipes. I need a raincoat. What am I supposed to do?'

'Get wet,' Julie suggested.

'Get stoned,' said Gretchen. 'And then get wet. You'll hardly notice.'

Lauren had volunteered herself for the university's media watchdog committee. Her job was to monitor three news shows daily and report on the coverage they gave to the war and to the student movement. The idea was that we would apply whatever pressure we could on those stations whose coverage seemed slanted in favor of the Administration. The fallacy was that we had any meaningful pressure that could be brought to bear. We wrote letters. We added their sponsors to the boycott. Nobody cared.

I know that Nixon felt undermined and attacked by the media. We did not see it this way. None of the major networks met with our approval. Only the local public station reported the news in Berkeley the way we saw it happening. One of their reporters was a young man who covered those stories felt to be of particular interest to the black community. He was handsome, moustached, broad-shouldered. He had the same dark, melting eyes as Lauren's dog. His name was Poncho Taylor. Lauren fell in love with him.

Well, you didn't expect us to give up love, did you? Just because there was a war on? I never expected you to.

Poncho was politically impeccable. He was passionate, he was committed. He was gorgeous. Any one of us could have

fallen in love with him. But Lauren was the first to announce
her passion and we were content to provide support. We
took turns with her transcribing duties during his airtime so
she wouldn't miss a moment of his face. We listened patiently
while she droned on about his cheekbones, his hair, the sexy
tremor in his voice when a story had an unhappy conclusion,
and we agreed. We saw it all. He was wonderful.

I remember a night when we made chocolate chip cookies
and ate the dough. Nestlé had just made the boycott list, but
the chips were old. 'The sooner we eat them, the better,'
Julie had suggested.

Gretchen had just returned from an organizational meeting
with new instructions for us. We had been told to band
together into small groups like the revolutionaries in *The
Battle of Algiers*. These were to be called affinity groups and
we were to select for them people we trusted absolutely. We
were to choose those people we would trust with our lives.
We smiled at one another over the bowl of dough as it
suddenly occurred to us that, for us, this choice had already
been made. Just as Gretchen said, when we could find our
happiness nowhere else, we were able to put it into each
other's hands and hold it there.

'There's more,' Gretchen continued. 'We're supposed to
arm ourselves.' Julie took another spoonful of dough, heavy
on the chips. I used the handle of my spoon to reach inside
my cast and scratch myself. Nobody said anything for a long
time.

Finally Julie indicated the boycott list. 'The pen is mightier
than the sword,' she suggested. She didn't sound sure.

Gretchen did. 'The boycott list is liberal bullshit,' she said.
'It's too easy. What good will it possibly do?'

Lauren cleared her throat and tapped the air with the back
of her spoon. 'It's a capitalist country. Money matters.'

'You can't destroy the system from within the system.'
Gretchen was very unhappy. 'We're too safe.'

We sent Nixon a telegram. Gretchen composed it. 'End

this obscene war at once Stop Pull out the way your father should have Stop.' It didn't make us feel better.

We should have done more. I look back on those years and it's clear to me that we should have done more. It's just not clear to me *what* more we should have done.

Perhaps we lacked imagination. Perhaps we lacked physical courage. Perhaps our personal stakes were just not high enough. We were women. We were not going to Vietnam. We were privileged. Our brothers, our lovers were not going to Vietnam. But you do us an injustice if you doubt our sincerity. Remember that we watched the news three times a day. Three times a day we read the body count in the upper right-hand corner of the screen like the score of a football game. This is how many of them we killed today. They killed this many of us. Subtract one figure from the other. Are we winning?

Could anyone be indifferent to this? Always, I added the two numbers together. My God, I would think. Dear God. Look how many people died today! (What if one of them was you?)

You are on a plane, an ordinary plane. You could be en route to Denver from Chicago or going home for Christmas if you just close your eyes and believe only your ears. But you are really between Japan and Vietnam. The plane has a stewardess dressed in a bathing suit like Miss America. This is designed as a consolation for you. If you are very, very frightened, she may agree to wear rabbit ears and a tail when she brings you your drink. But you must not touch her. She is a white woman and looks familiar to you – her height, her build quite ordinary. This will change. When you remember her later she will seem exotic. It will seem odd to you that a woman should be so big. You will remember that she came and tightened your seat belt as if she were your mother. What was she keeping you safe for? Whose body is it anyway? You look at your legs, at your hands, and wonder what your body will be like when it is returned to you. You wonder who will want it then.

The immediate threat is the plane's descent. You make a sudden decision not to descend with it. You spread your arms to hold yourself aloft. You hover near the top of the plane. But it is hopeless. If they have to shoot you down, they will. Friendly fire. You return to your seat. The plane carries your body down into Vietnam.

You think of me. How I will hate you if you don't live through this. How you must protect me. And during your whole tour, every time you meet someone returning home, you will give him a message for me. You will write your message on the casts of the wounded. You will print it on the foreheads of those who return walking, on the teeth of those who return bagged. *I am here, I am here, I am here.* So many messages. How are you to know that none will get through?

My affinity group was very kind about you. I would tell them frequently how the war would be over by Christmas, how you were responsible for the growing dissatisfaction among servicemen. Vets against the war, I said to them, was probably one of your ideas. They never mentioned how you never wrote. Neither did I. You were my wound. I had my broken ankle and I had you. It was so much more than they had. It made them protective of me.

They didn't want me at any more demonstrations. 'When you *could* run,' Lauren pointed out, 'look what happened to you.' But I was there with them when the police cordoned off Sproul Plaza, trapping us inside, and gassed us from the air. You don't want to believe this. Governor Ronald Reagan and all the major networks assured you that we had been asked to disperse, but had refused. Only Poncho Taylor told the truth. We had not been allowed to leave. Anyone who had tried to leave was clubbed. A helicopter flew over the area and dropped teargas on us. The gas went into the hospital and into the neighboring residential areas. When the police asked the city to buy them a second helicopter so that they could enlarge operations, many people not of the radical persuasion objected. A committee was formed to prevent this purchase, a committee headed by an old Bay Area activist. She happened to be Poncho Taylor's grandmother. Lauren took it as a sign from God.

Lauren's passion for Poncho had continued to grow and we had continued to feed it. It's difficult to explain why Poncho had become so important to us. Partly it was just that Lauren loved him and we loved Lauren. Whatever Lauren wanted she should have. But partly it was the futility of our political work. We continued to do it but without energy, without hope. Poncho began to seem attainable when peace was not. Poncho began to represent the *rest* of our lives, outside the words.

Lauren told everyone how she felt. Our friends all knew and soon their friends knew and then the friends of their friends. It was like a message Lauren was sending to Poncho. And if it didn't reach him, then Lauren could combine useful political effort with another conduit. She called Poncho's grandmother and volunteered us all for the Stop the Helicopter campaign.

We went to an evening organizational meeting. (We did more organizing than anything else.) Though now I remember that Julie did not come with us, but stayed at home to rendezvous in the empty apartment with her teaching assistant.

The meeting was crowded, but eventually we verified Poncho's absence. After interminable discussion we were told to organize phone trees, circulate petitions, see that the city council meeting, scheduled for the end of the month, was packed with vocal opponents. Lauren couldn't even get close to Poncho's grandmother.

When we returned home, Julie was drunk. Her lover had failed to show, but Mike, a friend of mine, had come by with a bottle of wine. Julie had never known Mike very well or liked him very much, but he had stayed the whole evening and they had gotten along wonderfully. Julie had a large collection of Barbra Streisand records we refused to let her play. Mike had not only put them on but actually cried over them. 'He's a lot more sensitive than I thought,' Julie told me.

Mike denied it all. He was so drunk he wove from side to side even sitting down. He tried to kiss me and landed on my shoulder. 'How did the meeting go?' he asked and snorted when we told him. 'Phone trees.' He lifted his head to grin at me, red-faced, unshaven, wine-soaked breath. 'The old radicals are even less ballsy than the young ones.'

I picked up one of his hands. 'Do you think it's possible,' I asked him, 'for a revolution to be entirely personal? Suppose we all concentrated on our own lives, filled them with revolutionary moments, revolutionary relationships. When we had enough of them, it would be a revolution.'

'No.' Mike removed his hand from mine. 'It wouldn't. That's cowardice talking. That's you being liberal. That's you saying, let's make a revolution, but let's be nice about it. People are dying. There's a real war going on. We can't be incremental.'

'Exactly,' said Gretchen. 'Exactly. Time is as much the issue as anything else.'

'Then we should all be carrying guns,' said Julie. 'We should be planning political assassinations.'

'We should be robbing banks,' said Mike. 'Or printing phony bills.' Mike had been known to pass a bad check or two. Though he never needed the money. He was an auto mechanic by day, a dope dealer by night. He was the richest person we knew. 'Lauren,' he called and Lauren appeared in the doorway to the kitchen. 'I came here tonight because I have a surprise for you.' He was grinning.

'If it's dope, I'm not interested,' said Lauren. 'Nor am I solvent.'

'What would you say,' Mike asked, 'if I told you that right now, right at this very moment, I have Poncho Taylor's car sitting in my garage waiting for repairs?' Lauren said we would go right over.

Poncho had a white convertible. Lauren loved it. She sat in the driver's seat, because Poncho had sat there. She sat on the passenger side, because that was where she would be sitting herself. I discovered an old Valentine in the glove compartment. Lauren was torn between the despair of thinking he already had a girlfriend and the thrill of finally discovering something personal. She opened it.

' "Love and a hundred smooches, Deborah." ' Lauren read it aloud disapprovingly. 'This Deborah sounds like a real sap.'

'Poncho seems more and more to be the perfect match for you,' I added. The Valentine had one feature of incontrovertible value. It had Poncho's address on it. Lauren began to copy it, then looked at us.

'What the hell,' she said and put the whole thing in her purse.

I had no address for you, you know. I mean, in the beginning I did and I probably should have written you first. Since I hardly talked to you when you came to say goodbye. Since I didn't cry. I *did* miss you. I kept thinking you would write *me*. And then later, when I saw you wouldn't, it was too late. Then I had no address. I couldn't believe you would *never* write me. What happened to you?

Even our senators sent me form letters. More than I got from you.

Dear (fill in name),

Well, here I am in Vietnam! The people are little and the bugs are big, but the food is Army and that means American. As far as I can see, Saigon has been turned into one large brothel. I go there as often as I can. It beats my other way of interacting with the locals, which is to go up in planes and drop 'Willie Peter' on them. Man, those suckers burn forever!

I made my first ground kill yesterday. Little guy in a whole lot of pieces. You have to bring the body for the body count and the arm came off right in my hand. We were able to count him six times, which everybody said was really beautiful. Hey, he's in so many pieces he's never going to need any company but his own again. The dope is really heavy-duty here, too. I've lost my mind.

Listen, I got to go. We're due out tonight on a walk-through with ARVN support and you know what they say here about the ARVN – with friends like these . . . Ugly little buggers.

Dust off the women. I'll be home by Christmas. Love you all.

(Fill in name)

Now you're angry. I hope. Who am I to condemn you? What do I know about the real war? Absolutely nothing. Gretchen says you're a running-dog imperialist. She thinks she met you once before you left, before she knew me, at a party at Barbara Meyer's. In Sausalito? I don't think it was you. She waited a long time to tell me about it. I was married before she told me. I don't think it was you. So . . .

So, it took Lauren two days to formalize her final plan. It was audacious. It was daring. It had Lauren's stamp all over it. Mike called when Poncho came in and picked up his car. This was our signal to start.

It was Lauren's night to cook dinner and she saw no reason to change this. She had bought the ingredients for cannelloni, a spectacular treat she made entirely from scratch. It required long intervals, she claimed, when the dough must be allowed to rest. During one of these rest periods, she fixed herself up and Julie drove her to San Francisco, where Poncho lived. Julie returned in forty minutes. She had only stayed long enough to see Lauren safely inside.

Lauren came home perhaps a half an hour later. She changed her clothes again, dropping the discarded ones on to the living room floor, and went into the kitchen to roll out the cannelloni dough. We sat around her at the kitchen table, chopping the onions, mixing the filling, stuffing the rolls while she talked. She was very high, very excited.

'I knocked on the door,' she said. 'Poncho's roommate let me in. Poncho was lying on the couch, reading. Poncho Taylor! He was there!'

'Can I come in?' Lauren had asked. She made her voice wobble. She showed us how. 'A man in a car is following me.'

'What was the roommate like?' Julie asked hopefully. 'Pretty cute?'

'No. He wears big glasses and his hair is very short. James. His name is James. He asked me why I came to their apartment since they live on the second floor?'

'Good question,' I admitted. 'What did you say?'

'I said I saw their Bobby Seale poster and I thought they might be black.'

'Good *answer*,' said Julie. 'Lauren thinks on her feet. All right!'

'There's nothing wrong with glasses,' Gretchen objected. 'Lots of attractive people wear glasses.' She cut into an onion with determined zeal. 'Maybe he's gay,' she said.

'No,' said Lauren. 'He's not. And it wasn't the glasses. It was the competition. Poncho is *so* . . .' We waited while she searched for the word worthy of Poncho. 'Magnetic,' she concluded.

Well, who could compete with Poncho? Gretchen let the issue drop.

Lauren had entered the apartment and James and Poncho had gone to the window. 'What make was the car?' James had asked. 'I don't see anybody.'

'Green VW bug,' said Lauren.

'*My* car,' said Julie. 'Great.'

'They wanted me to call the police,' Lauren said. 'But I was too upset. I didn't even get the license.'

'Lauren,' said Gretchen disapprovingly. Gretchen hated women to look helpless. Lauren looked back at her.

'I was distraught,' she said evenly. She began picking up the finished cannelloni and lining the pan with neat rows. Little blankets. Little corpses. (No. I am being honest. Of course I didn't think this.)

Poncho had returned immediately to the couch and his books. 'Chicks shouldn't wander around the city alone at night,' he commented briefly. Lauren loved his protectiveness. Gretchen was silent.

'Then I asked to use the phone,' Lauren said. She wiped her forehead with her upper arm since her hands were covered with flour. She took the pan to the stove and ladled tomato sauce into it. 'The phone was in the kitchen. James took me in, then he went back. I put my keys on the floor, very quietly, and I kicked them under the table. Then I pretended to phone you.'

'All your keys?' Julie asked in dismay.

Lauren ignored her. 'I told them no one was home. I told them I'd been planning to take the bus, but by now, of course, I'd missed it.'

'All your keys?' I asked pointedly.

'James drove me home. Damn! If he hadn't been there . . .' Lauren slammed the oven door on our dinner and came to sit with us. 'What do you think?' she asked. 'Is he interested?'

'Sounds like James was interested,' said Gretchen.

'You left your name with your keys?' I said.

'Name, address, phone number. Now we wait.'

We waited. For two days the phone never rang. Not even our parents wanted to talk to us. In the interests of verisimilitude Lauren had left all her keys on the chain. She couldn't get into the apartment unless one of us had arranged to be home and let her in. She couldn't drive, which was just as well since every gas company had made the boycott list but Shell. Shell was not an American company, but we were still investigating. It seemed likely there was war profiteering there *somewhere*. And, if not, then we'd heard rumors of South African holdings. We were looking into it. But in the meantime we could still drive.

'The counterculture is going to make gas from chicken shit,' said Julie.

'Too bad they can't make it from bullshit,' Lauren said. 'We got plenty of that.'

Demonstrators had gone out and stopped the morning commuter traffic to protest the war. It had not been appreciated. It drove something of a wedge between us and the working class. Not that the proletariat had ever liked us much. I told our postman that more than two hundred colleges had closed. 'BFD,' he said, handing me the mail. Nothing for me.

You are on the surface of the moon and the air itself is a poison. Nothing moves, nothing grows, there is nothing, but ash. A helicopter has left you here and the air from its lift-off made the ash fly and then resettle into definite shapes, like waves. You don't move for fear of disturbing these patterns, which make you think of snow, of children lying on their backs in the snow until their arms turn into wings. You can see the shadows of winged people in the ash.

Nothing is alive here, so you are not here, after all, on this man-made moon where nothing can breathe. You are home and have been home for months. Your tour lasted just over a year and you only missed one Christmas. You have a job and a wife and you eat at restaurants, go to baseball games, commute on the bus. The war is over and there is nothing behind you but the bodies of angels flying on their backs in the ash.

Poncho never called. We went to the city meeting on the helicopter, all four of us, to help the city make this decision. The helicopter was item seven on the agenda. We never got to it. Child care had been promised, but not provided. Angry parents dumped their children on the stage of the Berkeley Community Theater to sit with the council members. A small girl with a sun painted on her forehead knocked over a microphone. The conservative council members went home. Berkeley.

Lauren found Poncho and James in the dress circle. Poncho was covering the meeting. Lauren introduced us all. 'By the way,' she said carefully, 'you didn't find a set of keys at your house, did you? I lost mine and that night is the last I remember having them.'

'Keys?' asked Poncho. 'No.' Something in his smile told me Lauren must have overplayed herself that evening. He knew exactly what was going on.

'If you do find them, you will call me?'

'Of course.'

Julie drove us home and I made Lauren a cup of tea. She held my hand for a moment as she took it from me. Then she smiled. 'I thought we were boycotting Lipton's,' she said.

'It's a British tea.' I stirred some milk into my own cup. 'That should be all right, shouldn't it?'

'Have you ever heard of Bernadette Devlin?' Gretchen asked.

We never saw Poncho again except on TV. On 29 June he told us all American forces had been withdrawn from Cambodia. Your birthday, so I remember the date. Not a bad lottery number either. So I always wondered. Were you really drafted? Did you enlist?

Poncho lost his job about the same time Nixon lost his. Some network executive decided blacks didn't need special news so they didn't need special reporters to give it to them. Let them watch the same news as the rest of us. And apparently Poncho's ability to handle generic news was doubtful. The network let him go. Politically we regretted this decision. Privately we thought he had it coming.

God, it was years ago. Years and years ago. I got married. Lauren went to Los Angeles and then to Paris and now she's in Washington writing speeches for some senator. Hey, we emerged from the war of the words with *some* expertise. Gretchen and Julie had a falling-out and hardly speak to each other now. Only when I'm there. They make a special effort for me.

Julie asked me recently why I was so sure there ever had been a real war. What proof did I have, she asked, that it wasn't a TV movie of the decade? A miniseries? A maxiseries?

It outraged Gretchen. 'Don't do that,' she snapped. 'Keep it real.' She turned to me. She said she saw you about a month ago at Fisherman's Wharf in San Francisco. She said you had no legs.

It doesn't alarm me as much as you might think. I see you all the time, too. You're in the park, pushing your kids on the swings and you've got one hand and one hook. Or you're sitting in a wheelchair in the aisle of the movie theater watching *The Deer Hunter*. Or you're weighing vegetables at the supermarket and you're fine, you're just fine, only it's never really you. Not any of them.

So what do you think of my war? At the worst I imagine you're a little angry. 'My God,' I can imagine you saying. 'You managed a clean escape. You had your friends, you had your games. You were quite happy.' Well, I promised you the truth. And the truth is that some of us went to jail. (Damn few. I know.) Some of us were killed. (And the numbers are irrelevant.) Some of us went to Canada and to Sweden. And some of us had a great time. But it wasn't a clean escape, really, for any of us.

Look at me. I'm operating all alone here with no affinity group and it seems unnatural to me. It seems to me that I should be surrounded by people I'd trust with my life. Always. It makes me cling to people, even people I don't care for all that much. It makes me panic when people leave. I'm sure they're not coming back. The war did this to me. Or you did. Same thing. What did the war do to you?

Look how much we have in common, after all. We both

lost. I lost my war. You lost your war. I look today at Vietnam and Cambodia and Laos and I feel sick inside. Do you ever ask yourself who won? Who the hell won?

Your war. I made it up, of course. It was nothing, *nothing* like that. Write me. Tell me about it. Please. If I have not heard from you by Christmas, I have decided to ask Lauren to go to the monument and look for your name. *I don't want to do this.* Don't make me do this. Just send me some word.

I am thirty-five years old. I am ready to believe anything you say.

Lily Red

One day Lily decided to be someone else. Some-one with a past. It was an affliction of hers, wanting this. The desire was seldom triggered by any actual incident or complaint, but seemed instead to be related to the act or prospect of lateral movement. She felt it every time a train passed. She would have traded places instantly with any person on any train. She felt it often in the car. She drove on to the freeway that ran between her job and her house and she thought about driving right past her exit and stopping in some small town wherever she happened to run out of gas and the next thing she knew, that was exactly what she had done.

Except that she was stopped by the police instead. She was well beyond the city; she had been through several cities, and the sky had darkened. The landscape flattened and she fell into a drowsy rhythm in which she and the car were both passengers in a small, impellent world defined by her head-lights. It was something of a shock to have to stop. She sat in her car while the police light rotated behind her and at regular intervals she watched her hands turn red on the steer-ing wheel. She had never been stopped by the police before. In the rearview mirror she could see the policeman talking to his radio. His door was slightly open; the light was on inside his car. He got out and came to talk to her. She turned her motor off. 'Lady,' he said and she wondered if policemen on television always called women *lady* because that was what real policemen did, or if he had learned this watching

television just as she had. 'Lady, you were flying. I clocked
you at eighty.'

Eighty. Lily couldn't help but be slightly impressed. She
had been twenty-five miles per hour over the limit without
even realizing she was speeding. It suggested she could handle
even faster speeds. 'Eighty,' she said contritely. 'You know
what I think I should do? I think I've been driving too long
and I think I should just find a place to stay tonight. I think
that would be best. I mean, eighty. That's too fast. Don't
you think?'

'I really do.' The policeman removed a pen from the pocket
inside his jacket.

'I won't do it again,' Lily told him. 'Please don't give me
a ticket.'

'I could spare you the ticket,' the policeman said, 'and I
could read in the paper tomorrow that you smashed yourself
into a retaining wall not fifteen miles from here. I don't think
I could live with myself. Give me your license. Just take it
out of the wallet, please. Mattie Drake runs a little bed and
breakfast place in Two Trees. You want the next exit and
bear left. First right, first right again. Street dead-ends in
Mattie's driveway. There's a sign on the lawn. *Mattie's*.
Should be all lit up this time of night. It's a nice place and
doesn't cost too much in the off season.' He handed Lily
back her license and the ticket for her to sign. He took his
copy. 'Get a good night's sleep,' he said and in the silence
she heard his boots scattering gravel from the shoulder of
the road as he walked away.

She crumpled the ticket into the glove compartment and
waited for him to leave. He shut off the rotating light, turned
on the headlights, and outwaited her. He followed all the
way to the next exit. So Lily had to take it.

She parked her car at the edge of Mattie's lawn. Moths
circled the lights on the sign and on the porch. A large white
owl slid through the dusky air, transformed by the lights
beneath it into something angelic. A cricket landed on the
sleeve of her linen suit. The sprinklers went on suddenly; the

watery hiss erased the hum of insects, but the pathway to the door remained dry. Lily stood on the lighted porch and rang the bell.

The woman who answered wore blue jeans and a flannel shirt. She had the angular hips of an older woman, but her hair showed very little gray, just a small patch right at the forehead. 'Come in, darling,' she said. There was a faint southern softness in her voice. 'You look tired. Do you want a room? Have you come to see the caves? I'm Mattie.'

'Yes, of course,' Lily told her. 'I need a room. I met some people who were here last year. You really *have* to see these caves, they told me.'

'I'll have Katherine pack you a lunch if you like,' Mattie offered. 'It's beautiful hiking weather. You won't get nearly so hot as in the summer. You can go tomorrow.'

Lily borrowed the phone in the living room to call David. It sat on a small table between a glass ball with a single red rosebud frozen inside and a picture of the Virgin praying. The Virgin wore a blue mantilla and appeared to be suspended in a cloudless sky. The phone had a dial which Lily spun. She was so used to the tune their number made on the touch phone at work that she missed hearing it. She listened to the answering machine, heard her voice which sounded nothing like her voice, suggesting that she leave a message. 'I'm in Two Trees at Mattie's bed and breakfast,' she said. 'I had this sudden impulse to see the caves. I may stay a couple of days. Will you call Harriet and tell her I won't be in tomorrow? It's real slow. There won't be a problem.' She would have told David she missed him, but she ran out of time. She would have only said it out of politeness anyway. They had been married nine years. She would miss him later. She would begin to miss him when she began to miss herself. He might be missing her, too, just about then. It would be nice if all these things happened at the same time.

She took the key from Mattie, went upstairs, used the bathroom at the end of the hall, used someone else's toothbrush, rinsing it out repeatedly afterwards, unlocked her door, removed all her clothes and cried until she fell asleep.

In the morning Lily lay in bed and watched the sun stretch over the quilt and onto the skin of her arms and her hands. She looked around the room. The bed was narrow and had a headpiece made of iron. A pattern of small pink flowers papered the walls. On the bookcase next to the bed a china lady held a china umbrella with one hand and extended the other, palm up, to see if the rain had stopped. There were books. *Beauty's Secret*, one of them said on the spine. Lily opened it, but it turned out to be about horses.

A full-length mirror hung on the back of the bedroom door. Lily didn't notice until the sunlight touched its surface, doubling in brightness. She rose and stood in front of it, backlit by the sunny window, frontlit by the mirror so that she could hardly see. She leaned in closer. Last night's crying had left her eyes red and the lids swollen. She looked at herself for a long time, squinting and changing the angle. Who was she? There was absolutely no way to tell.

The smell of coffee came up the stairs and through the shut door. Lily found her clothes on the desk chair where she had left them. She put them on: stockings, a fuchsia blouse, an eggshell business suit, heels. She used the bathroom, someone else's hairbrush as well as someone else's toothbrush, and came downstairs.

'You can't go hiking dressed like that,' Mattie told her and, of course, Lily couldn't. 'You have nothing else? What size shoe do you wear? A six and a half? Six? Tiny little thing, aren't you? Katherine might have something that will do.' She raised her voice. 'Katherine? Katherine!'

Katherine came through the doorway at the bottom of the stairs, drying her hands on a dish towel. She was somewhat younger than Mattie though older than Lily, middle forties, perhaps, and heavier, a dark-skinned woman with straight black hair. On request she produced jeans for Lily, a sleeveless T-shirt, a red sweatshirt, gray socks, and sneakers. Everything was too big for Lily. Everything was wearable.

Mattie took her through the screen door and out the back porch after breakfast. Beyond the edge of Mattie's sprinklers, the lawn stopped abruptly at a hill of sand and manzanita. Mattie had stowed a lunch and a canteen into a yellow day-pack. She began to help Lily into it. 'You go up,' Mattie said. 'All the way up. And then down. You can see the trail from the other side of the fence. Watch for rattlers. You hiked much?' Lily was having trouble slipping her left arm under the second strap. It caught at the elbow, her arm pinned behind her. Mattie eased the pack off and began again.

'Oh, yes,' Lily assured her. 'I've hiked a lot.' Mattie looked unconvinced. 'I'm a rock-climber,' said Lily. 'That's the kind of hiking I'm used to. Crampons and ropes and mallets. I don't usually wear them on my back. I wear them on my belt. I take groups out. Librarians and school teachers and beauticians. You know.'

'Well, there's just a trail here,' said Mattie doubtfully. 'I don't suppose you can get into trouble as long as you stay on the trail. Your shoes don't really fit well. I'm afraid you'll blister.'

'I once spent three days alone in the woods without food or shelter and it snowed. I was getting a merit badge.' The daypack was finally in place. 'Thank you,' Lily said.

'Wait here. I'm going to get some moleskin for your feet. And I'm going to send Jep along with you. Jep has a lot of common sense. And Jep knows the way. You'll be glad of the company,' Mattie told her. She disappeared back into the house.

'It was in Borneo,' Lily said softly, so that Mattie wouldn't hear. 'You want to talk of blisters. You try walking in the snows of Borneo.'

Jep turned out to be a young collie. One ear flopped over in proper collie fashion. One pointed up like a shepherd's. 'I've heard some nice things about you,' Lily told him. He followed Lily out to the gate and then took the lead, his tail and hindquarters moving from side to side with every step. The weather was cool when they started. In an hour or so,

Lily removed her sweatshirt and Jep's tongue drooped from his mouth. Everyone felt good.

The sun was not yet overhead when Lily stopped for lunch. 'Eleven twenty-two,' she told Jep. 'Judging solely by the sun.' Katherine had packed apple juice and cold chicken and an orange with a seam cut into the peel and a chocolate Hostess cupcake with a cream center for dessert. Lily had not seen a cupcake like that since she had stopped taking a lunch to school. She sat with her back against a rock overhang and shared it with Jep, giving him none of the cream filling. There was a red place on her left heel and she covered it with moleskin. Jep lay on his side. Lily felt drowsy. 'You want to rest a while?' she asked Jep. 'I don't really care if we make the caves and you've seen them before. I could give a damn about the caves, if you want to know the truth.' She yawned. Somewhere to the left a small animal scuttled in the brush. Jep hardly lifted his head. Lily made a pillow out of Katherine's red sweatshirt and went to sleep, leaning against the overhang.

When she woke, the sun was behind her. Jep was on his feet, looking at something above her head. His tail wagged slowly and he whined once. On the ground, stretching over him and extending several more feet, lay the shadow of a man, elongated legs, one arm up as though he were waving. When Lily moved away from the overhang and turned to look, he was gone.

It unsettled her. She supposed that a seasoned hiker would have known better than to sleep on the trail. She turned to go back to Mattie's and had only walked a short way, less than a city block, when she saw something she had missed coming from the other direction. A woman was painted on to the flat face of a rock which jutted up beside the trail. The perspective was somewhat flattened, and the image had been simplified, which made it extraordinarily compelling somehow. Especially for a painting on a rock. When had Lily ever seen anything painted on a rock other than 'Kelly loves Eric' or 'Angela puts out'? The woman's long, black hair fell straight down both sides of her face. Her dark eyes were half-closed; her skin was brown. She was looking down at her hands, which she held cupped together, and she was dressed all in red. Wherever the surface of the rock was the roughest, the paint had cracked, and one whole sleeve had flaked off entirely. Lily leaned down to touch the missing arm. There was a silence as if the birds and the snakes and the insects had all suddenly run out of breath. Lily straightened and the ordinary noises began again. She followed Jep back down the trial.

'I didn't get to the caves,' she admitted to Mattie. 'I'll go again tomorrow. But I did see something intriguing. The painting. The woman painted on the rock. I'm used to graffiti, but not this kind. Who painted her?'

'I don't know,' said Mattie. 'She's been here longer than I have. We get a lot of farm labor through, seasonal labor, you know. I always thought she looked Mexican. And you see paintings like that a lot in Mexico. Rock Madonnas. I read somewhere that the artists usually use their own mother's faces for inspiration. The writer said that you see these paintings by the roadside all the time and that those cultures in which men idolize their own mothers are the most sexist cultures in the world. Interesting article. She's faded a lot over the years.'

'You don't often see a Madonna dressed in red,' Lily said.

'No, you don't,' Mattie agreed. 'Blue usually, isn't it?' She helped Lily out of the pack. 'Did you get blisters?' she asked. 'I was worried about you.'

'No,' said Lily, although the spot on her heel had never stopped bothering her. 'I was fine.'

'You know who might be able to tell you about the painting? Allison Beale. Runs the county library, but lives here in Two Trees. She's been here forever. You could run over tonight and ask her if you like. I'll give you the address. She likes company.'

So Lily got back in her car with Allison Beale's address in her pocket and a map to Allison's house. She was supposed to go there first and then pick up some dinner at a little restaurant called The Italian Kitchen, but she turned left instead of right and then left again to a bar she'd noticed on her way into Two Trees, with a neon martini glass tipping in the window. The only other customer, a man, stood with his back to her, studying the jukebox selections, but choosing nothing. Lily sat at the counter and ordered a margarita. It came without salt and the ice floated inside it uncrushed. 'You're the lady staying with Mattie,' the bartender informed her. 'My name is Egan. Been to the caves?'

'Lily,' Lily said. 'I don't like caves. I can get lost in the supermarket. Wander for days without a sweater in the frozen foods. I'm afraid to think what would happen to me in a cave.'

'These caves aren't deep,' the bartender said, wiping the counter in front of her with the side of his hand. 'Be a shame to come all the way to Two Trees and not even see the caves.'

'Take a native guide,' the other man suggested. He had come up behind her while she ordered. She slid around on the bar stool.

'Henry,' he told her. He wore a long, black braid and a turquoise necklace. The last time Lily had seen him he had been dressed as a policeman. She'd had no sense of his hair being long like this.

'You're an Indian,' Lily said.

'Can't put anything past you.' He sat down on the stool next to hers. Lily guessed he was somewhere in his thirties, just about her own age. 'Take off your wedding ring and I'll buy you a drink.'

She slid the ring off her finger. Her hands were cold and it didn't even catch at the knuckle. She laid it on the napkin. 'It's off,' she said. 'But that's all I'm taking off. I hope we understand each other.'

The bartender brought her a second margarita. 'The first one was on the house,' he said. 'Because you're a guest in

Two Trees. The second one is on Henry. We'll worry about the third when you get to it.'

Lily got to it about an hour later. She could easily have done without it. She was already quite drunk. She and Henry and the bartender were still the only people in the bar.

'It just intrigued me, you know?' she said. The bartender stood draped across the counter next to her. Henry leaned on one elbow. Lily could hear that she was slurring her words. She tried to sharpen them. 'It seemed old. I thought it intrigued me enough to go talk to the librarian about it, but I was wrong about that.' She laughed and started on her third drink. 'It should be restored,' she added. 'Like the Sistine Chapel.'

'I can tell you something about it,' the bartender said. 'I can't swear any of it's true, but I know what people say. It's a picture of a miracle.' He glanced at Henry. 'Happened more than a hundred years ago. It was painted by a man, a local man, I don't think anyone remembers who. And this woman appeared to him one day, by the rock. She held out her hands, cupped, just the way he drew them, like she was offering him something, but her hands were empty. And then she disappeared again.'

'Well?' said Lily.

'Well, what?' Henry answered her. She turned back to him. Henry was drinking something clear from a shot glass. Egan kept it filled; Henry never asked him, but emptied the glass several times without appearing to be affected. Lily wondered if it might even be water.

'What was the miracle? What happened?'

There was a pause. Henry looked down into his drink. Egan finally spoke. 'Nothing happened that I know of.' He looked at Henry. Henry shrugged. 'The miracle was that she appeared. The miracle was that he turned out to be the kind of person something like this happened to.' Lily shook her head in dissatisfaction. 'It's kind of a miracle the painting has lasted so long, don't you think?' Egan suggested. 'Out there in the wind and the sand for all those years?' Lily shook her head again.

'You are a hard woman,' Henry told her. He leaned closer. 'And a beautiful one.'

It made Lily laugh at him for being so unoriginal. 'Right.' She stirred her drink with her finger. 'How do Indians feel about their mothers?'

'I loved mine. Is that the right answer?'

'I'll tell you what I've always heard about Indians.' Lily put her elbows on the counter between them, her chin in her hands.

'I bet I know this.' Henry's voice dropped to a whisper. 'I bet I know exactly what you've always heard.'

'I've heard that sexual technique is passed from father to son.' Lily took a drink. 'And you know what I've always thought? I've always thought a lot of mistakes must be perpetuated this way. A culture that passed on sexual techniques from *mother* to son would impress me.'

'So there's a middle man,' said Henry. 'Give it a chance. It could still work.' The phone rang at the end of the bar. Egan went to answer it. Henry leaned forward, staring at her intently. 'You have incredible eyes,' he said and she looked away from him immediately. 'I can't decide what color they are.'

Lily laughed again, this time at herself. She didn't want to respond to such a transparent approach, but she couldn't help it. The laugh had an hysterical edge. She got to her feet. 'Take off your pants, and I'll buy you a drink,' she said and enjoyed the startled look on Henry's face. She held on to the counter, brushing against him by accident on her way to the back of the bar.

'End of the counter and left,' the bartender told her, hanging up the telephone. She gripped each stool and spun it as she went by, hand over hand, for as long as they lasted. She made it the last few steps to the bathroom on her own. The door was marked with the silhouette of a figure wearing a skirt. Lily fell through it and into the stall. On one side of her 'Brian is a fox' was scratched into the wall. On the other side were the words 'Chastity Chews.' A picture accompanied the text, another picture of a woman, presumably chewing chastity. She had many arms like Kali and a great many teeth. A balloon rose from her mouth. 'Hi,' she said simply.

Lily spent some time at the mirror, fixing her hair. She blew a breath into her hand and tried to smell it, but all she could smell was the lavatory soap. She supposed this was good. 'I'm going home,' she announced, back in the bar. 'I've enjoyed myself.'

She felt around in her purse for her keys. Henry held them up and rang them together. 'I can't let you drive home. You hardly made it to the bathroom.'

'I can't let you take me. I don't know you well enough.'

'I wasn't going to suggest that. Looks like you have to walk.'

Lily reached for the keys and Henry closed his fist about them. 'It's only about six blocks,' he said.

'It's dark. I could be assaulted.'

'Not in Two Trees.'

'Anywhere. Are you kidding?' Lily smiled at him. 'Give me the keys. I already have a blister.'

'I could give you the keys and you could hit a tree not two blocks from here. I don't think I could live with myself. Egan will back me up on this.' Henry gestured with his closed fist towards the bartender.

'Damn straight,' said Egan. 'There's no way you're driving home. You'll be fine walking. And, anyway, Jep's come for you.' Lily could see a vague doggy shape through the screen door out of the bar.

'Hello, Jep,' Lily said. The figure through the screen wagged from side to side. 'All right.' Lily turned back to the men at the bar. 'All right,' she conceded. 'I'm walking. The men in this town are pitiless, but the dogs are fine. You've got to love the dogs.'

She swung the screen door open. Jep backed out of the

way. 'Tomorrow,' Egan called out behind her, 'you go see those caves.'

Jep walked beside her on the curbside, between her and the street. Most of the houses were closed and dark. In front of one a woman sat on a porch swing, holding a baby and humming to it. Some heartbreak song. By the time Lily reached Mattie's she felt sober again.

Mattie was sitting in the living room. 'Egan called,' she said. 'I made you some tea. I know it's not what you think you want, but it has some herbs in it, very effective against hangover. You won't be sorry you drank it. It's a long hike to the caves. You want to be rested.'

Lily sat on the couch beside her. 'Thank you. You're being very good to me, Mattie. I don't deserve it. I've been behaving very badly.'

'Maybe it's just my turn to be good,' said Mattie. 'Maybe you finished your turn. Did you ever get any dinner?'

'I think I may have had some pretzels.' Lily looked across the room to the phone, wondering if she were going to call David. She looked at the picture of the Madonna. It was not a very interesting one. Too sweet. Too much sweetness. 'I should call my husband,' she told Mattie and didn't move.

'Would you like me to leave you alone?'

'No,' said Lily. 'It wouldn't be that sort of call. David and I, we don't have personal conversations.' She realized suddenly that she had left her wedding ring back at the bar on the cocktail napkin beside her empty glass.

'Is the marriage a happy one?' Mattie asked. 'Forgive me if I'm prying. It's just – well, here you are.'

'I don't know,' said Lily.

Mattie put her arm around Lily and Lily leaned against her. 'Loving is a lot harder for some people than for others,' she said. 'And being loved can be hardest of all. Not for you, though. Not for a loving woman like you.'

Lily sat up and reached for her tea. It smelled of chamomile. 'Mattie,' she said. She didn't know how to explain. Lily felt that she always appeared to be a better person than she was. It was another affliction. In many ways Mattie's analysis was true. Lily knew that her family and friends wondered how she lived with such a cold, methodical man. But there was another truth, too. Often, Lily set up little tests for David, tests of his sensitivity, tests of his commitment. She was always pleased when he failed them, because it proved the problems between them were still his fault. Not a loving thing to do. 'Don't make me out to be some saint,' she said.

She slept very deeply that night, dreaming on alcohol and tea, and woke up late in the morning. It was almost ten before she and Jep hit the trail. She watched for the painting on her way up this time, stopping to eat an identical lunch in a spot where she could look at it. Jep sat beside her, panting. They passed the rock overhang where she had eaten lunch the day before, finished the climb uphill and started down. The drop-off was sharp; the terrain was dusty and uninviting, and Lily, who was tired of walking uphill, found it even harder to descend. When the trail stopped at a small hollow in the side of a rock, she decided she would rest and then go back. Everyone else might be excessively concerned that she see the caves, but she couldn't bring herself to care. She dropped the daypack on the ground and sat beside it. Jep raised his collie ear and wagged his tail. Turning, Lily was not at all surprised to see Henry coming down the hill, his hair loose and hanging to his shoulders.

'So,' he said. 'You found the caves without me.'

'You're kidding.' Lily stood up. 'This little scrape in the rock? This can't be the famous Two Trees caves. I won't believe it. Tell me there are real caves just around the next bend.'

'You need something more?' Henry asked. 'This isn't enough? You are a hard woman.'

'Oh, come on.' Lily flicked her hair out of her eyes. 'Are you telling me people come from all over to see this?'

'It's not the caves.' Henry was staring at her. She felt her face reddening. 'It's what happens in the caves.' He moved closer to her. 'It's what happens when a beautiful woman comes to the caves.' Lily let herself look right at his eyes. Inside his pupils, a tiny Lily looked back out.

'Stay away from me,' said Lily. Was she the kind of woman who would allow a strange man in a strange place to kiss her? Apparently so. Apparently she was the kind of woman who said no to nothing now. She reached out to Henry; she put one hand on the sleeve of his shirt, one hand on his neck, moved the first hand to his back. 'I gave you my car and my wedding ring,' she told him. 'What do you want now? What will satisfy you?' She kissed him first. They dropped to their knees on the hard floor of the cave. He kissed her back.

'We could go somewhere more comfortable,' said Lily.

'No,' said Henry. 'It has to be here.'

They removed their clothes and spread them about as padding. The shadow of the rock lengthened over them. Jep whined once or twice and then went to sleep at a safe distance. Lily couldn't relax. She let Henry work at it. She touched his face and kissed his hand. 'Your father did a nice job,' she told him, moving as close to his side as she could, holding herself against him. 'You do that wonderfully.' Henry's arm lay underneath her back. He lifted her with it, turning her so that she was on top of him, facing down. He took hold of her hair and pulled her face to his own, put his mouth on her mouth. Then he let go, staring at her, holding the bits of hair about her face in his hands. 'You are so beautiful,' he said and something broke inside her.

'Am I?' She was frightened because she suddenly needed to believe him, needed to believe that he might love her, whoever she was.

'Incredibly beautiful.'

'Am I?' Don't say it if you don't mean it, she told him silently, too afraid to talk and almost crying. Don't make me want it if it's not there. Please. Be careful what you say.

'Incredibly beautiful.' He began to move again inside her. 'So beautiful.' He watched her face. 'So beautiful.' He touched her breasts and then his eyes closed and his mouth rounded. She thought he might fly apart, his body shook so and she held him together with her hands, kissed him until he stopped and then kissed him again.

'I don't want to hurt you,' Henry said.

It hurt Lily immediately, like a slap. So now she was the sort of woman men said this to. Well, she had no right to expect anything different from a man she didn't even know. She could have said it to him first if she'd thought of it. That would have been the smart thing to do. Nothing would have been stupider than needing him. What had she been thinking of? 'But you will if you have to,' she finished. 'Right? Don't worry. I'm not making anything of this. I know what this is.' She sat up and reached for Katherine's sweatshirt. She was cold and afraid to move closer to Henry. She was cold, and she didn't want to be naked any more.

'You sound angry,' Henry said. 'It's not that I couldn't love you. It's not that I don't already love you. Men always disappoint women. I'm not sure we can escape it.'

'Don't be ridiculous,' Lily told him sharply. She put her head into the red tent of the sweatshirt and pulled it through. 'I should have gotten your sexual history first,' she added. 'I haven't done this since the rules changed.'

'I haven't been with a woman in ten years,' Henry said. Lily looked at his face in surprise.

'Before that it was five years,' he said. 'And before that three, but that was two at once. That was the sixties. Before that it was fifteen years. And twenty before that. And two. And two. And before that almost a hundred.'

Lily stood up, pulling on Katherine's jeans. 'I should have gotten your psychiatric history first,' she said. The faster she tried to dress, the more difficulties she had. She couldn't find one of Katherine's socks. She was too angry and frightened to look among Henry's clothes. She put on Katherine's shoes without it. 'Come on, Jep,' she said.

'It can't mean anything,' Henry told her.

'It didn't. Forget it.' Lily left without the daypack. She hurried up the trail. Jep followed somewhat reluctantly. They made the crest of the hill; Lily looked behind her often to see if Henry was following. He wasn't. She went past the painting without stopping. Jep preceded her through the gate into Mattie's backyard.

Mattie and Katherine were waiting in the house. Katherine put her arms around her. 'You went to the caves,' Katherine said. 'Didn't you? I can tell.'

'Of course she did,' said Mattie. She stroked Lily's hair. 'Of course she did.'

Lily stood stiffly inside Katherine's arms. 'What the hell is going on?' she asked. She pushed away and looked at the two women. 'You sent me up there, didn't you? You did! You and Egan and probably Allison Beale, too. Go to the caves, go to the caves. That's all I've heard since I got here. You dress me like some virginal sacrifice, fatten me up with Hostess cupcakes and send me to him. But why?'

'It's a miracle,' said Mattie. 'You were chosen. Can't you feel it?'

'I let some man pick me up in a bar. He turns out to be a nut.' Lily's voice rose higher. 'Where's the miracle?'

'You slept with Henry,' said Mattie. 'Henry chose *you*. Just like the woman in the painting chose him. That's the miracle.'

Lily ran up the stairs. She stripped Katherine's clothes off and put her own on. Mattie came and stood in the doorway. Lily walked around her and out of the room.

'Listen to me, Lily,' Mattie said. 'You don't understand. He gave you as much as he can give anyone. That's why in the painting the woman's hands are empty. But that's *his* trap. *His* curse. Not yours. When you see that, you'll forgive him. Katherine and Allison and I all forgave him. I know you will, too. A loving woman like you.' Mattie reached out, grabbing Lily's sleeve. 'Stay here with us. You can't go back to your old life. You won't be able to. You've been chosen.'

'Look,' said Lily. She took a deep breath and wiped at her eyes with her hands. 'I wasn't chosen. Quite the opposite. I was picked up and discarded. By a man in his thirties and not the same man you slept with. Maybe you slept with a god. You go ahead and tell yourself that. What difference does it make? You were still picked up and discarded.' She shook loose of Mattie and edged down the stairs. She expected to be stopped, but she wasn't. At the front door, she turned. Mattie stood on the landing behind her. Mattie held out one hand. Lily shook her head. 'I think you're pretty pathetic, if you want to know the truth. I'm not going to tell myself a lot of lies or listen to yours. I know who I am. I'm going. I won't be back. Don't expect me.'

Her car waited at the front of the house, just where she had parked it the first night. She ran from the porch. The keys were inside. Left and left again, past the bar where the martini glass tipped darkly in the window, and on to the freeway. Lily accelerated way past eighty and no one stopped her. The foothills sped by and became cities. When she felt that she was far enough away to be safe from small town Madonnas and men who were cursed to endure centuries of casual sex with as many loving women as possible, which was damn few, in fact, if you believed the numbers they gave you, she slowed down. She arrived home in the early evening. As she was walking in the door, she noticed she was wearing her wedding ring.

David was sitting on the couch reading a book. 'Here I am, David,' Lily said. 'I'm here. I got a speeding ticket. I never looked to see how much it was for. I lost my ring playing poker, but I mortgaged the house and won it back. I lost a lot more, though. I lost my head. I'm half-hearted now. In fact, I'm not at all the woman I was. I've got to be honest with you.'

'I'm glad you're home,' said David. He went back to his book.

Contention

Some of us are dreamers.
Kermit the Frog

At dinner Claire's son asks her if she knows the name of the man who is on record as having grown the world's largest vegetable, not counting the watermelon, which may be a fruit, Claire's son is not sure. Claire says that she doesn't. Her son is eight years old. It is an annoying age. He wants her to guess.

'I really don't know, honey,' Claire says.

So he gives her a hint. 'It was a turnip.'

Claire eliminates the entire population of Lapland. 'Elliot,' she guesses.

'Nope.' His voice holds an edge of triumph, but no more than is polite. 'Wrong. Guess again.'

'Just tell me,' Claire suggests.

'Guess first.'

'Edmund,' Claire says, and her son regards her with narrowing eyes.

'Guess the last name.'

Claire remembers that there are more Chinese in the world than anything else. 'Edmund Li,' she guesses, but the correct answer is Edmund Firthgrove and the world's most common surname is Chang. So she is not even close.

'Guess who has the world's longest fingernails,' her son suggests. 'It's a man.'

Well, Claire is quite certain it's not going to be Edmund Firthgrove. Life is a bifurcated highway. She points this out to her son, turns to make sure her daughter is listening as well. 'We live in an age of specialization,' she tells them. 'You can make gardening history or you can make fingernail history, but there's no way in hell you can make both. Remember this. This is your mother speaking. If you want to be great, you've got to make choices.' And then immediately Claire wonders if what she has just said is true.

'We're having hamburgers again.' Claire's husband makes this observation in a slow, dispassionate voice. Just the facts, ma'am. 'We had hamburgers on Sunday and then again on Thursday. This makes three times this week.'

Claire tells him she is going for a personal record. In fact it is a headline she saw while waiting with the ground meat for the supermarket checker that is making her rethink the issue of choices now. 'Meet the laziest man in the world,' it said. 'In bed since 1969 . . . his wife even shaves and bathes him.'

Claire imagines that a case like this one begins when a man loses his job. He may spend weeks seeking employment and never even make it to the interview. He's just not a self-starter. Thoroughly demoralized, on a Monday in 1969, at the height of the Vietnam War, he refuses to get out of bed. 'What's the point?' he asks his wife. She is tolerant at first. He needs his rest. Fine. She leaves him alone for a couple of days, even brings in trays of food, changes the channel on the TV for him.

This is no bid for greatness, this is a modified suicide. 'Man collapses watching game show.' But staying in bed turns out to have pleasant associations for him. He begins to remember a bout of chicken pox he had as a child, how his mother would bring him glasses of orange juice. He feels warm and cared for. His despair begins to dissipate. 'I've got such a craving for orange juice,' he tells his wife.

Months pass, he has been in bed an entire year before he realizes what he has become. He's not just some schlub who can't find work. Suddenly he's a *contender*. With stamina, perseverance, and support he can turn tragedy into triumph.

He tells his wife that the only thing they have to fear now is a failure of nerve.

How does she feel about this? In the picture which accompanied the story she was shown plumping up his pillow and smiling, a beefy sort of woman, a type that is never going to be fashionable. She may feel, like him, that this is her only shot. His greatness is her greatness; his glory is her glory.

Or her motives may be less pure. Out in the world more, she is bound to be more worldly than he is. He has a vision. He is extending the boundaries of human achievement. She is speculating on the possibility of a movie made for TV. She may suggest that, as long as he is just lying there, he could be growing his fingernails, too.

She is an ignorant woman. You don't just grow your fingernails because you happen to have time on your hands. It requires commitment, a special, gelatinous diet, internal and external fortification. A person's nails, in fact, are at most risk during those precise hours a person spends in bed. She has her own motives, of course. She is tired of clipping his nails. 'Why don't you grow your beard out?' she suggests, rouging her cheeks and donning a feathery hat before slipping out to a three-martini lunch with the network executives. She will order lobster, then sell the exclusive rights to the tabloids instead. 'Why don't you make a ball out of twine?' The largest recorded string ball is more than twelve feet in diameter. *That* will keep him in bed for a while.

At the restaurant she meets Solero don Guillermo, the world's fastest flamenco dancer. She forgets to come home. Her husband grows hungrier and hungrier. He makes his way to the kitchen five days later, a smashed man. He contemplates cutting his wrists. Instead, while preparing his own breakfast, he manages, in twelve seconds, to chop a cucumber into 250 slices, beating Hugh Andrews of Blackpool by four cuts. The rounds of cucumber are so fine you could watch TV through them.

Forty-two years later – a good twenty-four years off the

record – he gets his wife's note, placed in a bottle and tossed off the *Queen Mary*. 'Kiss my ass,' it says.

'You *know*,' Claire's son's voice is accusing, 'how much I hate raw hamburgers. This is all pink in the middle. It's gross. I can't eat this.'

'I'm tired of hamburgers,' Claire's daughter says.

'Is there anything else to eat?' Claire's husband asks.

Claire smiles at them all. She sends them a message, tapping it out with her fork on the side of her plate. It may take years, but she imagines it will get there eventually.

The Faithful Companion at Forty

*This one is also for Queequeg, for
Kato, for Spock, for
Tinkerbell, and for Chewbacca*

His first reaction is that I just can't deal with the larger theoretical issues. He's got this new insight he wants to call the Displacement Theory, and I can't grasp it. Your basic, quiet, practical minority sidekick. The *limited* edition. Kato. Spock. Me. But this is not true.

I still remember the two general theories we were taught on the reservation that purported to explain the movement of history. The first we named the Great Man Theory. Its thesis was that the critical decisions in human development were made by individuals, special people gifted in personality and circumstance. The second we named the Wave Theory. It argued that only the masses could effectively determine the course of history. Those very visible individuals who appeared as leaders of the great movements were, in fact, only those who happened to articulate the direction that had already been chosen. They were as much the victims of the process as any other single individual. Flotsam. Running Dog and I used to be able to debate this issue for hours.

It is true that this particular question has ceased to interest me much. But a correlative question has come to interest me more. I spent most of my fortieth birthday sitting by myself, listening to Pachelbel's *Canon*, over and over, and I'm asking myself: are some people special? Are some people more special than others? *Have I spent my whole life backing the wrong horse?*

I mean, it was my birthday and not one damn person called.

Finally, about four o'clock in the afternoon, I gave up and called him. 'Eh, Poncho,' I say. 'What's happening?'

'Eh, Cisco,' he answers. 'Happy birthday.'

'Thanks.' I tell him. I can't decide whether I am more pissed to know he remembered but didn't call than I was when I thought he forgot.

'The big four-o,' he says. 'Wait a second, buddy. Let me go turn the music down.' He's got the *William Tell Overture* blasting on the stereo. He's always got the *William Tell Overture* blasting on the stereo. It makes him feel like an adventure is about to begin. Sort of like Pavlov's dogs.

I'm not saying the man has a problem, but the last time we were in Safeway together he claimed to see a woman being kidnapped by a silver baron over in frozen foods. He pulled the flip top off a Tab and lobbed the can into the ice cream. 'Cover me,' he shouts, and runs an end pattern with the cart through the soups. I had to tell everyone he was having a Vietnam flashback.

And the mask. There are times and seasons when a mask is useful; I'm the first to admit that. It's Thanksgiving, say, and you're an Indian so it's never been one of your favorite holidays, and you've got no family because you spent your youth playing the supporting role to some macho creep who couldn't commit, so here you are, *standing in line* to see *Rocky IV*, and someone you know walks by. I mean, I've been there. But for everyday, for your ordinary life, a mask is only going to make you *more* obvious. There's an element of exhibitionism in it. A large element. If you ask me.

So now he's back on the phone. He sighs, 'God,' he says. 'I miss those thrilling days of yesteryear.'

See? We haven't talked twenty seconds and already the subject is *his* problems. *His* ennui. *His* angst. 'I'm having an affair,' I tell him. Two years ago I wouldn't have said it.

Two years ago he'd just completed his Est training and he would have told me to take responsibility for it. Now he's into biofeedback and astrology. Now we're not responsible for anything.

'Yeah?' he says. He thinks for a minute. 'You're not married,' he points out.

I can't see that this is relevant. 'She is,' I tell him.

'Yeah?' he says again, only this 'yeah' has a nasty quality to it, this 'yeah' tells me someone is hoping for sensationalistic details. This is not the 'yeah' of a concerned friend. Still, I can't help playing to it. For years I've been holding this man's horse while he leaps on to its back from the roof. For years I've been providing cover from behind a rock while he breaks for the back door. I'm forty now. It's time to get something back from him. So I hint at the use of controlled substances. We're talking peyote *and* cocaine. I mention pornography. Illegally imported. From Denmark. Of course, it's not really *my* affair. Can you picture me? My affair is quiet and ardent. I borrowed this affair from another friend. It shows you the lengths I have to go to before anyone will listen to me.

I may finally have gone too far. He's really at a loss now. 'Women,' he says finally. 'You can't live with them and you can't live without them.' Which is a joke, coming from him. He had that single-man-raising-his-orphaned-nephew-all-alone shtick working so smoothly the women were passing each other on the way in and out the door. Or maybe it was the mask and the leather. What do women want? Who has a clue?

'Is that it?' I ask him. 'The sum total of your advice? She won't leave her husband. Man, my *heart* is broken.'

'Oh,' he says. There's a long pause. 'Don't let it show,' he suggests. Then he sighs. 'I miss that old white horse,' he tells me. And you know what I do? I hang up on him. And you know what he *doesn't* do? He doesn't call me back.

It really hurts me.

So his second reaction, now that I don't want to listen to him explaining his new theories to me, is to say that I seem to be sulking about something, he can't imagine what. And this is harder to deny.

The day after my birthday I went for a drive in my car, a little white Saab with personalized license plates. KEMO, they say. Maybe the phone is ringing, maybe it's not. I feel better when I don't know. So, he misses his horse. Hey, *I've* never been the same since that little pinto of mine joined the Big Round-up, but I try not to burden my friends with this. I try not to burden my friends with *anything*. I just nurse them back to health when the Cavendish gang leaves them for dead. I just come in the middle of the night with the medicine man when little Britt has a fever and it's not responding to Tylenol. I just organize the surprise party when a friend turns forty.

You want to bet even Attila the Hun had a party on his fortieth? You want to bet he was one hard man to surprise? And who blew up the balloons and had everyone hiding under the rugs and in with the goats? This name is lost forever.

I drove into the country, where every cactus holds its memory for me, where every outcropping of rock once hid an outlaw. Ten years ago the terrain was still so rough I would have had to take the International Scout. Now it's a paved highway straight to the hanging tree. I pulled over on the shoulder of the road, turned off the motor, and I just sat there. I was remembering the time Ms Emily Cooper stumbled into the Wilcox bank robbery looking for her little girl who'd gone with friends to the swimming hole and hadn't bothered to tell her mama. We were on our way to see Colonel Davis at Fort Comanche about some cattle rustling. We hadn't heard about the bank robbery. Which is why we were taken completely by surprise.

My pony and I were eating the masked man's dust, as usual, when something hit me from behind. Arnold Wilcox, a heavy-set man who sported a five o'clock shadow by eight in the morning, jumped me from the big rock overlooking the Butterfield trail and I went down like a sack of potatoes.

I heard horses converging on us from the left and the right and that hypertrophic white stallion of his took off like a big bird. I laid one on Arnold's stubby jaw, but he cold-cocked me with the butt of his pistol and I couldn't tell you what happened next.

I don't come to until it's after dark and I'm trussed up like a turkey. Ms Cooper is next to me and her hands are tied behind her back with a red bandanna and there's a rope around her feet. She looks dishevelled, but pretty; her eyes are wide and I can tell she's not too pleased to be lying here next to an Indian. Her dress is buttoned up to the chin so I'm thinking, at least, thank God, they've respected her. It's cold, even as close together as we are. The Wilcoxes are all huddled around the fire, counting money, and the smoke is a straight white line in the sky you could see for miles. So this is more good news, and I'm thinking the Wilcoxes were always a bunch of dumb-ass honkies when it came to your basic woodlore. I'm wondering how they got it together to pull off a bank job, when I hear horse's hooves and my question is answered. Pierre Cardeaux, Canadian French, hops off the horse's back and goes straight to the fire and stamps it out.

'Imbeciles!' he tells them, only he's got this heavy accent so it comes out 'Eembeeceeles.'

Which insults the Wilcoxes a little. 'Hold on there, hombre,' Andrew Wilcox says. 'Jess because we followed your plan into the bank and your trail for the getaway doesn't make you the boss here,' and Pierre pays him about as much notice as you do an ant your horse is about to step on. He comes over to us and puts his hand under Ms Cooper's chin, sort of thoughtfully. She spits at him and he laughs.

'Spunk,' he says. 'I like that.' I mean, I suppose that's what he says, because that's what they always say, but the truth is, with his accent, I don't understand a word.

Andrew Wilcox isn't finished yet. He's got this big chicken leg that he's eating and it's dribbling on to his chin, so he wipes his arm over his face. Which just spreads the grease around more, really, and anyway he's got this hunk of chicken stuck between his front teeth, so Pierre can hardly keep a straight face when he talks to him. 'I understand why we're keeping the woman,' Andrew says. ''Cause she has – uses. But the Injun there. He's just going to be baggage. I want to waste him.'

'Mon ami,' says Pierre. 'Even pour vous, thees stupiditee lives me spitchless.' He's kissing his fingers to illustrate the point as if he were really French and not just Canadian French and has probably never drunk really good wine in his life. I'm lying in the dust and whatever they've bound my wrists with is cutting off the circulation so my hands feel like someone is jabbing them with porcupine needles. Even now, I can remember smelling the smoke, which wasn't there anymore, and the Wilcoxes who were and the lavender eau de toilette that Ms Cooper used. And horses and dust and sweat. These were the glory days, but *whose* glory, you may well ask, and even if I answered, what difference would it make?

Ms Cooper gets a good whiff of Andrew Wilcox and it makes her cough.

'He's right, little brother,' says Russell Wilcox, the runt of the litter at about three hundred odd pounds and a little quicker on the uptake than the rest of the family. 'You ever heared tell of a man who rides a white horse, wears a black mask, and shoots a very pricey kind of bullet? This here Injun is his compadre.'

'Oui, oui, oui, oui,' says Pierre agreeably. The little piggie. He indicates me and raised his eyebrows one at a time. 'Avec le sauvage we can, how you say? Meck a deal.'

'Votre mere,' I tell him. He gives me a good kick in the ribs and he's wearing those pointy-toed kind of cowboy boots, so I feel it all right. Finally I hear the sound I've been waiting for, a hoot-owl over in the trees behind Ms Cooper, and then *he* rides up. He hasn't even got his gun out yet. 'Don't move,' he tells Pierre. 'Or I'll be forced to draw,' but he hasn't finished the sentence when Russell Wilcox has his arm around my neck and the point of his knife jabbing into my back.

'We give you the Injun,' he says. 'Or we give you the girl. You ain't taking both. You comprendez, pardner?'

Now, if he'd *asked* me, I'd have said, hey, don't worry about *me*, rescue the woman. And if he'd hesitated, I would have insisted. But he didn't ask, and he didn't hesitate. He just hoisted Ms Cooper up on to the saddle in front of him and pulled the bottom of her skirt down so her legs didn't show. 'There's a little girl in Springfield who's going to be mighty happy to see you, Ms Cooper,' I hear him saying, and I've got a suspicion from the look on her face that they're not going straight to Springfield anyway. And that's it. Not one word for me.

Of course, he comes back, but by this time the Wilcoxes and Pierre have fallen asleep around the cold campfire and I've had to inch my way through the dust on my side like a snake over to Russell Wilcox's knife, which fell out of his hand when he nodded off, whittling. I've had to cut my own bonds, and my hands are behind me so I carve up my thumb a little, too. The whole time I'm right there beneath Russell and he's snorting and snuffling and shifting around like he's waking up so my heart nearly stops. It's a wonder my hands don't have to be amputated, they've been without blood for so long. And then there's a big shoot-out and I provide a lot of cover. A couple of days pass before I feel like talking to him about it.

'You rescued Ms Cooper first,' I remind him. 'And that was the right thing to do; I'm not saying it wasn't; don't misunderstand me. But it seemed to me that you made up your mind kind of quickly. It didn't seem like a hard decision.'

He reaches across the saddle and puts a hand on my hand. Behind the black mask, the blue eyes are sensitive and caring. 'Of course, I wanted to rescue you, old friend,' he says. 'If I'd made the decision based solely on my own desires, that's what I would have done. But it seemed to me I had a higher responsibility to the more innocent party. It was a hard choice. It may have felt quick to you, but believe me, I struggled with it.' He withdraws his hand and kicks his horse a little ahead of me because the trail is narrowing. I duck under the branch of a Prairie Spruce. 'Besides,' he says, back over his shoulder, 'I couldn't leave a woman with a bunch of animals like Pierre Cardeaux and the Wilcoxes. A pretty woman like that. Alone. Defenseless.'

I start to tell him what a bunch of racists like Pierre Cardeaux and the Wilcoxes might do to a lonely and defenseless Indian. Arnold Wilcox wanted my scalp. '*I* remember the Alamo,' he kept saying and maybe he meant Little Big Horn; I didn't feel like exploring this. Pierre kept assuring him there would be plenty of time for 'trophies' later. And Andrew trotted out that old chestnut about the only good Indian being a dead Indian. None of which was pleasant to lie there listening to. But I never said it. Because by then the gap between us was so great I would have had to shout, and anyway the ethnic issue has always made us both a little touchy. I wish I had a nickel for every time I heard him say that some of his best friends are Indians. And I know that there are bad Indians; I don't deny it and I don't mind fighting them. I just always thought I should get to decide which ones were the bad ones.

I sat in that car until sunset.

But the next day he calls. 'Have you ever noticed how close the holy word "om" is to our Western word "home"?' he asks. That's his opening. No hi, how are you? He never asks how I am. If he did, I'd tell him I was fine, just the way you're supposed to. I wouldn't burden him with my problems. I'd just like to be asked, you know?

But he's got a point to make and it has something to do with Dorothy in the *Wizard of Oz*. How she clicks her heels together and says, over and over like a mantra, 'There's no place like home, there's no place like home,' and she's actually able to travel through space. 'Not in the book,' I tell him.

'I *know*,' he says. 'In the movie.'

'I thought it was the shoes,' I say.

And his voice lowers; he's that excited. 'What if it was the *words*,' he asks. 'I've got a mantra.'

Of course, I'm aware of this. It always used to bug me that he wouldn't tell me what it was. Your mantra, he says, loses its power if it's spoken aloud. So by now I'm beginning to guess what his mantra might be. 'A bunch of people I know,' I tell him, 'all had the same guru. And one day they decided to share the mantras he'd given them. They each wrote their mantra on a piece of paper and passed it around. And you know what? They all had the *same* mantra. So much for personalization.'

'They lacked faith,' he points out.

'Rightfully so.'

'I gotta go,' he tells me. We're reaching the crescendo in the background music and it cuts off with a click. Silence. He doesn't say goodbye. I refused to call him back.

The truth is, I'm tired of always being there for him.

So I don't hear from him again until this morning when he calls with the Great Displacement Theory. By now I've been forty almost ten days, if you believe the birth certificate the reservation drew up; I find a lot of inaccuracies surfaced when they translated moons into months. So that I've never been too sure what my rising sign is. Not that it matters to me, but it's important to him all of a sudden; apparently you can't analyze personality effectively without it. He thinks I'm a Pisces rising; he'd love to be proven right.

'We can go *back*, old buddy,' he says. 'I've found the way back.'

'Why would we want to?' I ask. The sun is shining and it's cold out. I was thinking of going for a run.

Does he hear me? About like always. 'I figured it out,' he says. 'It's a combination of biofeedback *and* the mantra "home". I've been working and working on it. I could always leave, you know, that was never the problem, but I could never *arrive*. Something outside me stopped me and forced me back.' He pauses here and I think I'm supposed to say something, but I'm too pissed. He goes on. 'Am I getting too theoretical for you? Because I'm about to get more so. Try to stay with me. The key word is *displacement*.' He says this like he's shivering. 'I couldn't get back because there was no room for me there. The only way back is through an exchange. Someone else has to come forward.'

He pauses again and this pause goes on and on. Finally I grunt. A redskin sound. Noncommittal.

His voice is severe. 'This is too important for you to miss because you're sulking about god knows what, pilgrim,' he says. 'This is travel through space *and* time.'

'This is baloney,' I tell him. I'm uncharacteristically blunt, blunter than I ever was during the primal-scream-return-to-the-womb period. If nobody's listening, what does it matter?

'Displacement,' he repeats, and his voice is all still and important. 'Ask yourself, buddy, *what happened to the buffalo?*'

I don't believe I've heard him correctly. 'Say what?'

'Return with me,' he says, and then he's gone for good and this time he hasn't hung up the phone; this time I can still hear the *William Tell Overture* repeating the hoofbeat part. There's a noise out front so I go to the door, and damned if I don't have a buffalo, shuffling around on my ornamental strawberries, looking surprised. 'You call this grass?' it asks me. It looks up and down the street, more and more alarmed. 'Where's the plains, man? Where's the railroad?'

So I'm happy for him. Really I am.

But I'm not going with him. Let him roam it alone this time. He'll be fine. Like Rambo.

Only then another buffalo appears. And another. Pretty soon I've got a whole herd of them out front, trying to eat my yard and gagging. And whining. 'The water tastes funny. You got any water with locusts in it?' I don't suppose it's an accident that I've got the same number of buffalo here as there are men in the Cavendish gang. Plus one. I keep waiting to see if any more appear; maybe someone else will go back and help him. But they don't. This is it.

You remember the theories of history I told you about. Back in the beginning? Well, maybe somewhere between the great men and the masses, there's a third kind of person. Someone who listens. Someone who tries to *help*. You don't hear about these people much so there probably aren't many of them. Oh, you hear about the failures, all right, the shams: Brutus, John Alden, Rasputin. And maybe you think there aren't any at all, that nobody could love someone else more than he loves himself. Just because *you* can't. Hey, I don't really care what you think. Because I'm here and the heels of my moccasins are clicking together and I couldn't stop them even if I tried. And it's OK. Really. It's who I am. It's what I do.

I'm going to leave you with a bit of theory to think about. It's a sort of riddle. There are good Indians, there are bad Indians, and there are dead Indians. Which am I?

There can be more than one right answer.

Duplicity

They took Alice out every single day. Sometimes she was crying when she came back. Sometimes she was limp and had to be carried. This was not much like Alice.

Alice had been Alice the day she and Tilly had returned to the base camp and found it violated. The tent had been ransacked. The camp lantern had been taken and some of their more brightly coloured clothes were gone. A box of tampons had been opened and several unwrapped. Alice picked one up, holding it by its long tail like a dead mouse. She laughed. 'What do you suppose they made of these?' she asked Tilly. She stuck the tampon into one of her ears, plugging the other ear with her finger. 'Very useful,' she said. 'Yes? Sleep late in the mornings. Miss the birds.'

Alice's cheerfulness was so marked it required explanation. Alice, who was an artist and amateur cartographer, had told Tilly that the blank spaces in maps were often referred to as *sleeping beauties*. This surprised Tilly, who had never given it any thought. She could not imagine anyone actually functioning with this optimistic attitude toward the unknown. Not without a lot of effort. Here be dragons, was Tilly's philosophy. Expect the worst and you'll still be disappointed. Her reaction to the intrusion into their camp had been one of barely controlled alarm. She had known this trip would be dangerous. They had come so casually. They had been very stupid.

But Alice had been Alice. 'It was clearly investigative,' she told Tilly calmly. 'And not malicious. Nothing was broken. If they had wanted us to go, they would have found an unambiguous way to suggest it. This was just curiosity. Though I do wish they hadn't taken our light.' Alice had been sitting outside the tent in the sun since she could no longer work at night. Propped open on her knees, she'd had a lap desk which folded and unfolded; she'd been pencilling a curve in the Nhamunda River on to her graph.

The map Alice and Tilly had brought was based on high-altitude infrared pictures. The maps Alice was doing would be much more detailed. On that day she had been working on something whimsical, partly map, partly picture. She had noted the turn in the river and then, in the water, had added the head of a large river turtle – the *tracaja*. On the day of their arrival, a turtle like this had watched them for hours while they emptied the boat and set up camp. Alice had sung the turtle song from Sesame Street to it, bringing civilization, she said, to the backwards turtles of Brazil who could have no knowledge of the advances other turtles had made glo-bally. Alice had nieces and nephews and a predilection for information there was no reasonable way she could know anyhow. Tilly didn't know that song.

Two untidy brown braids rested on Alice's shoulders. A slight breeze blew the unrestrained wisps of hair into her face. She held them back with her left hand, added an arrow to the map with her right. 'You are here,' she'd said to Tilly. Brightly.

You are here.

The sun was up. Dim green light filtered through the walls of the tent which smelled of sleeping bags and hiking boots and moisture. They opened the flaps every day but the tent never lost its hothouse feel. Tilly woke this morning missing Steven. Not memories, she wasn't *thinking*. The surface of her body missed him. Her skin. Where's Steven, it asked. Where's his mouth. Where're his hands. She substituted her own hands, but her body knew the difference. And there was another difference, which she recognized, that she would do this in front of Alice now. As if Alice had become part of her like an arm, like Tilly's left arm, less intimate than the right, but part of her all the same.

Although really she believed Alice was still asleep. Sleep was the only escape for Alice now. Tilly would have felt very guilty if she woke Alice from it early. She listened to Alice breathe and tried to guess if Alice were awake or not. Alice moved so seldom; her body was landscape.

Tilly would have liked to get up, but this would have woken Alice for sure and, anyway, the tent was clogged with the sleeping mats and bags, with the unused stove, with Tilly's camera cases, and with Alice's maps. Tilly could only stand up straight in the very middle of the tent. She had bouts of claustrophobia. Everything Tilly knew, everything Tilly could imagine, was either inside or outside this tent. The two sets were infinitely inclusive. The two sets were mutually exclusive. Except for Alice. Alice could belong to both.

The size of the tent had never bothered her before, when she could come and go as she pleased. In actual fact the tent was probably no smaller than the bedroom she had had as a child and it had never seemed small to her either, although you couldn't even open the bedroom door completely; the chest of drawers was behind it. The bedroom was a safe place, a place where you were cared for and protected. You could depend on this so confidently you didn't even notice it. As Tilly grew older she began to see the shapes and shadows of another world. A girl in the sixth grade at Tilly's school was followed home by a man in a white car. Tilly was told at the dinner table that she mustn't talk to strangers. Angela Ruiz, who lived next door, had heard from her cousin in Chicago how some boy she knew was beaten with a pair of pliers by his own father while his mother watched. In *Life* magazine Tilly saw a picture of a little boy and his two sisters, but there was something wrong about the way they looked, and the article said that their mother hadn't wanted anyone to know she had children so she'd hidden them in the basement for five years. Without sunshine, without exercise, their growth had been stunted. They were bonsai children. In the last week their vaguely misshapen bodies returned to Tilly's dreams.

In Obidos, where children at twelve play soccer and have sex, the man who sold them supplies had told them a story. A cautionary tale – Tilly could see this in retrospect. It involved the fresh water dolphin called the *boto*. The boto could take a woman, penetrating her in the water or in human male form on shore, or even in her dreams. She would grow pale and die in childbirth, if she lasted that long, and her child would be deformed – having the smooth face of the father, his rubber skin, a blow hole on the top of the head where the fontanel should be.

Tilly had moved her pad so that it was, in relation to the door, in the same spot as her bed was in her bedroom. Alice never mentioned it, though she'd had to move Alice's pad, too. Alice was gone at the time. They took Alice out every single day. It was hard not to envy Alice for this no matter how she looked when she came back.

An unseen bird, a trogon, began to shriek nearby. The sound rose above the other rain forest noises in the same way a police siren always buried the sounds of normal traffic. Shhh. The door was a curtain of nylon which whispered when the wind blew. The faint smell of mimosa, just discernible over the smell of sleep and sweat and last night's urine, passed through the tent and was gone. Alice's pad was as far away from the door as it could be. Tilly propped herself on one elbow to look at Alice, who was staring up at the ceiling. 'Alice,' Tilly said. Any word you spoke in this little room was spoken too loudly. Shhhh, said the door.

'I'm still here,' said Alice. 'Did you think I might not be?' She moved and caught herself in mid-movement. Her hair was snarled in the back. She had stopped braiding it weeks ago when her last rubber band had snapped. 'My back is sore,' she said. 'I ache all over.' She looked directly at Tilly. 'I thought of another one. The boy in the bubble.'

This was a game Alice had made up to pass the time. She

and Tilly were making a list of famous prisoners. The longer the game went on the more flexible the category became. Tilly wanted to count Howard Hughes. You could be self-imprisoned, Tilly argued. But Alice said no, you weren't a prisoner if there wasn't a jailor and the jailor had to be someone or some *thing* on the outside. Outside the tent something shifted and coughed.

When the camp was violated, Alice and Tilly had assumed the trespassers were Indians, although it had surprised them. What else would they think? A number of the local tribes would be considered low contact, if hardly untouched. There were the Hixkaryana, the Kaxuiana, the Tirio. They had shotguns and motorboats. They had been to the cities. If you mentioned Michael Jackson to them they would nod and let you know you were not the first. The man who advised them on supplies in Obidos had been from the Tirio tribe. His advice, though lengthy, had been essentially indifferent; the spectacle of two women on holiday in the rain forest had aroused less comment than they expected. He had made one ominous observation in Portuguese. 'It is quite possible,' he had said, 'to go into the forest as a young woman and come out very old.'

Alice and Tilly should have gone to FUNAI for permission to visit the Indians, who were protected by the Brazilian government from curious tourists. But Alice was only interested in the terrain. She had hardly given the Indians a thought when she planned the trip. Steven had asked about them, but then Steven asked about everything. He was in New York City riding the subways and worrying about Tilly out here with the savages. Steven had been mugged twice last year.

Tilly had insisted on moving the camp after the intrusion, back from the river, but not too far since they still needed water and Alice was still taking measurements. It was a lot of work for nothing. Tilly was setting up the tent again when she realized she was being watched.

From a distance they still looked like Indians. Tilly saw

shadows of their shapes between the trees. They paced her when she went to the river for water. She wondered how she'd ever be able to bathe again, knowing or not knowing they were there. She wouldn't even brush her teeth. She went back to camp and argued with Alice about setting a watch at night. By then it was afternoon. Alice had made lunch. 'We can decide that later,' she said. 'There will be plenty of time to decide that later.' But later they came right into the camp and they didn't look like Indians at all. Their heads were hairless and flattened uniformly in the back. The features on their faces were human enough to be recognizable; two eyes deep set into pockets of puffy skin and two nostrils flush with the rest of the face, expanding and contracting slightly when they breathed. Their mouths were large and mobile. They had a human mix of carnivorous and herbivorous teeth. If Tilly had only seen one she might have thought it a mutation of some sort, or the result of disease or accident. In books she had seen pictures of humans deformed to a similar degree. But these were all the same. They were aliens. She told Alice so.

Alice was not sure. There was nothing off-world about their clothing, drapes of an undyed loose weave, covering the same parts of the body that humans felt compelled to conceal. She pointed to the tampons which dangled by their strings from cloth belts. 'They've taken trophies,' said Alice. 'They've got our scalps. Doesn't that strike you as rather primitive for a race with interstellar capabilities?' Alice *invited* them into the tent. Tilly did not follow. Tilly had the sense to be terrified. She was ready to run, had a clear path to the river, hardly stopped to notice that flight would have meant abandoning Alice. But there were more and more of them. She never had the chance. On the way into the tent one veered toward Tilly. She ducked away, but the arm was longer than she expected; the hand landed on her shoulder. There was an extra flexibility in the fingers, an additional joint, but Tilly didn't notice it then. The hand was cooler than her own skin. She could feel it through her cotton shirt and it pulsed, or else that was her own heartbeat she felt. She was so frightened she fainted. It was a decision she made; she remembered this later. A blackening void behind her eyes and her own voice warning her that she was going to faint. Shall we stop? the voice asked, and Tilly said no, no, let's do it, let's get out of here.

The clasps of the tent door clicked together like rosary beads as it was brushed to one side. Breakfast had arrived. The dishes were from Tilly and Alice's own kits. Tilly's was handed to her. Alice's was set on the floor by the door. One of them stayed to watch as Alice and Tilly ate.

Tilly's plate had a tiny orange on it, porridge made of their own farinha and a small, cooked fish. There were crackers from their own store. Alice was given only the crackers and less of them. From the very first there had been this difference in their treatment. Of course, Tilly shared her food with Alice. Tilly had to move on to Alice's pad to do this; Alice would never come to Tilly. She made Tilly beg her to eat some of Tilly's breakfast, because there was never enough food for two people. 'What kind of fish do you think this is?' Tilly asked Alice, taking a bit of it and making Alice take a bite.

'It's a dead fish,' Alice answered. Her voice was stone.

Tilly was very hungry afterwards. Alice was hungry, too, had to be, but she didn't say so. 'Thank you, Tilly,' Alice would say. And then two more would come and the three of them would take Alice.

Tilly was always afraid they would not bring her back. It was a selfish thing to feel, but Tilly could not help it. Tilly cared about Alice and Alice should belong to the set of things inside the tent. Everything else Tilly cared about did not. Like Steven. She missed Steven. He was so nice. That's what everyone said about Steven. Alice was always pointing this out to Tilly. The thing about Steven, Alice was always saying, was that he was just so nice. Alice didn't quite believe in him. 'And women don't want nice men anyway,' said Alice. 'Let's be honest.'

'I do,' said Tilly.

'Then why aren't you married to Steven?' Alice asked. 'Why are you here in the rain forest instead of home married to your nice man? Because there's no adventure with Steven. No intensity. The great thing about men, the really appealing thing, is that you can't believe a word they say. They fascinate. They compel.' Alice knew a variety of men. Some of them had appeared to be nice men initially. Alice always found them out, though. Occasionally they turned out to be married men. 'I don't know why so many women complain that they can't find men willing to commit,' Alice said. 'Mine are always overcommitted.'

Steven must be just starting to wonder if everything was all right. A small worry at first, but it would grow. No sight of them in Obidos, he would hear. Where they were expected four weeks ago. Perhaps the boat would be found, covered by then in the same purple vines that choked the rest of the riverbank. Would Steven come himself to look for her? Steven had taken her to the plane and at just the last minute, with his arms around her, he had asked her not to go. Tilly could feel his arms around her arms if she tried very hard. He could have asked earlier. He could have held her more tightly. He had been so nice about the trip. Tilly thought of him all day long and it made her lonely. She never dreamed of him at night, though; her dreams had shadows with elongated arms and subtly distorted shapes. Steven had no place in that world. And even without him, even with the dreams, night was better.

A storm of huge green dragonflies battered themselves against the walls of the tent, but they couldn't get in. It sounded like rain. All around her, outside, her jailors grunted as they drove the insects away with their hands. They were in front of the tent and they were behind the tent; there would be no more escape attempts. Alice was no longer even planning any. Alice was no longer planning anything. To convince herself that Alice would be coming back, Tilly played Alice's game. She sat still with her legs crossed, combing out her hair with her fingers, and tried to think of another prisoner for their list. Her last suggestion had come from a story she suddenly remembered her father telling her. It was about a mathematician who'd been sentenced to death for a crime she didn't recall. On the night before his execution he'd tried to write several proofs out, but very quickly. The proofs were hard to read and sometimes incomplete. Generations of mathematicians had struggled with them – some of these problems were still unsolved. Tilly's father had been a mathematician. Steven was an industrial artist.

Alice had told Tilly she had the story wrong. 'He wasn't a prisoner and he wasn't sentenced to death,' Alice said. 'He was going to fight a duel and he was very myopic so he knew he'd lose.' She wouldn't count Tilly's mathematician. The last prisoner of Tilly's Alice had been willing to count was Mary, Queen of Scots. This was way back when they were first detained. Tilly was just the tiniest bit irritated by this.

The river drummed, birds cried, and far away Tilly heard the roaring of the male howler monkeys, like rushing water or wind at this distance. Bugs rattled and clicked. Each ordinary sound was a betrayal. How quickly the forest accepted an alien presence. It was like plunging a knife into water; the water reformed instantly about the blade, the break was an illusion. Of course, the forest had responded to Tilly and Alice in much the same way. And now they were natives, local fauna to an expedition from the stars. Or so Tilly guessed. 'Our only revenge,' she had told Alice, 'is that they're bound to think we're indigenous. We're going to wreak havoc with their data. Centuries from now a full-scale invasion will fail because all calculations will have been based on this tiny error.'

Alice had offered two alternative theories. Like Tilly's, they were straight from the tabloids. The first was that their captors were the descendants of space aliens. Marooned in the forest here they had devolved into their current primitive state. The second was that Tilly and Alice had stumbled into some Darwinian detour on the evolutionary ladder. Something about this particular environment favored imbedded eyes and corkscrew fingers. It was a closed gene pool. 'And let's keep it closed,' Alice had added . She smiled and shook her head at Tilly. Her braids flew. 'South American Headshrinking Space Aliens Forced Me to Have Elvis's Baby,' Alice said.

At first Alice had kept diary entries of their captivity. She did a series of sketches, being very careful with the proportions. She told Tilly to take pictures but Tilly was afraid, so Alice took them herself with Tilly's cameras. The film sat curled tightly in small, dark tubes, waiting to make Alice and Tilly's fortunes when they escaped or were let go or were rescued. Alice had tallied the days in the tent on her graphs and talked as if they would be released soon. There was no way to guess how soon because there was no way to guess why they were being held. Alice fantasized ways to escape. Tilly would have liked to ink the days off on the wall of the tent; this would have been so much more in the classical tradition. Four straight lines and then a slash. A hieroglyphic of the human hand. A celebration of the opposable thumb. Anne Boleyn had six fingers. Tilly wondered how she had marked the walls of her cell.

The door clicked to the side. Tilly sat up with a start. One of them was entering, bent over, her dish in its hands. It was one of the three who had taken Alice. There was no mistaking it, because it wore Tilly's green sweater, the two arms tied round its neck in mock embrace, the body of the sweater draped on its back. The face belonged to a matinee horror monster – maybe the Phantom of the Opera. From the neck to the waist, largely because of her sweater, it could have been any freshman at any Eastern university. From the waist down Tilly saw the rest of the sacklike gown, bare legs, bare feet. Monklike, only the legs were hairless. On the dish was a duplication of Tilly's breakfast. She stared at it, hardly able to believe in it. She had never been offered additional food before. The door rattled again as she was left alone. She took a tiny bit of the fish in her fingers. She looked at it. She put it in her mouth. She took another bite. And then another. The food was here, after all. Why shouldn't she eat it just because Alice was so hungry? How would it help Alice not to eat this food? Alice would *want* her to eat it. She ate faster and faster, licking her fingers. She ate the rind and seeds of the orange. She scraped the fish bones under her sleeping pad.

Alice was pale and tearful when she came back. She lay down, and her breath was a ragged series of quick inhalations. There were no marks on her. There never were. Just an agony about her face. 'What did they do to you?' Tilly asked her, and Alice closed her eyes. 'I mean, was it different today?' Tilly said. She sat beside Alice and stroked her hair until Alice's breathing had normalized.

Alice had her own question. 'Why are they doing this?' Alice asked. Or she didn't ask it. The question was still there. 'They don't try to talk to me. They don't ask me anything. I don't know what they want. They just hurt me. They're monsters,' said Alice.

And then there was a silence for the other questions they asked only deep inside themselves. Why to me and not to you? Why to you and not me?

When dinner came that night there was nothing but crackers for both of them. Alice was given more than Tilly. This had never happened before. 'Look at that,' she said with the first lilt Tilly had heard in her voice in a long time. 'Why do you suppose they are doing that?' She equalized the portions. 'They will see that we always share,' she told Tilly. 'No matter what they do to us.'

'I don't want any,' Tilly said. 'Really. After what they did to you today I'm sure you need food more than I do. Please. You eat it.'

It made Alice angry. 'You've always shared with me,' Alice insisted. 'Always. We share.' She directed these last words toward the one who stayed to watch them eat. Tilly took the crackers. The sun went down. The birds quieted and the bugs grew louder. Tree frogs sang, incessantly alto. The world outside maintained a dreadful balance. Inside, the tent walls darkened, and they were left alone. Alice lay still. Tilly undressed completely. She climbed into her bag, which smelled of mildew, and missed Steven.

She had to urinate during the night. She waited and waited until she couldn't wait anymore, afraid she would wake Alice. Finally she slid out of her bag and crawled to the empty bucket that sat by the tent door. She tried to tilt the bucket so that the urine would make less noise hitting the bottom, but every sound she made was too loud in this room. Of course Alice would hear her and wonder. Alice rarely used the bucket at all now. Tilly wished she could empty the bucket before Alice saw it. She got back into her sleeping bag and missed Steven until she finally fell asleep, sometime in the morning.

When she woke up, she missed him again. Alice's eyes were open. 'That teacher who killed that doctor,' Tilly said. 'The diet doctor.'

'Jean Harris,' said Alice. 'I already said her.'

'No, you didn't,' said Tilly.

'I don't want to play anymore. It was a stupid game and it just upsets me. Why can't you forget it?' Of course the mornings were always tense for Alice. The day's ordeal was still ahead of her. Tilly tried not to mind anything Alice said in the mornings. But the truth was that Alice was often rather rude. Maybe that was why she was treated like she was. Tilly was not rude and nobody treated Tilly like they treated Alice.

'I have another one,' said Tilly. There was already a film of sweat on her forehead; the day was going to be hot. She climbed out of her sleeping bag and lay on top it, wiping her face with the back of her hand. 'And you certainly haven't said her. I can't remember her name, but she lived in Wales in the 1800s and she was famous for fasting. She lived for two years without eating food and without drinking water

and people said it was a miracle and came to be blessed and
brought her family offerings.'

Alice said nothing.

'She was a little girl,' Tilly said. 'She never left her bed.
Not for two years.' Alice looked away from her.

'There was a storm of medical controversy. A group of
doctors finally insisted that no one could live for two years
without food and water. They demanded a round-the-clock
vigil. They hired nurses to watch every move the little girl
made. Do you know this story?'

Alice was silent. 'The little girl began to starve. It was
obvious that she had been eating secretly all along. I mean,
of course, she had been eating. The doctors all knew this.
They begged her to eat now. But they wouldn't go away
and let her do it in secret. They were not really very nice
men. She refused food. She and her parents refused to admit
that it had all been a hoax. The little girl starved to death
because no one would admit it had all been a hoax,' said
Tilly. 'What was she a prisoner of? Ask me. Ask me who
her jailors were.'

Shhh, said the door.

'You must be very hungry,' said Alice. 'Diet doctors and
fasting girls. I'm hungry, too. I wish you'd shut up.' It wasn't
a very nice thing for Alice to say.

Alice was given crackers for breakfast. Tilly had a Cayenne
banana and their own dried jerky and some kind of fruit
juice. Tilly sat beside Alice and made Alice take a bite every
time Tilly took a bite. Alice didn't even thank her. When
they finished breakfast, two more of them came and took
Alice.

They brought Tilly coffee. There was sugar and limes
and tinned sardines. There was a kind of bread Tilly didn't
recognize. The loaf was shaped in a series of concentric circles
from which the outer layers could be torn one at a time until
the loaf was reduced to a single simple circle. It was very
beautiful. Tilly was angry at Alice so she ate it all and while
she was eating it, she realized for the first time that they

loved her. That was why they brought her coffee, baked bread for her. But they didn't love Alice. Was this Tilly's fault? Could Tilly be blamed for this?

Tilly was not even hungry enough to eat the seeds of the limes. She lifted her pad to hide them with the fish bones. Many of the tiny bones were still attached to the fish's spine, even after Tilly had slept on them all night. It made her think of fairy tales, magic fish bones, and princesses who slept on secrets and princes who were nice men or maybe they weren't, you really never got to know them *at home*. She could imagine the fish alive and swimming, one of those transparent fish with their feathered backbones and their trembling green hearts. No one should know you that well; no one should see inside you like that, Tilly thought. That was Alice's mistake, wearing her heart outside like she did. Telling everybody what she thought of everything. And she was getting worse. Of course she didn't speak anymore, but it was easier and easier to tell what she was thinking. She had a lot of resentment for Tilly. Tilly couldn't be blind to this. And for what? What had Tilly ever done? This whole holiday had been Alice's idea, not Tilly's. It was all part of Alice's plan to separate Tilly from Steven.

Tilly got out Alice's papers, looking to see if she'd written anything about Tilly in them. But Alice hadn't written anything for a couple of weeks. PD, the last entry ended. PD. Tilly traced it with her index finger. What did that mean?

When Alice came back Tilly was shocked by the change in her. She was carried in and left, lying on her back on Tilly's mat, which was closest to the door, and she didn't move. She hardly looked like Alice anymore. She was fragile and edgeless as if she had been rubbed with sandpaper. The old Alice was all edges. The new Alice was all bone. Her bones were more and more evident. It was a great mistake to show yourself so. 'What does PD mean?' Tilly asked her.

'Get me some water,' Alice whispered.

They kept a bucket full by the door next to the empty bucket which functioned as the toilet. A bug was floating in the drinking water, a large white moth with faint circles painted on its furry wings. If Tilly had seen it fall she would have rescued it. She doubted that Alice would have bothered. Alice was so different now. Alice would have enjoyed seeing the moth drown. Alice wanted everyone to be as miserable as she was. It was the only happiness Alice had. Tilly scooped the dead moth into the cup of water for Alice, to make Alice happy. She held the cup just out of Alice's reach. 'First tell me what it means,' she said.

Alice lay with her head tilted back. The words moved up and down the length of her throat. Her voice was very tired and soft. Shhh, said the door. 'It's a cartographer's notation.' Her eyes were almost closed. In the small space between the lids Tilly could just see her eyes. Alice was watching the water. 'It means *position doubtful*.' Tilly helped her sit up, held the cup so she could drink. Alice lay back on the mat. 'Prospects doubtful,' said Alice. 'Presumed dead,' said Alice.

Outside Tilly heard the howler monkeys, closer today. She could almost distinguish one voice from the rest, a dominant pitch, a different rhythm. She had once stood close enough to a tribe of howler monkeys to connect each mouth with its own deafening noise. This was at the zoo in San Diego. In San Diego, Tilly had been the one on the outside.

It was so like Alice to just give up, thought Tilly. Not like Alice before, but certainly like Alice now. Alice now was completely different from Alice before. Living together like this had shown her what Alice was *really* like. This was probably what the South American Headshrinking Space Alien Children of the Boto had wanted all along, to see what people were really like.

Well, what did they know now? On the one hand, they had Alice. Alice was completely exposed. No wonder they didn't love Alice.

But on the other hand, they had Tilly. And there was no need to change Tilly.

They loved Tilly.

Lieserl

Einstein received the first letter in the afternoon post. It had travelled in bags and boxes all the way from Hungary, sailing finally through the brass slit in Einstein's door. *Dear Albert*, it said. *Little Lieserl is here. Mileva says to tell you that your new daughter has tiny fingers and a head as bald as an egg. Mileva says to say that she loves you and will write you herself when she feels better.* The signature was Mileva's father's.

The letter was sent at the end of January, but arrived at the beginning of February, so even if everything in it was true when written, it was entirely possible that none of it was true now. Einstein read the letter several times. He was frightened. Why could Mileva not write him herself? The birth must have been a very difficult one. Is the baby really as bald as all that? He wished for a picture. What kind of little eyes did she have? Did she look like Mileva? Mileva had an aura of thick, dark hair.

Einstein was living in Bern, Switzerland, and Mileva had returned to her parents' home in Titel, Hungary for the birth. Mileva was hurt because Einstein sent her to Hungary alone, although she had not said so. The year was 1902. Einstein was twenty-two years old. None of this is as simple as it sounds, but one must start somewhere even though such placement inevitably involves the telling of a lie.

Outside Einstein's window, large star-shaped flakes of snow swirled silently in the air like the pretend snow in a glass globe. The sky darkened into evening as Einstein sat on his bed with his papers. The globe had been shaken and

Einstein was the still, ceramic figure at its swirling heart, the painted Father Christmas. Lieserl. How I love her already, Einstein thought, dangerously. Before I even know her, how I love her.

The second letter arrived the next morning. *Liebes Schatzerl*, Mileva wrote. *Your daughter is so beautiful. But the world does not suit her at all. With such fury she cries! Papa is coming soon, I tell her. Papa will change everything for you, everything you don't like, the whole world if this is what you want. Papa loves Lieserl. I am very tired still. You must hurry to us. Lieserl's hair has come in dark and I think she is getting a tooth.* Einstein stared at the letter.

A friend of Einstein's will tell Einstein one day that he, himself, would never have the courage to marry a woman who was not absolutely sound. He will say this soon after meeting Mileva. Mileva walks with a limp although it is unlikely that a limp is all this friend means. Einstein will respond that Mileva has a lovely voice.

Einstein had not married Mileva yet when he received this letter, although he wanted to very badly. She was his Liebes Dockerl, his little doll. He had not yet found a way to support her. He had just run an advertisement offering his services as a tutor. He wrote Mileva back. *Now you can make observations*, he said. *I would like once to produce a Lieserl myself, it must be so interesting. She certainly can cry already, but to laugh she'll learn later. Therein lies a profound truth.* On the bottom of his letter he sketched his tiny room in Bern. The sketch resembled the drawings he will do later to accompany his Gedanken, or thought experiments, how he would visualize physics in various situations. In this sketch, he labelled the features of his room with letters. Big B for the bed. Little b for the picture. He was trying to figure a way to fit Mileva and Lieserl into his room. He was inviting Mileva to help.

In June he will get a job with the Swiss Civil Service. A year after Lieserl's birth, the following January, he will marry Mileva. Years later, when friends ask him why he married her, his answer will vary. Duty, he will say sometimes. Sometimes he will say that he has never been able to remember why.

A third letter arrived the next day. *Mein liebes, boses Schatzerl! it said. Lieserl misses her Papa. She is so clever, Albert. You will never believe it. Today she pulled a book from the shelf. She opened it, sucking hard on her fingers. Can Lieserl read? I asked her, joking. But she pointed to the letter E, making such a sweet, sticky fingerprint beside it on the page. E, she said. You will be so proud of her. Already she runs and laughs. I had not realized how quickly they grow up. When are you coming to us? Mileva.*

His room was too small. The dust collected over his books and danced in the light with Brownian-like movements. Einstein went out for a walk. The sun shone, both from above him and also as reflected off the new snowbanks in blinding white sheets. Icicles shrank visibly at the roots until they cracked, falling from the eaves like knives into the soft snow beneath them. *Mileva is a book, like you,* his mother had told him. *What you need is a housekeeper. What you need is a wife.*

Einstein met Mileva in Zürich at the Swiss Federal Polytechnical School. Entrance to the school required the passage of a stiff examination. Einstein himself failed the General Knowledge section on the first try. *She will ruin your life,* Einstein's mother said. *No decent family will have her. Don't sleep with her. If she gets a child, you'll be in a pretty mess.*

It is not clear what Einstein's mother's objection to Mileva was. She was unhappy that Mileva had scholastic ambitions and then more unhappy when Mileva failed her final examinations twice and could not get her diploma.

Five days passed before Einstein heard from Mileva again. *Mein liebes Schatzerl. If she has not climbed on to the kitchen table, then she is sliding down the banisters,* Mileva complained. *I must watch her every minute. I have tried to take her picture for you as you asked, but she will never hold still long enough. Until you come to her, you must be content with my descriptions. Her hair is dark and thick and curly. She has the eyes of a doe. Already she has outgrown all the clothes I had for her and is in proper dresses with aprons. Papa, papa, papa, she says. It is her favorite word. Yes, I tell her. Papa is coming. I teach her to throw kisses. I teach her to clap her hands. Papa is coming, she says, kissing and clapping. Papa loves his Lieserl.*

Einstein loved his Lieserl whom he had not met. He loved Mileva. He loved science. He loved music. He solved scientific puzzles while playing the violin. He thought of Lieserl while solving scientific puzzles. Love is faith. Science is faith. Einstein could see that his faith was being tested.

Science feels like art, Einstein will say later, but it is not. Art involves inspiration and experience, but experience is a hindrance to the scientist. He has only a few years in which to invent, with his innocence, a whole new world that he must live in for the rest of his life. Einstein would not always be such a young man. Einstein did not have all the time in the world.

Einstein waited for the next letter in the tiny cell of his room. The letters were making him unhappy. He did not want to receive another so he would not leave, even for an instant, and risk delaying it. He had not responded to Mileva's last letters. He did not know how. He made himself a cup of tea and stirred it, noticing that the tea leaves gathered in the center of the cup bottom, but not about the circumference. He reached for a fresh piece of paper and filled it with drawings of rivers, not the rivers of a landscape, but the narrow, twisting rivers of a map.

The letter came only a few hours later in the afternoon post, sliding like a tongue through the slit in the door. Einstein caught it as it fell. *Was treibst Du, Schatzerl?* it began. *Your little Lieserl has been asked to a party and looks like a princess tonight. Her dress is long and white like a bride's. I have made her hair curl by wrapping it over my fingers. She wears a violet sash and violet ribbons. She is dancing with my father in the hallway, her feet on my father's feet, her head only slightly higher than his waist. They are waltzing. All the boys will want to dance with you, my father said to her, but she frowned. I am not interested in boys, she answered. Nowhere is there a boy I could love like I love my papa.*

In 1899 Einstein began writing to Mileva about the electro-dynamics of moving bodies, which became the title of his 1905 paper on relativity. In 1902 Einstein loved Mileva, but in 1916 in a letter to his friend Besso, Einstein will write that he would have become mentally and physically exhausted if he had not been able to keep his wife at a distance, out of sight and out of hearing. You cannot know, he will tell his friends, the tricks a woman such as my wife will play.

Mileva, trained as a physicist herself, though without a diploma, will complain that she has never understood the special theory of relativity. She will blame Einstein who, she will say, has never taken the time to explain it properly to her.

Einstein wrote a question along the twisting line of one river. Where are you? He chose another river for a second question. How are you moving? He extended the end of the second river around many curves until it finally merged with the first.

Liebes Schatzerl! the next letter said. It came four posts later. *She is a lovely young lady. If you could only see her, your breath would catch in your throat. Hair like silk. Eyes like stars. She sends her love. Tell my darling papa, she says, that I will always be his little Lieserl, always running out into the snowy garden, caped in red, to draw angels. Suddenly I am frightened for her, Albert. She is as fragile as a snowflake. Have I kept her too sheltered? What does she know of men? If only you had been here to advise me.* Even after its long journey, the letter smelled of roses.

Two friends came for dinner that night to Einstein's little apartment. One was a philosophy student named Maurice Solovine. One was a mathematician named Konrad Habicht.

The three together called themselves the Olympia Academy, making fun of the serious bent of their minds.

Einstein made a simple dinner of fried fish and bought wine. They sat about the table, drinking and picking the last pieces of fish out with their fingers until nothing remained on their plates but the spines with the smaller bones attached like the naked branches of winter trees. The friends argued loudly about music. Solovine's favorite composer was Beethoven whose music, Einstein suddenly began to shout, was emotionally overcharged, especially in C minor. Einstein's favorite composer was Mozart. Beethoven created his beautiful music, but Mozart discovered it, Einstein said. Beethoven wrote the music of the human heart, but Mozart transcribed the music of God. There is a perfection in the humanless world which will draw Einstein all his life. It is an irony that his greatest achievement will be to add the relativity of men to the Newtonian science of angels.

He did not tell his friends about his daughter. The wind outside was a choir without a voice. All his life, Einstein will say later, all his life, he tried to free himself from the chains of the *merely personal*. Einstein rarely spoke of his personal life. Such absolute silence suggests that he escaped from it easily or, alternatively, that its hold was so powerful he was afraid to ever say it aloud. One or both or neither of these things must be true.

Let us talk about the merely personal. The information received through the five senses is appallingly approximate. Take sight, the sense on which humans depend most. Man sees only a few of all the colors in the world. It is as if a curtain has been drawn over a large window, but not drawn so that it fully meets in the middle. The small gap at the center represents the visual abilities of man.

A cat hears sounds that men must only imagine. It has an upper range of 100,000 cycles per second as opposed to the 35,000 to 45,000 a dog can hear or the 20,000 which marks the upper range for men. A cat can distinguish between two sounds made only eighteen inches apart when the cat itself is at a distance of sixty feet.

Some insects can identify members of their own species by smell at distances nearing a mile.

A blindfolded man holding his nose cannot distinguish the taste of an apple from an onion.

Of course man fumbles about the world, perceiving nothing, understanding nothing. In a whole universe, man has been shut into one small room. Of course, Einstein could not begin to know what was happening to his daughter or to Mileva deprived of even these blundering senses. The postman was careless with Mileva's next letter. He failed to push it properly through the door slit so that it fell back into the snow where it lay all night and was ice the next morning. Einstein picked the envelope up on his front step. It was so cold it burnt his fingers. He breathed on it until he could open it.

Another quiet evening with your Lieserl. We read until late and then sat together talking. She asked me many questions tonight about you, hoping, I think, to hear something, anything I had not yet told her. But she settled, sweetly, for the old stories all over again. She got out the little drawing of your room you sent just after her birth; have I told you how she treasures it? When she was a child she used to point to it. Papa sits here, she would say, pointing. Papa sleeps here. I wished that I could gather her into my lap again. It would have been so silly, Albert. You must picture her with her legs longer than mine and new gray in the black of her hair. Was I silly to want it, Schatzerl? Shouldn't someone have warned me that I wouldn't be able to hold her forever?

Einstein set the letter back down into the snow. He had not yet found it. He had never had such a beautiful daughter. Perhaps he had not even met Mileva yet, Mileva whom he still loved, but who was not sound and liked to play tricks.

Perhaps, he thought, he will find the letter in the spring when the snow melts. If the ink has not run, if he can still read it, then he will decide what to do. Then he will have to decide. It began to snow again. Einstein went back into his room for his umbrella. The snow covered the letter. He could not even see the letter under the snow when he stepped over it on his way to the bakery. The snow filled his footprints behind him. He did not want to go home where no letter was hidden by the door. He was twenty-two years old and he stood outside the bakery, eating his bread with gloved hands, reading a book in the tiny world he had made under his umbrella in the snow.

Several years later, after Einstein has married Mileva and neither ever mentions Lieserl, after they have two sons, a colleague will describe a visit to Einstein's apartment. The door will be open so that the newly washed floor can dry. Mileva will be hanging dripping laundry in the hall. Einstein will rock a baby's bassinet with one hand and hold a book open with the other. The stove will smoke. How does he bear it? the colleague will ask in a letter that still survives, a letter anyone can read. That genius. How can he bear it?

The answer is that he could not. He will try for many years and then Einstein will leave Mileva and his sons, sending back to them the money he wins along with the Nobel Prize.

When the afternoon post came, the postman had found the letter again and included it with the new mail. So there were two letters, only one had been already opened.

Einstein put the letter aside. He put it under his papers. He hid it in his bookcase. He retrieved it clumsily because his hands were shaking. He had known this letter was coming, known it perhaps with Lieserl's first tooth, certainly with her first dance. It was exactly what he had expected, worse than he could have imagined. *She is as bald as ice and as mad as a goddess, my Albert*, Mileva wrote. *But she is still my Liebes Dockerl, my little doll. She clings to me, crying if I must leave her for a minute. Mama, mama! Such madness in her eyes and her mouth. She is toothless and soils herself. She is my baby. And yours, Schatzerl. Nowhere is there a boy I could love like my papa, she says, lisping again just the way she did when she was little. She has left a message for you. It is a message from the dead.*

You will get what you really want, Papa, she said. I have gone to get it for you. Remember that it comes from me. She was weeping and biting her hands until they bled. Her eyes were white with madness. She said something else. The brighter the light, the more shadows, my papa, she said. My darling papa. My poor papa. You will see.

The room was too small. Einstein went outside where his breath came in a cloud from his mouth, tangible, as if he were breathing on glass. He imagined writing on the surface of a mirror, drawing one of his Gedanken with his finger in his own breath. He imagined a valentine. Lieserl, he wrote across it. He loved Lieserl. He cut the word in half, down the *s* with the stroke of his nail. The two halves of the heart opened and closed, beating against each other, faster and faster, like wings, until they split apart and vanished from his mind.

Pat Murphy

His Vegetable Wife

Fynn planted her with the tomatoes in the green-house on the first day of spring. The instructions on the package were similar to the instructions on any seed envelope. Vegetable Wife: Prefers sandy soil, sunny conditions. Plant two inches deep after all danger of frost has passed. When seedling is two feet tall, transplant. Water frequently.

A week later, a fragile seedling sprouted in the plastic basin beside the tomatoes: two strong shoots that grew straight with little branching. The seedling grew quickly and when the shoots were two feet tall, Fynn transplanted the seedling to a sunny spot near the entrance to his living dome, where he would pass it on his way to the fields each day.

After transplanting the seedling, he stood beneath the green sky and surveyed his empire: a hastily assembled pre-fabricated living dome that marked the center of his homestead; a greenhouse built of plexiglass slabs, tilted to catch the sun; and the fields, four fertile acres which he had tilled and planted himself. Most of the farm's tilled area was given over to cash crops: he was growing cimmeg, a plant that bore seeds valued for their flavor and medicinal properties. Row after row of dark green seedlings raised their pointed leaves to the pale sky.

Beyond the fields grew the tall grasses native to the planet, a vast expanse of swaying stalks. When the wind blew, the stalks shifted and moved and the grasses hissed. The soft sound of the wind in the grasses irritated Fynn; he thought it sounded like people whispering secrets. He had enjoyed hacking down the grass that had surrounded the living dome, churning its roots beneath the mechanical tiller, planting the straight rows of cimmeg.

Fynn was a square-jawed man with coarse brown hair and stubby, unimaginative fingers. He was a methodical man. He liked living alone, but he thought that a man should have a wife. He had chosen the seed carefully, selecting a hardy stock, bypassing the more delicate Vegetable Maiden and Vegetable Bride, selecting a variety noted for its ability to thrive under any conditions.

The seedling grew quickly. The two shoots met and joined forming a thicker trunk. By the time the cimmeg was knee-high, the wife had reached the height of his shoulders, a pale green plant with broad soft leaves and a trunk covered with downy hairs. The sun rose earlier each morning, the cimmeg grew to waist high, filling the air with an exotic spicy scent, and the Vegetable Wife's stem thickened and darkened to olive green. The curves of her body began to emerge: swelling hips pinching in to form a thin waist; rounded breasts covered with fine pale down; a willowy neck supporting the rounded knob that would become her head. Each morning, Fynn checked the dampness of the soil around the seedling and peered through the leaves at the ripening trunk.

In late spring, he first saw her pubic hair, a dark triangle just above where the twin trunks joined to form her body. Hesitantly, he parted the leaves and reached into the dimness to stroke the new growth. The smell of her excited him: rich and earthy and warm, like the smell of the greenhouse. The wood was warm beneath the hair and it yielded slightly to his touch. He moved closer, moving his hands up to cup the breasts, running his thumbs over the unevenness that promised to become nipples. The rustle of the wind in her leaves made him look up.

She was watching him: dark eyes, a suggestion of a nose, a mouth that was little more than a slit, lips barely parted.

He backed away hastily, noticing only then that he had broken the stalks of several leaves when he stepped in to fondle the trunk. He touched the broken leaves guiltily, then reminded himself that she was only a plant, she felt no pain. Still, he watered the wife generously that day, and when he went to work in the cimmeg fields, he hummed to himself so that he would not hear the grasses whispering.

The instructions had said that she would ripen at two months. Each morning, he checked on her progress, parting the leaves to admire the curves of her body, the willowy stalk of her neck, the fine bright gleam of her eyes. She had a full body and a softly rounded face. Though her eyes were open, her expression was that of a sleep-walker, an innocent young girl who wanders in the darkness unawares.

The expression excited him as much as her body, and sometimes he could not resist pushing close to her, running his hands along the gentle curve of her buttocks and back, stroking the fine dark hair that topped her head, still short like a little boy's hair, but growing, maturing like the rest of her.

It was late spring when he first felt her move under his touch. His hand was on her breast, and he felt her body shift as if she were trying to pull away. 'Ah,' he said with anticipation, 'It won't be long.' Her hand, which had formed recently from a thickened stalk, fluttered in the wind as if to push him away. He smiled, as she swayed in a puff of wind and her leaves rustled.

That afternoon, he brought a thick rope, looped it around her ankle, and knotted it carefully in place. Smiling at her angelic face, framed in dark hair, he spoke softly. 'Can't have you running off. Not now that you're almost ripe.' He tied the other end of the rope firmly to the frame of the dome, and after that he checked on her three times each day, rather than just once.

He cleaned the inside of the dome for the first time in months, washing the blankets of his bachelor bed, opening the windows to banish the mustiness. He could look out the open window and see her swaying in the breeze. Sometimes, she seemed to be struggling against the rope, and when she did that he checked the knots to make sure they were secure.

The cimmeg grew tall, its sharp glossy leaves catching the sunlight and glittering like obsidian blades. Her leaves withered and fell away, leaving her naked olive-green body exposed to the sun and to his gaze. He watched her carefully, returning from the fields several times each afternoon to check the knots.

He woke one morning to find her crouched at the end of her tether, pulling at the knot with soft fingers that bled pale sap where the coarse rope had cut her. 'Now, now,' he said, 'leave that alone.' He squatted beside her in the dust and put his hand on her sun-warmed shoulder, thinking to reassure her. She turned her head toward him slowly, majestically, with the stately grace of a flower turning to face the sun. Her face was blank; her eyes, expressionless. When he tried to embrace her, she did not respond except to push at his shoulders weakly with her hands.

Excitement washed over him, and he pushed her back on the hard ground, his mouth seeking her breast where the rough nipple tasted like vanilla, his hand parting her legs to open the mysteries of that dark downy triangle of hair.

When he was done, she was crying softly, a high faint sound like the singing of the small birds that nested in the tall grass. The sound woke compassion in him. He rolled off her and buttoned his pants, wishing that he could have been less hasty.

She lay in the dust, her dark hair falling to hide her face. She was silent, and he could hear the wind in her hair, like the wind in the tall grass.

'Come now,' he said, torn between sympathy and annoyance. 'You are my wife. It can't be that bad.'

She did not look at him.

He cupped her chin in one hand and tilted her head so that he could see her expression. Her face was serene, expressionless, blank. He patted her shoulder, reassured by her expression. He knew she felt no pain; the instructions had said so.

He untied the rope from the frame of the dome and

brought her inside. By the window, he set a basin of water for her. He secured the rope to the leg of the bed, leaving the tether long enough so that she could stand in the window or the doorway and watch him work in the fields.

She was not quite what he expected in a wife. She did not understand language. She did not speak language. She paid little attention to him unless he forced her to look at him, to see him. He tried being pleasant to her – bringing her flowers from the fields and refilling her basin with cool clean water. She took no notice. Day and night, she stood in the window, her feet in the basin of water. According to the instructions, she took her nourishment from the sun and the air and the water that she absorbed through pores in her skin.

She seemed to react only to violence, to immediate threats. When he made love to her, she struggled to escape, and sometimes she cried, a wordless sound like the babble of the irrigation water flowing in a ditch. After a time, her crying came to excite him – any response was better than no response.

She would not sleep with him. If he dragged her to bed, she would struggle free in the night, and when he woke she was always at the window, gazing out at the world.

He beat her one afternoon, when he returned from the fields and caught her sawing at the rope with a kitchen knife. He struck her on the back and shoulders with his belt. Her cries and the sight of the pale sap excited him and he made love to her afterwards. The rough blankets of his bed were sticky with her sap and his sperm.

He kept her as a man keeps a Vegetable Wife, as a man keeps a wild thing that he has taken into his home. Sometimes, he sat in the dome and watched darkness creep over his homestead as he listened to the wind in the grasses. He watched his Vegetable Wife and brooded about all the women who had ever left him. It was a long list, starting with his mother, who had given him up for adoption.

One day, a government agent came in a copter to inspect the cimmeg fields. Fynn did not like the man. Though Fynn directed his attention to the cimmeg, the government agent kept glancing toward the dome. The wife stood in the window, her naked skin glistening in the sun, smooth and clear and inviting. 'You have good taste,' said the agent, a young man dressed in khaki and leather. 'Your wife is beautiful.'

Fynn kept his temper with an effort.

'They're quite sensitive, I hear,' said the young man.

Fynn shrugged.

The apple tree that he had planted near the dome entrance bore fruit: a basketful of small hard green apples. Fynn had crushed them into a mash and fermented a kind of applejack, a potent liquor smelling of rotten apples. Late in the afternoon after the agent had left, he sat beneath the apple tree and drank until he could barely stand. Then he went to his wife and dragged her away from the window.

Fynn whipped his wife for flaunting her nakedness. He called her a tramp, a whore, a filthy prostitute. Though the sap flowed from the welts on her back, her eyes were dry. She did not fight back, and her passivity inflamed him. 'Goddamn you!' he cried, striking her repeatedly. 'Goddamn you.'

He grew tired and his blows grew softer, but his fury was not abated. She turned on the bed to face him, and his hands found her throat. He pressed on her soft skin, thinking somehow, in the confusion of drunkenness, that strangling her would stop the whispers that he heard, the secrets that were everywhere.

She watched him, impassive. Since she absorbed air through the skin, the pressure at her throat did not disturb her. Nevertheless, she lifted her hands and put them to his throat, applying slow steady pressure. He struggled drunkenly, but she clung to him until his struggles stopped.

He was quiet at last, quiet like a plant, like a tree, like the grasses outside. She groped in his pocket and found a jackknife. With it, she cut away the rope that bound her. The skin of her ankle was scarred and hardened where the rope had rubbed her.

She stood in the window, waiting for the sun. When it warmed the earth, she would plant the man, as she had seen him plant seeds. She would stand with her ankles in the mud and the wind in her hair and she would see what grew.

On a Hot Summer Night
in a Place Far Away

Gregorio is a hammock vendor in the ancient Mayan city of T'hoo, known to the Mexicans as Merida. He is a good salesman – *el mejor*, the best salesman of hammocks. He works in Parque Hidalgo and the Zocalo, T'hoo's main square, hailing tourists as they pass, calling in English, 'Hey, you want to buy a hammock?'

Gregorio is short – only about five feet tall – but he is strong. His hands are strong and the nails are rimmed with purple from the plant dyes that he uses to tint the hammocks. Two of his front teeth are rimmed with gold. He is, most of the time, a good man. He was married once, and he has two little daughters who live far away in the village of Pixoy, near the city of Valladolid, on the other side of the Yucatan peninsula. Gregorio's wife threw him out because he drank too much and slept with other women. When she married another man, Gregorio left his village and travelled to Merida. He sold hammocks and lived in the nearby village of Tixkokob. Once, he went back to his village to visit his daughters, but they looked at him as if he were a stranger and they called the other man Papa. He did not go back to visit again.

Gregorio was sad when his wife threw him out, and he misses his village and his daughters, but he knows that drinking and sleeping with women do not make him a bad man. He has stopped drinking so much, but he has not stopped sleeping with women. He believes in moderation in virtue as well as vice.

Gregorio met the very thin woman in the sidewalk café beside the Parque Hidalgo. She was watching him bargain with an American couple: the bearded man in the Hawaiian shirt had been determined to get a good deal, and the bargaining took about an hour. Gregorio won, though the tourist never knew it: the final price was slightly higher than Gregorio's lowest, though lower than he would usually drop for a tourist. The gringo was pleased and Gregorio was pleased.

Gregorio noticed the woman when he was tying up his bundle of hammocks. She was a thin woman with pale blonde hair cropped close to her head and small breasts and long thin legs that she had stretched underneath the table. She held a notebook on her lap and a pen in one hand. She wore white pants and a white shirt and dark glasses that hid her eyes.

'Hey, you want to buy a hammock?'

She shook her head slightly. 'No, *gracias.*'

'*¿Porqué no*? Why not? You ever try sleeping in a hammock?'

'No.' She was watching him, but he did not know what was going on behind the dark glasses. There was something strange about her face. The eyebrows, the cheekbones, the mouth – all looked fine. But there was something strange about the way that they were put together.

Gregorio set down his bundle of hammocks and looked around. It was late in the morning on a sunny Sunday. Chances were that most tourists were out visiting Uxmal or some other ancient site. He pulled out a chair. 'OK if I rest here a while?'

She shrugged again, setting her notebook on the table. Her fingers, like her legs, were long and thin. Gregorio noticed that she wore no rings. And even though there was something strange about her face, she was a good-looking woman.

He whistled for the waiter and ordered *café con leche*, coffee with milk. When it came, he poured six teaspoons of sugar into the cup and sat back in the chair. 'Where are you from?'

'Here and there,' she said. And then, when he kept looking at her, 'California, most recently. Los Angeles.'

She did not act like a Californian – Californians talked too much and were very friendly – but he let that pass. 'You on vacation?' he asked.

'More or less,' she said. 'Always a tourist.'

They talked about the weather for a time, about Merida, about the surrounding ruins. Gregorio could not put this woman in a category. She did not seem like a tourist. She was not relaxed. Her long fingers were always busy – twisting the paper napkin into meaningless shapes, tapping on the table, tracing the lines of checks on the tablecloth.

He asked her if she had been to visit Uxmal and Chichen Itza.

'Not this trip,' she said. 'I visited them before. A long time ago.'

The church bell at the nearby church rang to call the people to noon mass; the pajaritos screamed in the trees. The woman sipped her *café* and stared moodily into the distance. She made him think of the tall storks that stand in the marshes near Progresso, waiting. He liked her: he liked her long legs and the small breasts that he knew must be hidden in her baggy shirt. He liked her silences and moodiness. Quiet women could be very passionate.

'You would sleep well in one of my hammocks,' he said.

She smiled, an expression as fleeting as a hummingbird. 'I doubt that.'

'You will never know until you try it,' he said. 'Why don't you buy a hammock?'

'How much are your hammocks?'

Gregorio grinned. He quoted her his asking price, double the price he would accept. She bargained well. She seemed to know exactly when he was serious in his claim that he could accept no lower price, and she seemed, in a quiet way, to enjoy working him down to the lowest price he would accept. The hammock she bought was dyed a deep purple that shimmered in the sun.

Gregorio finished his coffee, hoisted his bundle of hammocks, and returned to work, hailing two blond gringos in university T-shirts. He lured them into a bargaining session before they realized what was what.

Tourists stroll through the Zocalo, stare up at the cathedral built from the ancient stones of Mayan temples, admire the colonial architectures of the buildings in the city. Many regard the hammock vendors as pests, like the pigeons that coo and make messes on the lintel above the cathedral door. Many tourists are fools.

The hammock vendors know what happens in T'hoo. They are a select company: only thirty men sell hammocks on T'hoo's streets, though often it seems like much more. Each man carries a bundle of hammocks, neatly bound with a cord. Each man carries one hammock loose, using it as a cushion for the cord looped over his shoulder. When he hails a tourist, he stretches the loose hammock open wide so that the tropical sun catches in the bright threads and dazzles the eyes.

Hammock vendors live at a different tempo than the tourists. They sit in the shade and talk, knowing that the luck will come when the luck comes. They can't rush the luck. Sometimes, tourists buy. Sometimes, they do not. A hammock vendor can only wander in the Zocalo and wait for the luck to come.

While they are waiting, the hammock vendors watch people and talk. The French tourists who are staying at the Hotel Caribe will never buy a hammock: they bargain but never buy. There are pretty women among the Texans who have come to study Spanish at the University of the Yucatan, but all of them have boyfriends. The tall thin woman with pale hair is always awake very early and goes to her hotel very late.

'There she is,' said Ricardo, looking up from the hammocks he was tying into a bundle. 'She was in Restaurant Express last night until it closed. Drinking aguardiente.'

Gregorio glanced up to see the thin woman sitting at the same table as the day before. She had a lost look about her, as if she waited for a friend who had not come.

'She was here at seven this morning,' observed Pich, a gray-haired, slow-moving hammock vendor. 'She needs a man.'

Ricardo looked sour and Gregorio guessed that he had suggested that to the thin woman the night before without success. The hammock vendors discussed the woman's probable needs for a time, then continued an earlier discussion of the boxing match to be held that evening. The woman was of passing interest only.

Still, when Gregorio wandered on to search for customers, he passed her table and said hello. Her notebook was on the table before her, but he could not read the writing. Not Spanish, but it did not look much like English either. Though the morning sun was not very bright, she wore the dark glasses, hiding her eyes behind them. '*Buenos dias,*' she said to him. '*¿Qué tal?*'

'Good,' he said. He sat down at her table. 'What are you writing?' He peered at the notebook on the table.

'Poetry,' she said. 'Bad poetry.'

'What about?'

She glanced at the notebook. 'Do you know the fairy tale about the princess who slept for a thousand years? I've written one about a woman who did not sleep for a thousand years.'

'Why do you look so sad today? You are on vacation and the sun is shining.'

She shrugged, the slightest movement of her shoulders. 'I am tired of being on vacation,' she said. 'But I can't go home. I am waiting for my friends. They're going to meet me here.'

'I understand.' He knew what it was like to be homesick. She looked at him long and hard and he wondered about the color of her eyes behind her dark glasses. 'Did you sleep in my hammock?' he asked her at last.

'I strung it in my hotel room.'

'But you did not sleep in it?'

She shook her head. 'No.'

'Why not?'

She shrugged lightly. 'I don't sleep.'

'Not at all?'

'Not at all.'

'Why not?'

'I slept at home,' she said. 'I can't sleep here.'

'Bad dreams? I know a *curandera* who can help you with that. She'll mix you a powder that will keep bad dreams away.'

She shook her head, a tiny denial that seemed almost a habit.

'Why not then? Why can't you sleep?'

She shrugged and repeated the head shake. 'I don't know.'

He stared at her face, wishing that she would remove her glasses. 'What color are your eyes?' he asked.

She moved her sunglasses down on her nose and peered at him over the frames with eyes as violet as the sky at dusk. Her eyes were underlined with darkness. A little lost, a little wary. She replaced her sunglasses after only a moment.

'You don't sleep really?' Gregorio asked.

'Really.'

'You need a man.'

'I doubt that.' Her tone was cool, distant curious. It did not match the lost look in the violet eyes he had seen a moment before. She gestured at two American women taking a table at the other end of the café. 'Those two look like they need a hammock,' she said.

Gregorio went to sell them a hammock.

Gregorio did not mention to the other hammock vendors that the thin woman did not sleep. Odd that he should forget to mention it – it was an interesting fact about a strange woman. Nevertheless, he forgot until he met her again, very late at night. He was wandering through the Zocalo, cursing his bad luck. He had missed the last bus to his village,

Tixkokob, because he had taken a pretty young woman to the movies. But the young woman had declined to share her bed with him and he had no way home. He was in the Zocalo looking for a friend who might have a spot to hang a hammock.

He noticed the thin woman sitting alone on a bench, watching the stars. 'What are you doing out here so late?' he asked.

She shrugged. 'The cafés are closed. What are you doing here? All your customers have gone home.'

He explained and she nodded thoughtfully and offered him a drink from the bottle of aguardiente that sat beside her on the bench. Aguardiente was a potent brandy and the bottle was half-empty. He sat beside her on the bench and drank deeply. With his foot, he nudged the paper bag that rested on the ground by her feet and it clinked: more bottles.

'I like this drink,' she said slowly, her head tilted back to look at the stars. 'It makes me feel warm. I am always cold here. I think, sometimes, if I found a place that was warm enough, then I would sleep.'

The guitarists who serenaded tourists were putting away their instruments, grumbling a little at the evening's take. The Zocalo was almost deserted. Gregorio shifted uneasily on the bench. 'I should go to Parque Hidalgo and see if Pich is still there. He would let me stay at his house.'

'Keep me company for a while,' she said. 'You can stay in my room.' She glanced at him. 'And don't bother looking at me like that. I plan to sit up by the hotel pool tonight. It's a good night to watch the stars.' She leaned back to look at the night sky. 'Tell me – have you always lived in Tixkokob?'

'I come from Pixoy. But it is better that I am not there now.'

'Better for you.' Her eyes were on the sky, but he felt vaguely uncomfortable, as if she were watching him closely.

'Better for everyone,' he said.

'I understand,' she said. She drank from the bottle and gave it back to him. They watched the moon rise.

Her room was on the bottom floor of the Hotel Reforma. It was a small dark room, very stuffy and hot. His hammock was strung from rings set in the walls. A stack of notebooks rested on the small table beside the bed. On the dresser, there was a strange small machine that looked a little like a cassette player, a little like a radio. 'What's this?' he asked, picking it up.

She took it from his hand and set it gently back on the table. The aguardiente made her sway just a little, like a tall tree in the wind. 'My lifeline. My anchor. And maybe an albatross around my neck.'

Gregorio shook his head, puzzled by her answer, but unwilling to pursue it. The brandy was warm in his blood, and he was very close to deciding that the thin woman had invited him here because she wanted a man. He came close to her and wrapped his arms around her, leaning his head against her chest. He could feel her small breasts and that excited him.

She pushed him away with surprising strength and he fell back against the bed. She picked up her notebook and the strange small machine, tucked the bottle of aguardiente under her arm, and stepped toward the door. 'Sleep,' she said.

He slept badly. The tendrils of someone else's thoughts invaded his dreams. He wandered through a warm humid place where the light was the deep purple color of his hammock. The place was crowded with men and women as tall and thin as the thin woman. He asked them where he was, and they looked at him curiously with dark violet eyes. He wanted to go home, but when he asked if they could tell him the way, they said nothing. He was tired, very tired, but he could not rest in that place. The air was too thick and hot.

He woke, sweating, in the thin woman's room, and went to the patio to find her. The first light of dawn was touching the eastern sky, but stars were still visible overhead. She sat in a lounge chair beside the pool, speaking softly into the machine. He could not understand the words. Two empty aguardiente bottles were at her feet and another was on the table by her side. He sat in a chair beside her.

Fireflies were dancing over the pool. She gestured at the bottle that rested on the table and Gregorio saw that a firefly had blundered inside the bottle and seemed unable to find its way out. It crawled on the inside of the glass, its feeble light flickering. 'I can't get her out,' the woman said in a harsh voice blurred with brandy and filled with uncertainty. 'And she can't find her way. She just keeps flashing her light, but no one answers. No one at all.'

Without speaking, Gregorio took the bottle to the ornamental flower bed by the side of the pool. He took a brick from the border, lay the bottle on the cement, and tapped it lightly with the brick – once, twice, three times. A starburst of fine cracks appeared from each place he struck the bottle, and when he pulled on the neck, the cracks separated and the bottle broke. The insect rose, sluggishly at first, then faster, dancing toward the other lights.

She smiled, and he could tell that the brandy had affected her. The smile was slow and full, like a flower unfolding. 'She returns to her place,' the woman said, blinking at the dancing lights. 'Sometimes I think that I have returned home and maybe I am asleep and dreaming of this place. Sometimes I try to think that. I go for days believing that I am asleep. Then I come to my senses and I know this is real.' She reached for the last bottle, but it was empty.

'Where do you come from?' Gregorio asked.

She lifted one thin arm and pointed up at a bright spot of light high in the sky. 'That one.'

Gregorio looked at her and frowned. 'Why are you here?'

She shrugged. 'Merida is as good a place to wait as any. It's warm here, warmer than most places. My friends are supposed to come get me. They're late.'

'How late?'

She looked down at her thin hands, now locked together in her lap. 'Very late. Just over one hundred years now.' Her hands twisted, one around the other. 'Or maybe they never intended to come back. That's what bothers me. I send out reports regularly, and maybe that was all they want. Maybe they will leave me here forever.'

'Forever?'

'Or for as long as I live.' She glanced at him. In the light of the rising sun, he could see her strange violet eyes – wide and mournful. 'I don't belong here. I don't . . .' She stopped and put her head in her hands. 'Why are they so late? I want to go home.' He did not understand what she said next – the language was not English and not Spanish. She was crying and he did not know what to say or do. She looked up at him with a face like an open wound. Her violet eyes were wet and the circles beneath them stood out like bruises. 'I want to go home,' she said again. 'I don't belong here.'

'Who are you?'

She closed her eyes for a moment and seemed to gather strength to her. 'The explorers brought us here,' she said. 'The ones in the space-craft. They left us to gather information about your people.' She looked down for a moment and he thought she would stop talking, but she looked up again. 'We travel with the explorers but we are a different people. When we meet with new ways, we adapt. We learn. We take on a little bit of the other, retaining a little bit of ourselves. We blend the two.' She spread her hands on her knees. 'We are diplomats, translators, go-betweens for merchants. We live on the border, neither fish nor fowl, not one thing and not another.' Her hands closed into fists. 'There were three of us, but Mayra died two years ago, Seena, last year. We grew tired, so tired. They left us here too long. I have lost myself. I don't know who I am.

'I should not speak, but it has been so long.' She shook her head and rubbed her eyes with her slender fingers. 'You will forget this. I will make you forget.' She leaned back in her chair and stared at the sky. The stars were gone now, washed out by the light of the rising sun. 'I send them poetry instead of reports, but still they do not come for me. Maybe they don't care. Maybe none of this matters.' Her voice had a high, ragged note of hysteria. 'It did not bother me at first,' she said. 'Not while the others were alive. Only recently. It bothers me now. I would like to curl up and sleep for days. For weeks.'

Gregorio took her long thin hand in his, squeezing it gently for comfort. This woman, she needed help. And he wanted her. She was aloof and foreign and he wanted to hold her. He wanted her because of her long thin legs, like a heron's legs, her long thin hands, like the cool hands of the Madonna.

He said nothing, but he was thinking of the place that the dream had brought to his mind, the dark, warm, limestone cavern just outside the nearby village of Homun. He had been thinking about seeing the thin woman naked, swimming in the waters of the cavern, alone with him.

She looked at his face and suddenly laughed, a small chuckle that seemed drawn from her against her will. 'Sometimes, I can find my way out of my own self-pity, and I see you, son of the strange men who built those cities, goggling at me for . . . what? What do you want?' She stared at him, her violet eyes filled with amusement, then suddenly widening as if she were trying to see something in the dim light. 'Wait . . . where is this . . . this place . . . where?'

Her thin fingers were playing over his face as if searching for something. She reached out and ran a cool finger along the back of one hand. She had moved closer to him, her eyes wide and eager.

The quiet ones, he thought to himself. They are always the most passionate. And he imagined her clearly again, a long pale naked woman stepping into the warm water and smiling at him in invitation.

But she pulled back then, leaning back in her chair and slipping the dark glasses over her violet eyes, hiding behind the tinted lenses.

Later that day, Gregorio could not remember all that had happened out by the pool. He remembered the woman's hand in his; he remembered telling the woman that he would take her to the caves of Homun, to a very private cave he knew. But there was a curiously incomplete blurred feel to his memory.

Gregorio liked the woman, but he did not like the vague feeling that he was being tricked and he acted to prevent such a thing from happening again. In his right pocket, for clarity of mind, he carried a clear polished stone that had been thrice blessed with holy water. In his left, for good luck, he carried a jade bead that had been carved on one side with the face of Kin Ahau, the sun god who watches by day, and on the other side with the face of Akbal, the jaguar-headed god who watches by night. With these talismans he was confident. His mind would not be clouded.

The bus to Homun was hot and crowded. It dropped them on the edge of the village and Gregorio led the woman through the monte, the scrubby brush that covers much of the Yucatan, to the entrance to the cavern.

The Yucatan peninsula is riddled with limestone caverns that lead to deep dark places beneath the Earth. Here and there, the caves dip beneath the water table, forming subterranean pools. Gregorio knew of such a cave, a secluded subterranean pool that was a fine place to bring cute American tourists for seduction.

A tunnel led deep into the underworld to a pool of clear water in a limestone cave. Shells – all that remained of ancient clams and oysters – were embedded in the rock. Another tunnel, extending back from the first pool, led to an even more secluded pool.

Gregorio took the woman to the most remote pool. Stalactites hung low over the pool. The air was close and humid, very hot and moist. He carried a small flashlight and shone it on the limestone to show her the way. She was smiling now, following close behind him.

Gregorio strung his hammock on the two hooks that he had set in the limestone walls long ago. As soon as he had it strung, the woman sat on the edge of the hammock and then lay back with a soft sigh.

'We can swim,' Gregorio said. He was quickly stripping off his clothing.

No reply from the woman in the hammock.

He went, naked, to the hammock. She was curled on her side, one hand tucked under her cheek, the other resting on her breast like a bird who has found her nest. Her eyes were closed and she breathed softly, gently, rhythmically. He touched her cheek, warm at last, brushing a stray tendril of hair back into place, and kissed her lightly. When he touched her, he felt a bright warm sensation, like the spreading warmth of brandy but quicker, cleaner, more pure. He saw in the darkness the tall thin people, holding out their long arms in welcome. He felt content and loved and very much at home.

He did not wake her. He swam alone in the warm water, dressed, and left her there, sleeping peacefully.

In a limestone cavern at Homun, a woman sleeps like a princess in a fairy tale. Gregorio knows she is there, but few others know the way to the hidden cave and if anyone does chance to find her, Gregorio knows that the person's mind will be clouded and he will forget. Gregorio visits her sometimes, touches her lightly on the cheek and feels the warm glow of homecoming. And he watches for the day when a tall thin man who does not sleep comes to town and sits in the cafés, sitting up late as if waiting for a friend. This one, Gregorio will take to the cavern to wake the woman who sleeps so soundly, wake her with a kiss and take her home.

Dead Men on TV

I stay up late each night, watching my dead father on TV. Tonight, he's in *Angels of the Deep*, a World War II movie about the crew of a submarine. My father plays Vinny, a tough New York kid with a chip on his shoulder. He was about twenty when the movie was made; he's darkly handsome, and an air of danger and desperation surrounds him.

I've seen the movie half-a-dozen times before, but I turn on the TV and curl up in my favorite easy chair with a glass of bourbon and a cigarette. The cream-colored velvet that covers the easy chair's broad arm is marked with cigarette burns and dark rings from other glasses of bourbon on other late nights. The maid told me that the stains won't come out, and I told her that I don't care. I don't mind the stains. The rings and burns give me a record of many late nights by the TV. They give me a feeling of continuity, a sense of history: I belong here. The television light flickers in the darkened room, warming me like a fire. My father's voice speaks to me from the set.

'Can't you feel it?' my father says to another sailor. His voice is hoarse: his shoulders are hunched forward, as if he were trying to make himself smaller. 'It's all around us – dark water pushing down. Trying to get in.' He shivers, wrapping his arms around his body, and for a moment his eyes meet mine. He speaks to me. 'I've got to get out, Laura. I've got to.'

On the TV screen, a man named Al shakes Vinny, telling him to snap out of it. Al dies later in the movie, but I know that the man who played Al is still alive. I saw his picture in the newspaper the other day: he was playing in a celebrity golf tournament. In the movie, he dies and my father lives. But out here, my father is dead and Al is alive. It seems strange to be watching Al shaking my dead father, knowing that Al is alive and my father is dead.

'I've got to get out,' my father moans.

He can't get out. For the next hour and a half, he'll be stuck in the submarine with the water pressing in. I watch with sympathy as my father cowers in his bunk.

Late at night I watch the movies, knowing that most of the men and women who move across the TV screen are dead. In my living room, they tell jokes and laugh, dance to big-band tunes played by dead musicians, lie and cheat and betray one another, argue and make love. And despite all that, they are dead. It seems strange to watch dead people on TV. Are they all being punished? What did the others do, who did they hurt, who must forgive them?

I never believed in heaven or hell or life after death until the day after my father's funeral. I was sitting alone in my father's house, and I turned on the television. My father's face stared out at me. He was surrounded by stone walls and darkness. It took me a moment to recognize the scene from *The Pharaoh's Tomb*. My father plays an archaeologist who is trapped in the tomb by a gang of criminals who want to steal the ancient artifacts.

'We're trapped in here,' said a woman's voice. She was on the edge of hysteria.

'There's got to be an escape route,' he said. 'We'll find it. There's got to be a way out.'

My father was right there on my TV screen, even though I knew he was dead. He spoke to me from the TV screen.

I figure it this way. The movie camera steals a person's soul. Just a little bit of the soul with each picture it takes. But if a person is in a great many movies – well then, his whole soul is sucked up into the camera and caught in the movies.

The way I figure it, I have my father's soul in a box.

The Grocery-on-Wheels truck delivers my supplies: TV *Guide*, bourbon, eggs for breakfast, cold cuts for lunch, steak to grill for dinner, a few canned soups, fresh vegetables for variety. I cook for myself these days. I don't eat much. The last cook disapproved of my drinking and pestered me to eat more, go out more. So I fired her and now I cook for myself, eating only when my body demands fuel.

As a child, I was overweight: a round-faced little girl who, in all the photos, wears a sullen expression. Now I am thin. My wristbones are enormous. I can count my ribs. My face is angular, and I can see the bones beneath the skin. I order my clothes from mail-order catalogs and they are always too large for me, but I don't mind. I wear them anyway, belting the pants tightly to keep them from falling.

After I put away the groceries, I don my bikini and lie by the pool, leafing through the TV *Guide*. My father left me this ranch house and the trust fund that supports me. The gardener tends the yard and the pool. The maid cleans the house. I keep my father's soul alive by watching his old movies. He's all I have left.

I was five years old when my mother died. I remember she had soft hands and dark curly hair. I have pictures of her: a soft-bodied woman tending to fat, with a round face and dark eyes.

She came to California from Georgia, a soft-spoken country girl with a slight southern drawl. She was working as a secretary at MGM, and she met my father there. At the time, my father was still taking bit parts in cut-rate monster movies and westerns.

The year I was born, my father landed his first big role – Vinny in *Angels of the Deep*. That movie was a hit, and he went on from there with a few more war movies. Then he played a hard-boiled detective in a series of movies, and made a name for himself.

My mother started drinking heavily. Every afternoon she would sit by the pool, a glass of bourbon by her side. Some nights, my father wouldn't come home. The next day, my mother would start drinking early in the morning, lying in a lounge chair in her black one-piece swimsuit, dark circles beneath her dark eyes. I remember sticky kisses that stank of bourbon. I remember her telling me, 'Your father's a no-good louse.'

Bourbon and sleeping pills killed her. The coroner called it accidental death: she left no suicide note. But I know better. She killed herself; my father drove her to it. After that, my father was home even less. And when he was home, he seemed to look through me, as if I weren't real. I hated that.

I don't hate my father for the things he did to me. He didn't do anything much to me. I hate him for the things he didn't do. He didn't love me, he didn't want me, he didn't care about me – and that's what I can't forgive.

He sent me to private boarding schools, where I waited desperately for summer break. Then, during summer break, he sent me to camp. I lived in dormitories and cabins, cared for by teachers and counsellors and housemothers. And I saw more of my father on the movie screen than I ever did in life.

He married again – three more times. Each marriage ended in divorce. But he had no more children. One was enough. One was too much. I don't think he ever wanted a daughter.

It's one in the morning, and I'm watching a videotape of *The Darkness Underground*. My father plays an impoverished coal miner, working the mine in a company town.

The living room is illuminated by the light from the TV screen. I love the light the TV casts – it makes everything seem unreal, fantastic, as if the living room had no substance. The couch and end table are dim outlines, barely visible. In this light, I'm not real. Only the world on the TV set is real.

The videotape is old: colored snow flickers on the screen. I watch the videotapes only when I have no choice; I'd much rather watch a broadcast and know that many people are watching my father. But the tapes have some advantages.

'I hate this life,' my father says. He slams his fist down on the rough wooden table. 'I hate it. I know why the fox gnaws off its leg to escape a trap.'

'Don't,' says the woman who plays his wife. I think her name is Mary. She dries her hands on her apron and hurries to his side.

I stop the tape, run it back, then play it again. 'I hate this life,' he says. Then he catches sight of me and stares from the television. 'Laura, listen to me. Please.' His face fills the screen. His skin is mottled with red and yellow snow that dances across his cheeks like flames. He slams his fist into the table. This time, I stop the tape before the woman can rush to comfort him.

I play the scene over and over, watching him strike the table and cry out in anger and frustration, unable to escape. 'I can't stand this life,' he says. 'Laura . . .' His eyes watch me from the screen.

At last I let the movie run to the end. My father leads the miners in a strike. They triumph against the company, but my father dies. It's a good movie, especially the cave-in that kills my father. I play that over a few times.

At my mother's funeral, I walked beside my father, holding his hand. I've seen pictures of us standing at the grave. My father looks handsome in a black suit; I'm wearing a black dress, black gloves, and a broad-brimmed black hat. The only spot of white is my face: round, pale, and mournful, with black smudges for eyes. I remember that the dew from the grass in the graveyard beaded up on my new patent leather shoes. The droplets caught the sun and sparkled like diamonds. Newspaper reporters took pictures of us, but I would not look at the photographers; I was watching my shoes. When we left the photographers behind, my father stopped holding my hand.

We rode back home in a big black car that stank of dying flowers. I sat on one side of the big back seat, and he sat on the other. His eyes were rimmed with red and his breath smelled of whiskey.

I can't watch my mother on TV; she was never in the movies. I wonder what happened to her soul when she died. Is there a heaven for people who were never in the movies?

On Sunday afternoon, the two o'clock movie is *Summer Heat*. I've seen it before: my father plays a prisoner in San Quentin who was framed for a crime he did not commit.

At about one-thirty, I pull the drapes so that the room is dark and I switch on the TV. Instead of a picture, I get jagged lines, like lightning across the screen. I thump the side of the TV and the lightning jerks, but the picture does not return. The sound is a hash of white noise.

It's the maid's day off. I'm alone in the house and panic sets in quickly. I have to see the movie. I always watch my father's movies. I smack the set again and again, bruising my hand. I switch desperately from channel to channel. Nothing.

I look under 'Television Repair' in the telephone book. In shop after shop, the phone rings unanswered. Sunday afternoon and no one is at work.

Finally, at a place called Pete's Repair-It, a man answers the phone. 'Pete's Repair-It. Pete speaking.'

'Thank God you're there,' I say quickly. 'My television's broken and I have to have it fixed.'

'Sure,' says the man. 'Drop it by on Monday and I'll have a look.'

'You don't understand,' I say shakily. 'It has to be fixed this afternoon. My father will be on at two and . . .' I glance at the clock. 'It's quarter to two now. I'll pay extra.'

'Sorry, ma'am,' he says politely. 'The shop's closed today. I just stopped by to – '

Then I break down. 'You have to help me,' I plead. 'You

just have to. My father's going to be on TV at two and I have to see him.' I start crying and I can barely speak.

'Hang on,' he mutters. 'Just calm down. What's the matter with the set?'

Between sniffles, I describe the TV's behavior. He gets my address and promises that he will come right away. I pace, watching the clock. At five to two, I hear a van in the driveway. I meet the man halfway down the walk. He's a broadly built man, middle-aged, with glasses and curly brown hair. Over the pocket of his red shirt, his name is embroidered: PETE. He carries a toolbox.

'Please hurry,' I beg him.

I watch him work: removing the back of the TV and inspecting the tangle of wires inside. 'Would you like something to drink?' I ask awkwardly.

'Sure. Have you got a beer?'

I shake my head. 'How about bourbon and lemonade? That's what I'm drinking.'

'All right,' he said. 'I'll try it.'

He is whistling softly as I come out of the kitchen. 'You could probably get yourself a new TV for the price of this house call,' he says.

I nod. 'Maybe I'd better get another. So I'll have one as a spare.'

He chats as he works, talking about what's wrong with the set, about how much a new set might cost me, but I pay little attention. I am watching the clock, waiting for the moment I can watch the movie. Finally, at two-thirty, he plugs in the set and the picture snaps into focus. 'Thank you,' I say. 'Oh, thank you.'

I curl up happily on the couch. On the TV screen, my father paces to and fro in his little cell. 'I don't belong here,' he says.

His cellmate, a wiry man with a thin face and cold eyes, lies back on his bunk and laughs. 'You and every other con in the joint.'

'You don't understand.' The screen shows a close-up of

my father's face, his tortured eyes, his square chin rough with stubble. 'I'm innocent.'

'This is a great movie,' I say to Pete.

'You've seen this before?' He picks up his drink and sits beside me on the couch.

'Of course,' I say. 'Five times before.'

'Sure, you're innocent,' my father's cellmate is saying. 'You and everyone else. We're all innocent.' The wiry man takes a drag on his cigarette, then blows the smoke at the ceiling. 'But we're all stuck here together.'

'If you've seen it before, then what was the big hurry to get the set fixed?' Pete growls. He is staring at me with puzzlement and frank curiosity. 'You got me out here on a Sunday with a sob story about your father being on TV and . . .'

'That's my father,' I say quickly, pointing to the TV, where my father is lighting a cigarette.

'He's your dad?' Pete stares at the set. 'I grew up watching his movies.'

'So did I,' I say. 'I watch all his movies. All of them.'

For a moment, Pete glances from the screen to my face and back again. 'Yeah, I can see it,' he says. 'You look like his daughter.'

I'm startled. 'You think so?'

'Of course,' he says. 'Especially the eyes. You got the same eyes. I should have recognized you.'

I notice that his glass is empty and I offer him another bourbon and lemonade. He accepts. I feel strangely comfortable watching the movie with him.

'He died about a year ago,' I say. 'But I watch all his movies. That keeps him with me.'

'What a great guy he must have been.' Pete hesitates a moment, then says soberly, 'You must miss him a lot.' He puts one arm around my shoulders as if to comfort me. I lean against his shoulder.

'Not really,' I say. 'These days, I've got him right where I want him. He can't get away.'

Pete frowns. 'What do you mean?'

'He's right here,' I say. 'I watch him every night.' I laugh and Pete smiles uncertainly. But he stays for another drink. And another. We both get a little drunk.

I seduce the TV repairman by the light of the television, that flickering uncertain light where nothing is quite real. My father watches from the screen.

The late movie is a musical. My father plays a gambler who falls in love with a society lady. Dead men and women sing songs about love, and Pete's snores blend with the music, a rumbling bass voice. A vigorous chorus startles Pete; he wakes and blinks at me myopically.

'You OK?' he mumbles. He scratches his head sleepily, waiting for my reply.

'I just can't sleep,' I say. 'It's OK.'

He struggles to a sitting position on the couch. 'It's my snoring,' he mutters gloomily. 'I'm keeping you awake.'

'No,' I say. 'Not at all. I just don't sleep much.'

He sighs and pushes a hand through his hair. Half the curls stand on end. The curly hair on his chest matches the hair on his head. 'My ex-wife always complained that I snored like a freight train.'

I study him with new interest. Knowing that he has an ex-wife who complained about his snoring somehow makes him more real. He is naked and that suits him better than the shirt embroidered with PETE'S REPAIR-IT.

On the TV, three dead women in tight, sequined dresses sing about summer nights, moonlight, and love.

'What happened to your ex-wife?' I ask.

'She found someone who didn't snore and moved to Phoenix, Arizona.'

'Do you hate her?'

'Naw. I figure living in Phoenix is punishment enough.' He shrugs. 'She's got what she wanted, but she still isn't happy. Some people just don't know how to be happy.' He yawns and lumbers to his feet. 'Want some hot milk to make you sleep?' Without waiting for my answer, he heads for the kitchen; I trail behind him. I watch him pour milk into a saucepan and rummage in the cupboards, a naked hairy man taking charge of my kitchen. 'You got any brown sugar? It's better with brown, but I guess white'll do.' He heats the milk to near boiling, sweetens it with sugar, and sprinkles cinnamon on top. Then he fills two mugs and leads me back to the living room. 'My mom used to make this when I couldn't sleep,' he says, giving me a mug.

The milk is sweet and soothing. I have never tasted anything so good. On the television, my father is dancing with the leading lady. Her head is resting on his shoulder and they look very good together.

'I hate my father,' I tell Pete.

'Yeah?' He stares at the couple on TV and shrugs. 'Why bother? He's dead.'

I shrug, watching my father's face on the TV.

'Come on,' Pete says. 'Lie down and sleep.' I lie beside him on the couch and he wraps his arms around me.

I dream myself into my father's movie. My father's arm encircles my waist and we waltz together beneath crystal chandeliers.

The ballroom's French doors open on to a clear summer night, but the room is cold and damp. The air stinks of decay, a charnel-house stench of rotting flesh and dying flowers.

My father and I spin together, and I catch a glimpse of the band. The bandleader is freshly dead; his body is bloated, the skin puffy and discolored. The dead musicians are in various stages of decay. A trumpet player presses the trumpet's mouthpiece to bare teeth; his head is a skull, precariously balanced on the column of vertebrae that rises from the collar of his tuxedo. The bass player plucks the strings with skeletal hands.

'Relax,' my father says to me. He has held up better than the band, but his corneas have turned milky white, and the hand that holds mine feels suspiciously soft, as if it has begun rotting from the inside. 'Isn't this where you've always wanted to be?'

At small tables around the dance floor, well-dressed men and women talk and laugh, but the laughter sounds like chattering teeth and rattling bones. A blond woman has lost clumps of hair and her sequined evening dress hangs limply on her shoulders, no flesh to fill it out.

'You can stay here with me,' my father says. His eyes are sunken; his smile is the expressionless grimace of a skull. 'I was never a good father. I can make it up to you now.'

I try to pull away, but he clings to me, clutching at me with soft decaying hands, staring with cloudy sightless eyes. I tear myself free and run from him, toward the open doors.

On the TV screen, a woman in an evening gown is running away across the dance floor. My father stares after her. A lock of dark hair has fallen into his eyes. He looks handsome and charming. The dance floor is filled with beautiful men and women.

I slip from Pete's arms and unplug the TV before I can change my mind. The old television is too heavy to lift, so I drag it across the living room. The wooden legs make a horrible scraping sound on the Italian tiles in the entryway, and Pete wakes up.

'What are you doing?' he mumbles.

'Give me a hand,' I say.

Half asleep, he helps me push the set down the hall and out the back door into the yard. He stops in the doorway, watching sleepily as I drag the set down the concrete walk toward the pool. Near the pool, I tip it off the path. It lies on its back in the damp grass, the screen reflecting the patio lights and the moon.

The VCR is light by comparison. I heap the videotapes on top of the TV. Then I clear the upstairs closets of my father's clothing: white suits, tuxedos, a trench coat, a drawerful of blue jeans. A tweedy jacket carries his smell even now: a hint of tobacco, a whiff of aftershave, a touch of whiskey. I stand in the wet grass for a moment, holding the jacket and fingering the rough fabric. Then I drape it over my shoulders to keep off the wind. Pete watches, shaking his head.

In the garage, I find the can of gasoline that the gardener keeps there for the power mower. I am generous, dousing the clothes repeatedly.

A single match, and the heap of clothing erupts with flames. It is like the Fourth of July, like orgasm, like the moment when the monster dies, like the happy ending when the credits roll. Pete is pulling me away from the fire, shouting something. I struggle away from him for long enough to strip the jacket from my shoulders and hurl it into the flames.

I stand in the circle of Pete's arms, leaning against his shoulder. The air smells of gasoline, flames, and wet grass. I watch the flames and listen to the distant sound of sirens. It's good to be free.

Prescience

       Katherine knew the future: she read it in the tarot cards, in the lines on a person's palm, in tea leaves, in horoscopes, in the way a man sat in a chair, in the way a woman placed her money on the counter when she paid for the fortune. She kept a dream journal, and her dreams, all too often, came true.

Though her predictions were accurate, her customers were usually dissatisfied. The futures that Katherine saw were never happy. In calm and measured tones, she told them of coming disasters: broken marriages, lost jobs, spoiled vacations, disappointments in love. People rarely returned for a second reading.

It was just after noon, and Katherine sat on a high stool at the counter of the occult store where she worked. The shelves behind her were filled with the paraphernalia of magic: vials of graveyard dust, bottles of holy water, cannisters filled with mandrake root, jimson seed, powdered bone, and incense. Her boss had gone out to lunch and she was eating her lunch, a container of lowfat yogurt.

The string of bells that hung on the doorknob jingled and a man walked into the store. She glanced at him, then returned to her yogurt. Generally, the customers did not wish to be observed too closely. This one prowled among the bookshelves for a time, then finally approached the counter.

'Hello,' he said. 'I'd like to have my fortune read.'

She looked up and met his eyes. Of course, she remembered his face. Last night, she had dreamed exactly this: he came into the shop, she read his palm, and then he asked her out for coffee.

'Can't be done,' she said briskly. 'Our fortune teller's gone. She ran off with the carnival.'

'Don't you read palms.'

'Nope. Sorry. Can't help you.'

He didn't look like a bad sort. But already, she knew too much about him. By the way he held his shoulders and the tilt of his head, she knew he was lonely and a little nervous about being in the shop. He had nice eyes: dark and wistful. But she knew better and she refused to be drawn in. She didn't need to see the lines on his palm to know that he was trouble. She could see the clouds and predict the coming storm. Going out with him would be a disaster.

'Sorry,' she said again. 'It's really too bad.'

She looked down at her yogurt, not wanting to know any more. 'Awfully sorry,' she said, and kept her eyes down until she heard the bells jingle and knew that he was gone.

After lunch, she had cup of jasmine tea. When she finished her tea, she thoughtlessly glanced into the bottom of the cup where the loose tea leaves had accumulated. His face was there, plain enough for anyone who knew how to see it.

Her boss was a toad of a man, a squat Hungarian who burned incense to gain power over women. He read palms, and whenever he could, he grabbed Katherine's hand and examined the lines of her palm. His hands were sweaty and he always held on a little too long.

'You're afraid,' he said. 'Your heart and your life line cross – a sign of uncertainty.' She peered unwillingly into her own palm. It seemed to her that there were more lines each day, crisscrossing her palm like bird tracks in the sand. The lines made her nervous: too many decisions, too many choices, too many fates. 'I think you are afraid of men,' he said.

She snatched her hand away and went to tidy the cannisters of herbs. She saw him staring at her from across the shop, but she ignored him. He was harmless enough. She never saw him in her dreams.

Two in the morning: she woke up and scrambled for the light, for a pen, for her dream journal. It was important to note the details quickly, before they blurred and lost their definition. She wrote:

'A coffee shop on Haight Street. The dark-haired man across the table takes my hand and asks me something. I can't hear him because the pounding of my heart is too loud. I am terrified, overcome by panic.'

She hesitated, groping for more details. With details, she can protect herself.

'I am wearing my favorite silver bracelet and a peasant blouse. There's a cup of coffee on the table in front of me. He strokes my hand gently; I like his touch on my skin.'

She scratched out the last line and got out of bed long enough to put her peasant blouse on the floor beside the door. The next day, she would give it to the Salvation Army. The bracelet, she would send to her sister in Texas as a present.

Even so, she lay awake for a long time before she could sleep again.

Katherine peered at the lines on her customer's palm. This woman had beautiful hands, with well-manicured nails. Compared to Katherine's, her palm was wonderfully clear: the lines were beautifully defined, expressways with highway markers and street signs to tell the way. On Katherine's palm, the lines resembled the trails left by rabbits in a meadow: faint tracks where the grass was beaten down, crossing and recrossing one another in nonsensical fashion.

Katherine followed the woman's love line and said that she would soon fall in love. The woman smiled, but Katherine tried to talk her out of it.

'I hate being in love,' Katherine said. 'It's like some kind of disease. It grabs you and turns your mind to jelly. Love always makes me stupid. Frankly, if I were you, I'd try to get out of it.'

Katherine caught her boss watching her from the other side of the shop. He was frowning.

The woman blinked at Katherine, startled by her vehemence.

'Your heart line is strong,' Katherine said, returning to the reading and dispensing with further editorial comment.

After work, she walked down Haight Street, heading up to the post office to mail the bracelet to her sister. She hated to give the bracelet up, but she knew better than to play games with fate.

As she walked past a coffee shop, she saw the man inside. He sat alone at a table, drinking coffee and reading the paper. Her eye registered the details that she did not want to know. From the way he held his coffee cup, she knew that he was protective and a little possessive. The angle of his newspaper revealed that he was shy, but he covered that up with an outward show of sociability. He was slow to express his emotions. He was uncomfortable in his body.

She hurried past, carrying her small package as if it held a bomb.

Because she knew the future, she often started saying good-bye before she said hello. In the blank hours before she fell asleep, she rehearsed farewell speeches. She was very skilled at saying goodbye. She could toss it off as if it didn't really matter: 'It's been nice.' 'So long.' 'See you around.'

That night, she sent out for Chinese food. It came with two fortune cookies. The first one said: 'Nothing ventured, nothing gained.' The second said: 'Watch your step.' She burned both scraps of paper in the incense burner by her bed. The smoke from the fortunes smelled faintly of jasmine.

A dream: the dark-haired man was walking toward her, and

she wanted to run away. She turned and ran, but she was running in slow motion, as if she were running through glue. She woke drenched in sweat and wrote the dream down, cursing the lack of detail.

She was working at the counter when her boss grabbed her hand and prised it open.

'You are avoiding something,' he said. 'But you can't avoid it much longer. The energy has to go somewhere.' She was dimly aware that he was stroking her hand and smiling.

'What should I do?' she murmured, half to herself.

He grinned at her as if he had thought she would never ask. 'Put yourself in my hands,' he said. 'I know what to do.' His grip on her wrist tightened.

She pulled away and stared him down with glacial eyes.

Whenever she was upset, she walked on the beach, trying to read the messages that the waves painted on the sand. She could not read the waves, and she liked that. People were too easy. They wore their futures on their faces, out where everyone could see. She could not help but read them, whether she wanted to or not.

The sand pipers ran ahead of her, leaving footprints on the sand. The waves always washed them away, wiping the beach clean again.

She was concentrating on the waves, and she looked up just in time to see him walking toward her. He was looking out to sea, where the sunset was smearing the clouds with color. She turned and ran, but the loose sand slowed her down.

She dreamed: she sat with him on a green park bench and held his hand. He looked at her and said 'I love you,' and then he kissed her. And she knew, sure as anything, that he would leave her.

She could not sleep again that night. She sat up and read

the tarot cards, thinking of him. In the cards, she found heartbreak, betrayal, and pain.

It is not good to read your own cards, she reminded herself. The accuracy is suspect. She shuffled and read again. Entrapment, confusion, destruction.

Yet again: happiness, contentment, peace. Too many futures.

She shuffled repeatedly, and laid the cards out on the table, searching in the brightly colored pictures for patterns in which she could believe.

At dawn, she reluctantly went for a stroll in Golden Gate Park, where the morning sun was just beginning to burn off the fog.

She found him on a green park bench, feeding popcorn to the pigeons. They flocked around him, running after the kernels that he tossed. Their footprints in the dust made an intricate pattern of crisscrossing lines. It was impossible to tell where the prints left by one bird left off and the prints of another began. She stood for a moment and watched him.

He looked at her – a quick sidelong glance – and then returned to the pigeons before she could meet his eyes. Still he did not speak.

'What bothers me is the inevitability of it all,' she said. 'Is my life a paint-by-numbers? Doesn't knowing the future set me free? Apparently not.'

He looked at her, bewildered. 'What?'

He didn't look so dangerous. A bold pigeon climbed on to his tennis shoe and reached for the popcorn in his hand. He squinted a little because the sun was in his eyes.

'Nice morning,' she said, and he nodded.

'About that reading,' she said, and against her better judgment she took his hand. 'Don't say it,' she told him before he could open his mouth. 'Just don't say it.'

Then she stole a quick look at her own palm. It seemed that the heart line was a little stronger and that maybe the life line did not cross it at all.

'I still think you'll leave me,' she said softly. She looked up and met his eyes. He was confused. She was doing things in the wrong order again. It wasn't time to say goodbye. Not yet.

'All right,' she said. 'I'll risk it.'

And then, despite it all, she kissed him.

Clay Devils

Dolores dreams of the devil one night. The devil of her dream is one of the many devils who live in the *malpais*, the bad lands outside the village. He is tall with a craggy face and a body covered with coarse dark hair, like the hair of a goat. Dark red horns grow from his head.

He leers at her, and his teeth are long and yellowed, like the teeth in a coyote skull that she once saw in the desert. He reaches for her with his long claws, but she wakes before he can catch her.

Tomas, her husband, and Esperanza, her daughter, are still sleeping when she slips silently from beneath the blanket and pulls on her thin cotton dress. The sun's first pale light is shining between the loosely woven branches that form three walls of the kitchen, a small shelter built on the back of the one-room adobe house. Dolores opens the door .to the wooden chicken coop, and the two chickens, skinny birds that never grow fat, ruffle their feathers, and peer nervously out the door.

In the hearth, a few coals from last night's fire still glow. She fans them to life and feeds them with tinder, saving the cost of a match. By the time Tomas wakes up, she has ground the corn meal on the grinding stone, cooked tortillas for breakfast, and packed a lunch of tortillas and beans for her husband to take with him to the fields where he will spend the day working.

Tomas uses a gourd bowl to scoop water from the aluminium can that stands just outside the kitchen. He splashes his face, dries it on his shirt, then stands for a moment in the kitchen doorway, gazing out at the hills. A few drops of water, caught in the hairs of his arm, glisten in the sunlight like bits of broken glass by the roadside.

'Soon, the American will come,' he says without looking at her.

Dolores, like many of the women in her village, makes clay toys and whistles that her husband sells to tourist shops in the city market. One man – an old American – was particularly pleased with Dolores' work: clever whistles shaped like doves, like owls, like chickens, like dogs baying at the moon; miniature clay men and women, dressed like the people of her village. The American had asked Tomas whether Dolores made other clay figurines, and Tomas, eager to do business, had said yes, she made many beautiful figures. The American had arranged with Tomas to come to their village and see the beautiful things that Dolores made.

'Yes,' says Dolores, putting another tortilla to cook. 'In a few days, I will fire the toys and paint them.'

Tomas nods. He is a good-looking young man and Dolores knows that he wants to do well at business. He has never been content to work in the fields – he complains that the afternoon sun makes his head hurt and using a short-handled hoe to knock down weeds makes his back ache. He wants to wear black store-made pants, rather than the homemade white trousers that village men wear when they work in the fields.

Esperanza toddles from her bed to stand by her mother, and Dolores gives her a warm tortilla to eat.

'Today, I will make many figures,' Dolores says, and Tomas nods his approval. Soon, he takes his lunch and goes to the fields to work.

The clay, which Tomas helped Dolores carry from the river, is wrapped in black plastic to keep it damp. Warmed by the sun, the clay feels good in her hands. It smells of the river: aromas of dark secrets and ancient places. Dolores kneads the clay like dough, squeezing out air bubbles that would make her pottery burst in the firing. After kneading the clay smooth, she breaks a handful away from the rest and begins smoothing it into shape, trying to think of something to make that will please an American.

Esperanza plays in the dirt and sings to herself, a series of notes without a tune. The chickens scratch in the dusty weeds, searching for insects to eat. On the roof, doves make small mournful sounds, grieving for some long forgotten loss.

The house is on the very edge of the village, and Dolores looks out on to the rolling pine-covered hills of the *malpais*, where devils live. Without thinking, Dolores shapes a little man with craggy face, deepset eyes, and horns that curl from his forehead.

When Dolores was a little girl, only a little older than Esperanza is now, her grandfather warned her about the devils in the *malpais*. 'Don't go walking there alone,' he said. 'Or the devils will take you with them to Hell.' Grandfather said that he heard the sounds of the devil snuffling around the house on the night that Pedro, Dolores' favorite brother, died of fever. When Dolores' father got drunk and could not work, grandfather blamed the devils. When Dolores was stung by a scorpion, grandfather knew that the devils were at fault. When she was a little girl, Dolores had feared the devils. She knew that they were responsible for the bad things that happened in the village.

Now, a grown woman, she refuses to be afraid of a clay doll that she can twist in her hands. She gives her toy devil grasping talons and a gaping smile that shows his sharp teeth. She bends his legs so that he is dancing and tilts his head back so that he is laughing. A silly devil, a child's toy.

Dolores puts him in the sun to dry and begins working another handful of clay. She finds herself making another laughing devil. This time, she gives him a guitar to strum with his long sharp claws, so that he may play while his brother dances. Together, they dry in the sun. Another devil, a trumpet player, joins them.

She does not like the look of the three devils, lying on their backs in the sun and laughing, probably at something evil. But she leaves them and hurries to make other figures: a whistle shaped like a frog and one shaped like a dove; a clay burro with its neck outstretched to bray; five clay goats and a man to tend them.

Finally, when the sun is high overhead, she wraps the rest of the clay in the black plastic, gives Esperanza a tortilla to eat, and begins her other chores: carrying water from the public fountain, gathering firewood from the *malpais*, pulling weeds from her small garden. She puts beans to soak for the evening meal and sweeps the dirt floor of the house with a twig broom.

Just before Tomas comes home, she checks her pottery. The figures are warm to the touch. The afternoon sun is red upon the devils, touching the dark clay with light the color of blood. The laughing figures make her uneasy, but she is not a little girl, to be so easily frightened.

When Tomas comes home, she shows him the figures. He picks up one of the devils – in the afternoon sun, the clay has already stiffened. He examines the figure casually, just as he might examine a whistle or a clay burro. 'The American will like these,' he predicts. And he pokes the devil lightly in the belly, as if tickling the small figure. 'Oh, how he dances.' Tomas' presence banishes her uneasiness and she smiles at her own fears.

That night, when Esperanza is sleeping, Tomas makes love to Dolores. The night is warm and they throw back the thin blanket. Their bed frame is built of wooden packing crates, and the slats creak beneath their shifting bodies, a rhythmic song that keeps time to her soft moans. With his arms around her, she falls asleep and has no dreams.

A few days later, she fires the pottery in a pit that she had dug on a barren patch of ground near the house. When she lights the wood and straw, flames crackle and the wood snaps like gunfire. The heat of the fire touches her face, hotter than the afternoon sun, and Esperanza crows with delight, clapping her hands to see the flames. Black smoke from the straw rises like thunderclouds.

Dolores goes about her chores while the fire burns: carrying water to her garden, fetching firewood to replace the wood she had burned, going to the market to buy a little rice, a little chilli. Late in the afternoon, the fire has burned low. With a green branch, she rakes away the ashes, uncovering the blackened figurines. Soot-colored dove whistles nestle in the ashes; baying dogs lift their blackened heads. Two goats have broken, cracking when air trapped within the clay expanded in the heat of the fire. But the devils are intact. Silently, they play their instruments with their inhuman hands, laughing and dancing on the smoking ground.

The next day, she paints the figures with the bright paints that Tomas brought her from the city. She leaves the devils until last, then gives them red horns and yellow teeth and flashing golden eyes. The bright colors shimmer in the afternoon sun, and the devils leer at her as she works, staring with their bulging eyes.

The American is a thin gray-haired man in a brightly flowered shirt and pale brown pants. His face and the top of his head, visible through his sparse hair, are reddened from the sun. He speaks Spanish well, and is very polite.

He is a very clean man: his hands are pale and soft. Dolores notices that his fingernails are clean and as neat as a woman's. He picks up a dove whistle with his soft hand and looks at it, turning the toy this way and that.

Tomas stands beside the American, his legs wide apart, his thumbs hooked in the waistband of his trousers. 'They are very good,' Tomas says. 'Very beautiful.' He is like a nervous rooster, strutting for show.

Dolores stands back, keeping her eyes down, her hands hidden in her apron. She is wearing her best dress, the newer of the two she owns, but she is ashamed of her looks. Her own fingernails are broken and stained with clay.

The American says nothing. He puts the dove down and

picks up the dancing devil. One by one, he examines each of the devils. 'The others are pleasant, but nothing special,' he says at last, dismissing the other toys with a wave. 'But these show imagination. I know a few folk art collectors in America who. . . .' He stops without finishing his sentence. 'I will buy these,' he says, pointing to the devils. 'And I would like to see more.'

Before he leaves, he and Tomas shake hands. They will do business.

That evening, Tomas buys tequila with money from the American. Other men from the village come to hear him brag of his success. Dolores watches from the doorway of the house.

The men sit on the rusting hulk of an old car that was abandoned on the edge of the *malpais*. The car's wheels were stolen long ago. Now the car rests on its belly, and men perch on its rusted hood. They drink tequila and laugh loudly. The light from the setting sun paints them red. Their shadows stretch away into the *malpais*.

Dolores dreams that night of devils. One is feathered like a rooster and he struts through the dream, puffing out his chest and preening his shiny horns. Another has a bulging belly, like an old sow with a litter. His ears are hairy, like the ears of a pig, and his horns curl like goat horns.

Tomas has little to say at breakfast. His eyes are red and weary-looking, and he complains that his head hurts. He pushes Esperanza away when she comes to kiss him good morning. 'Make more devils,' he tells Dolores before he goes to the fields.

She comforts Esperanza and makes devils of clay. In her hands, the fat devil becomes fatter. Her fingers smooth the round curve of his belly, a pig's belly supported by spindly legs. His ears droop mournfully as he dries in the sun. He is a ridiculous devil, a child's toy, but somehow she cannot laugh at him.

From a handful of clay, she makes the strutting rooster

devil, with his puffed out chest and his nose like a beak. The devil looks foolish, but Dolores is uneasy. The devils stink of dark and ancient places, and she remembers her grandfather's tales.

'Never call the evil one by name,' her grandfather told her. 'If you do, you will call him to you and give him power.'

She pats the clay, molding the delicate shapes of devil's horns and wondering what her grandfather would say about these toys. A breeze blows from the *malpais* and she feels ill, weak and feverish.

Tomas insists on bringing the devils into the house that evening. He says that someone might take them if they were left outside. He sets them on a shelf beside the bed, poked the fat one in the belly, and laughs.

Again, Tomas and his friends sit on the old car and drink tequila. Dolores goes to bed, but she does not sleep. She can hear Tomas talking and the laughter of his friends. And she hears other sounds – small sounds like mice searching for grains of corn on the dirt floor. She lies awake, knowing that the devils are moving on the shelf, their claws scratching against the wood.

She is awake when Tomas stumbles into the house. He brings his bottle of tequila with him: she hears the clink of glass as he sets the bottle down by the bed, the rustle of clothing as he takes off his shirt. He lies beside her in the bed, and she turns toward him. His breath stinks of tequila, and he pulls her toward him, pressing his lips against her throat. He makes love to her in the darkness, but she thinks of the devils, watching from the shelf. The bed sings, but she is silent. At last, Tomas sleeps.

While her husband and daughter sleep, Dolores listens to the devils moving on the shelf. In the morning, the devils are quiet, standing as if they had never moved. That morning, on her way to fetch water from the public fountain, Dolores stops at the house of the *curandera*, the village healer and herbalist.

Dona Ramon's house and yard have a pungent smell from the drying herbs in the rafters and the growing herbs in the yard. Esperanza stays close by her mother, her eyes wide, a little fearful of Dona Ramon.

Dolores tells Dona Ramon of the American who wants devils, of her terrible dreams, and of the sounds she hears at night.

The old woman nods. 'These devils will bring you bad luck,' she says. 'When you make them, you give the devil power. You call the devils from the *malpais* to your house.'

'What can I do?' Dolores asks.

'Stop making devils.'

'The American wants devils,' Dolores says.

Dona Ramon shrugs. 'Then you will have bad luck.'

That afternoon, Dolores makes whistles shaped like doves and owls and coyotes and frogs, simple toys that will make children happy and will bring no devils to her house. As she works, Esperanza plays beside her in the mud, making round balls of clay and patting them flat to make mud tortillas.

When Tomas comes home that evening and examines Dolores' new pottery. There is not a single devil. 'The American told you to make devils,' he says to her. 'Why do you make these toys?'

'I do not like the devils,' Dolores tells him softly. 'They will bring bad luck.'

Tomas scowls. 'These devils will bring us money. And money will bring us luck.'

She shakes her head. 'The *curandera* told me that these clay devils will bring real devils from the *malpais* to our house.'

Tomas laughs. It is wicked, hurting laughter with no joy in it. 'Why do I have such a stupid wife?' he asks. 'There are no devils in the *malpais*. Those are stories to scare children.'

Dolores shakes her head again, suddenly stubborn. 'I can't make devils,' she says. 'I. . . .'

Tomas strikes without warning, an open-handed slap that nearly knocks her down. 'Why do I have such a stupid wife?' he shouts. 'The American wants devils and you will make devils.' When he strikes her again, Dolores falls to her knees and clutches her head, weeping. He stands over her for a moment, his hand raised as if to strike again. When she looks up at him, he scowls at her, the expression of a young boy who has been denied something he wants. 'You must make devils,' he says. 'Then we will have money, and we can buy you a new dress.' Reluctantly, she nods her head. Then he tells her to dry her tears and helps her to her feet.

That night, Tomas drinks with his friends, finishing the tequila that he bought with the American's money. Dolores dreams of a bat-winged devil who dances on a platform of human skulls, a feathered devil who clutches two weeping children in its talons; a snake devil who has caught a naked women in his coils.

The next morning, Dolores makes devils: the snake with the captive woman; the bat-winged dancer; the bird devil and the children. Her head aches and she is weary before the day is half over.

When Tomas comes home, he sees her work and smiles. 'These will bring money,' he says, but she does not answer. He puts them on the shelf with the others and, because there is no more tequila, his friends do not come to visit. He sits alone on the rusting car and drowses in the setting sun. Dolores watches from the kitchen door; she does not like seeing him sitting so near the *malpais* when the night is coming. She goes to him. 'Come in the house,' she says. 'It is not good to be out here.'

He smiles, and his face looks unfamiliar in the red light of sunset. 'You shouldn't fear the devils,' he says. 'The devils will make us rich. The devils will buy you new dresses and build us a new house.'

She takes his hand and he follows her into the house, obedient as a sleepwalker. They go to bed and he sleeps; Esperanza sleeps. And Dolores hears whispering.

'Dolores,' they say. 'We will make you strong. We will give you money. We will give you power.' Tiny voices, dry as the wind from the desert. 'Listen to us.'

Tomas turns in his sleep, and Dolores hears him moan softly, as if crying out in a dream. He is a weak man, susceptible to the devils' promises. They have promised him riches, then tempted him with drink. He is weak, but she is strong. She hears the whispering voices, but she does not listen.

In the faint light of early dawn Dolores leaves her bed and carries the devils out to the edge of the *malpais*. She lines them up side by side on the hood of the old car. They stare at her with bulging eyes, threaten her with their claws.

She takes a large stick from the ground and clubs the snake devil who holds the woman captive, smashing the unfired clay into pieces. The light of the sun warms her as she lifts her club to strike again.

In the Abode of the Snows

In a hospital room with white walls, Xavier Clark held the hand of his dying mother. The chill breeze from the air-conditioner made him think of the snow-covered peaks of the Himalayas: Annapurna, Machhapuchhare, Dhaulagiri, Nilgiri. Places he had never been. His mother's shallow breathing could have been the whispering of snow crystals, blown by mountain breezes across a patch of ice. The veins beneath her pale skin were faintly blue, the color of glacial ice.

His mother's eyes were closed, and he knew she was dying. With each passing year, she had grown more frail, becoming as brittle as the delicate tea cups that she kept locked in the china cabinet. Her hair had grown paler, becoming so ethereal that her scalp showed through no matter how carefully she combed and arranged the white wisps.

His mother's breathing stopped, and he listened, for a moment, to the quick light sound of his own breathing and the pounding of his own heart. Closing his eyes, he clung to his mother's hand and savored a faint uneasy feeling of release, as if his last tie to earth had been cut and he could soar like a balloon, leaving the ordinary world behind.

Xavier returned from the hospital to his mother's house. Though he had lived in the house for all of his forty years, he still thought of it as his mother's house. Even when his father had been alive, the house had been his mother's. His father had always seemed like a visitor, stopping at the house to rest and write between expeditions to Nepal.

When Xavier was five, his father had died in a snowslide on the eastern slope of Dhaulagiri. When Xavier tried to remember his father, he could picture only the broad-shouldered man that he had seen in out-of-focus book-jacket photos, a lifeless black-and-white image.

More clearly than Xavier remembered his father, he remembered his father's possessions: an elaborately carved prayer wheel that reeked of incense, a small rug on which two dragons curled about one another in an intricate pattern, a brass bowl that sang when struck with a wooden rod, wooden masks with great empty eyes and grimacing mouths, round brass bells the size of his fist attached to a strip of brightly colored tapestry. Upon receiving word of his father's death, Xavier's mother had taken all these exotic treasures, wrapped them in newspaper, and packed them in a steamer trunk that she pushed into a corner of the attic. As a child, Xavier had yearned to look at his father's belongings, but the steamer trunk was locked and he had known better than to ask his mother for the key.

His mother had never talked of his father after his death. She never remarried, raising Xavier herself, living frugally on the proceeds of his father's insurance policies and on royalties from his books.

As a teenager, Xavier bought copies of his father's three books: *Adventures on the Roof of the World*, *Land of Yak and Yeti*, and *The Magic of Nepal*. He hid the books from his mother and read them in his room when he was supposed to be doing his homework. On the map in the flyleaf of one book, he traced his father's journeys in red pen. In his sleep, he muttered the names of mountains: Machhapuchhare, Annapurna, Dhaulagiri, Nilgiri. He remembered the names of Himalayan rivers, fed by monsoon rains and melting snows. He knew the names of his father's porters – the Sherpas who accompanied the mountaineering expeditions – better than he knew the names of his own schoolmates.

He was a shy teenager with few friends. After graduating from high school, he attended the local college and majored in biology. He had planned to base his thesis on observations of mountain sheep in the Rockies, but just before he was due to leave, his mother had taken ill. He cancelled his trip and spent the summer observing waterfowl in a local pond, writing a thesis on the behavior of coots in an urban environment.

At college graduation, he was offered a job as wildlife biologist in the Idaho National Forest. Upon receiving the good news, his mother suffered the first in a series of heart attacks. He accepted a position as biology teacher at the local high school and stayed home to nurse her.

Living in his mother's house with the silent memories of his father's glorious past, he had become a secretive and solitary man. His clothes hung loosely on his body, like the skin of a reptile preparing to molt. His students joked about him, saying that he looked like one of the thin dry lizards that he kept in the classroom's terrarium. He had grown prematurely old, never leaving town because his mother was never well enough to travel and never well enough to be left alone.

In the empty house, on the evening of his mother's death, Xavier was truly alone for the first time in decades. He felt strangely hollow – not lonely, but empty. He felt light, insubstantial, as if the slightest breeze could carry him away. He could do anything. He could go anywhere. He thought about his father's trunk and went to the attic.

The trunk had been pushed to the farthest corner, tucked under the eaves – behind a broken lamp, a dressmaker's dummy stuck with pins, a box of Xavier's old toys, and an overstuffed armchair with torn upholstery in which generations of mice had nested. The truck was locked and, for a moment, Xavier hesitated, considering retreat. Then he realized that the house and all its contents were his. With a screwdriver and hammer, he attacked the trunk's rusty hasp and tore it free of the lid.

On top of the newspaper-wrapped bundles in the trunk lay a package wrapped in brown paper and decorated with Nepali stamps. Xavier carefully unwrapped the package and found a leatherbound notebook filled with spidery hand-writing that looked curiously like his own.

Xavier opened the book and read a page: 'I have decided to leave the expedition and press on alone, following the Kali Gandaki to its source. In the bleak northern hills, I am certain I will find the man-ape that the Sherpa call the yeti. Winter is coming and many will call me foolish, but I cannot turn back. I miss my wife and son, but I like to think that my son, if he were here, would understand. I cannot turn back. The mountains will not let me.'

Mingling with the dusty air of the attic, Xavier thought he smelled incense, a foreign smell that awakened unfamiliar urges. Kneeling beside the trunk, his father's journal in his hands, he felt, in some strange way, that he had made a decision. He knew that he would not return to school for the fall term.

In a new backpack, purchased at the local sporting goods store, Xavier packed field notebooks, camera, and many rolls of film. He bought a kerosene stove and tested it in the backyard, boiling water for tea in a light-weight aluminium pot. He bought a plane ticket to Katmandu by way of Bangkok and converted $5000 cash into traveler's checks. He studied a book titled *Nepali Made Simple*, memorizing simple phrases. He haunted the local college library, reading all the accounts of yeti sightings that he could find.

Mountaineers described the beast as inhumanly tall and covered with shaggy hair. Some said it was nocturnal, prowling the barren slopes between the treeline and the permanent snows. Some said it was like a monkey; others, like a bear. Tibetans and Nepalis credited the beast with supernatural powers: its bones and scalp were valued as objects of great power.

He read his father's journal, lingering over descriptions of the terrain, the mountains, the wildlife. His father's books had maintained a heroic tone: men battled the wilderness, always fought fair, and usually triumphed. The journal gave a more realistic account: describing stomach upsets and bouts with dysentery, complaining of lazy porters, recording bribes given minor officials for quicker service. The journal told of superstitions: Tibetans believed that shamans could transform themselves into birds, that finding a hat was unlucky, that dogs howling at dawn were an inauspicious omen. Xavier read all this with great enthusiasm.

At night, Xavier dreamed of cold slopes, scoured clean by endless winds. He was filled with a feverish longing for the high country, where the snows never melt. He would find the yeti, track its movements, study its biology. He would finish the task that his father had begun and return to his mother's house to write of his success.

On his first day in Katmandu, Xavier wandered the narrow streets of the alien city, marveling at how strange and yet how familiar it seemed. It matched his father's descriptions, yet somehow, on some level, it seemed quite different.

A shy Hindu boy with a red tika dot painted on his forehead stared at Xavier from a dark doorway. The child wore no pants and his dark skin reflected a little light from the street, a subtle sheen on thin legs, thin buttocks. In the shade provided by a shrine to Ganesh, the elephant-headed son of Vishnu, a street dog rested and licked her sores.

The market smelled of incense, strong spices, and cow manure. Xavier shooed away the vendors who tried to sell him tourist trinkets, the rickshaw drivers who asked in broken English where he was going, the black market money changers who offered him a good rate, a very good rate, for American dollars. He was caught by the feeling that something was about to happen, something sudden and strange, something exotic and unanticipated. He stared about him with impassioned hungry eyes, watching for a secret signal that the adventure began here.

In a small square, bedsheets and other laundry flapped from the second floors of the surrounding houses. The wooden frames of the windows had been ornately carved sometime in the last three centuries. The faces of Hindu deities and demons stared from a complex background of twisting human bodies, vines, and flowers. In the square below, heaps of yellow grain dried in the autumn sun. Small children kept guard, stopping noisy games to chase away cows and dogs and pigs.

In a small street frequented only by Nepalis, Xavier ate lunch, crouching uncomfortably on a wooden bench just barely out of the street. The high clear piping of flutes played by flute sellers mingled with the honking of rickshaw horns and the jingling of bicycle bells.

Though the Nepalis ate with their hands, the shopkeeper insisted on giving Xavier a tarnished and bent fork and on showing the American how to sprinkle hot peppers on his daal baat, the rice and lentil dish that served as the staple of the Nepali diet. The shopkeeper, a wizened man in a high-crowned brimless hat, sat beside Xavier on the bench and watched him eat.

'You come from England?' the shopkeeper asked Xavier.

'No, from America.'

'You going trekking?'

'Well, yes,' he said. 'I plan to go up past a town called Jomsom. I . . .' He hesitated, then plunged on. 'I have read that yeti have been seen in that area.'

'Ah, you wish to find the yeti?'

'Very much.'

The shopkeeper studied him. 'Westerners do not have the patience to find the yeti. They hurry, hurry, and never find what they look for.'

'I have all the time in the world,' Xavier said.

The shopkeeper folded his hands in his lap, smiled and said, 'You will need a guide. My cousin, Tempa, can take you where you need to go.'

Xavier ate and listened to the shopkeeper praise the virtues of his cousin Tempa. Sitting in the open stall, he looked up at the thin strip of sky visible between the houses. A single bird flew over, heading north-west. Xavier watched it vanish from sight and knew, with the same certainty that had caused him to quit his job and come to Nepal, that he would go northwest to the Himalayas, to the high country where anything could happen.

On the fourth day on the trail, Xavier and Tempa were caught in a violent hailstorm that transformed the path into a running stream that splashed merrily around Xavier's boots. The water quickly penetrated the waterproof oil that Xavier had applied to the boots in Katmandu. His socks were soon soaked and his feet ached with the cold.

In a low stone hut that served as teahouse and provided primitive accommodations, they found shelter. The group of ragged porters that huddled by the fire looked up when Xavier ducked through the low doorway. The teahouse was filled with woodsmoke and the scent of unwashed clothing. The small fire that burned in the center of the single room seemed to provide more smoke than warmth.

Xavier blinked as his eyes adjusted to the dark interior. Not elegant accommodations, but better than a tent and no worse than the teahouses that had sheltered them for the past three days. Xavier propped his pack against the wall and hung his rain parka on a nail that jutted from the wooden doorframe.

The proprietress, a Tibetan woman, offered him rokshi, locally distilled wine, and he accepted gratefully. The clear liquor smelled faintly of apples and tasted overwhelmingly of alcohol. The first mouthful seared his mouth and throat with a bright, almost painful warmth that spread slowly to his chest. He sat on a wooden bench by the door and slowly unlaced his wet boots.

Tempa was already deep in conversation with the porters who crouched by the fire. He looked up at Xavier, his eyes reflecting the firelight. 'They say that snow has fallen in the pass to the north,' Tempa said to Xavier. 'And a big storm is coming.'

Xavier shrugged, pulled off his boots, and gingerly wiggled his toes. Since the very first day, Tempa had been complaining about the weight of his pack, the length of each day's hike, the perils of bad weather. 'Not much we can do about the weather,' he said.

Tempa frowned. 'Big storm,' he said. 'Too late in the season to go on. Tomorrow, we go back.'

Xavier shook his head and frowned at Tempa, trying to assume an air of authority. 'Go back? We've just started. If there's a storm, we'll wait it out.'

'Too cold,' Tempa said. 'Winter is here.'

'Tomorrow, we go on,' Xavier said. His father had written of stubborn porters and of the need to show them who was boss. 'Do you understand? I'm not ready to go back.'

Tempa returned unhappily to his friends by the fire. Xavier relaxed, loosened the collar of his damp flannel shirt, and leaned back against the stone wall of the teahouse. The warmth of the rokshi spread throughout his body. Outside, the rain had stopped and a rooster was crowing. Xavier closed his eyes and listened to the soft whispering of water flowing down the trail, the gentle clucking of the chickens that searched for edible insects in the scrubby weeds that grew just outside the teahouse door. The breeze that blew through the door smelled of mountains that had been washed clean by the rain. He took a deep breath, but caught a whiff of another scent, something stronger than the woodsmoke or the rokshi – an animal scent. He looked up to see an old man standing in the hut's open doorway.

Though the afternoon breeze was cold, the old man wore no shirt or jacket, only a loose loincloth of an indeterminate color. The cloth may once have been white, but it had become an uncertain shade of gray: the color of dust, of woodsmoke, of ashes and grime. The man's long gray-streaked hair was wound in a topknot. The ancient face was stern – a high forehead, a nose like a beak. Around the man's neck hung a string of round beads, each one a different shade of off-white. Xavier stared at the beads, recognizing them from a description in his father's journal. Each of the 108 beads had been carved from the bone of a different human skull. At the man's belt dangled a carved ivory phurba, the ritual dagger carried by all shamans of Bon, the ancient animalistic religion that had preceded Buddhism in the Himalayas.

In one hand, the man carried a metal bowl, which he held out to the Tibetan woman. She beckoned him in and he squatted beside the fire.

'*Namaste*,' Xavier said, the traditional Nepali greeting that meant 'I salute you.' His voice was suddenly unsteady. Here was adventure – a traveling shaman visiting the same tea-house.

The old shaman stared at Xavier, but did not return his greeting.

Xavier beckoned to Tempa. 'Who is the old man?' he whispered.

Tempa's small vocabulary deserted him when he did not find it convenient to speak English. Now, occupied with a glass of rokshi and eager to return to his friends, Tempa shrugged. '*Ta chaina.*' I don't know.

'Where is he from?'

Tempa frowned, seemingly reluctant to say anything about the old man. 'He lives alone.' Tempa waved an arm toward the hills.

'A hermit,' Xavier said.

Tempa shrugged and returned to his friends.

The Tibetan woman served dinner, scooping a serving of rice into the old man's bowl and moistening the grain with a spoonful of daal. The old man silently accepted the offering. The woman dished out a similar dinner for the others.

After his third glass of rokshi and a plate of daal baat, Xavier had relaxed. The old man, he noticed, ate alone, squatting in a corner of the hut. With rokshi-induced courage, Xavier went to the corner and endeavoured to begin a conversation with the old man.

'Rokshi?' Xavier said to the old man, and then he signaled

the woman for another glass. The old man studied Xavier
with impassive black eyes, then accepted the glass.

'*Timiko ghar ke ho?*' the old man asked Xavier. '*Timi kaha
jane?*' Where are you from? Where are you going?

Xavier replied in halting Nepali. I come from America.
Then he waved a hand to indicate his destination, pointing
northward toward the high cold mountains that filled his
dreams. '*Meh-teh hirne,*' he said. Which meant, more or less,
I look for the yeti.

The old man took Xavier's hand in a strong grip and
peered into the American's face with sudden intensity. He
spoke rapidly in Nepali, but Xavier could not follow his
words. When Xavier shrugged, looking bewildered, the old
man called to Tempa, who sat with the other porters by the
fire. Tempa responded in Nepali.

The old man broke into a grin, his stern face collapsing
into wrinkles. He reached out a withered hand and cupped
Xavier's chin, lifting the biology teacher's face as a doting
grandmother might lift the face of a shy child. The old man
threw back his head and laughed at something that he saw
in Xavier's face. He released his hold on Xavier, and said
something, but the only word Xavier could catch in the rapid
string of Nepali was '*meh-teh.*' Something about yeti.

Xavier smiled uneasily, wondering how his father would
have handled a situation like this. 'What's all that about?'
Xavier asked Tempa. Reluctantly, Tempa left his friends and
came to squat beside Xavier and the old man.

'He wants to know where you are going,' Tempa said. 'I
tell him you look for the yeti.'

Xavier nodded and smiled at the old man.

The old man said something else in rapid Nepali. Xavier
shook his head and asked him to speak more slowly.

Still grinning, the old man repeated himself, pausing after
each word and accompanying his words with gestures.
Xavier couldn't follow everything that the old man said, but
he thought he caught the gist of it: The old man had seen

the yeti many times. He was a powerful shaman and he had hunted the yeti many times.

Xavier poured the old man another cup of rokshi and asked him to tell about the yeti. Beside the fire, three porters played a noisy game of cards. Outside the door, by candlelight, the Tibetan woman washed the dinner dishes. Inside the smoky teahouse, Xavier leaned close to the old man, ignoring his animal scent, and listened to tales of the yeti.

The yeti looked like men, only different, the old man explained slowly. They hunted at night, and they were very strong. With only his hands a yeti could kill a yak, break the neck. (The old man brought his hands together like a man snapping a stick.) The yeti is fierce and cunning.

Xavier, with hand gestures and halting Nepali, asked the old man how he hunted such a fierce beast. With a dirty finger, the old man tapped his temple and nodded sagely. He called out to the woman, and she brought a stoneware crock and two tin cups. The old man filled the cups with a ladle and offered one to Xavier. 'Yo chang ho,' the old man said. This is chang.

Xavier had heard of chang, a thick beer brewed with rice and barley. Unwilling to offend the old man, he sipped the thick beverage. It tasted like a mixture of sour porridge and alcohol, but after the first few sips it wasn't too bad.

The old man tapped the cup and told Xavier that he hunted the yeti with chang. He launched into a long explanation which Xavier followed with difficulty. To catch a yeti, it seems, the old man found a village where a yeti had been bothering people, stealing their crops and killing their goats. On a night when the moon was new, the old man left a pot of chang in the path where the yeti would find it. The yeti drank the chang and fell asleep, and in the morning, the old man captured it easily. Yeti, said the old man, like chang.

More chang, more labored discussion of the habits of the yeti. Xavier grew accustomed to the smoke that filled the room. At some point, the Tibetan woman lit a candle, and the flickering light cast enormous shadows that danced on the walls. The old man's face, illuminated by the candle, seemed filled with sly amusement. Sometimes, it seemed to Xavier that the old man was laughing at him beneath the words, teasing him with some private joke. But the room seemed small and cozy and Xavier's Nepali improved with each cup of chang. It was a good life, a good place to be. With each cup of chang, the joke seemed less important. Xavier lost track of how many cups of chang he drank. The old man seemed like a good friend, a faithful companion.

Somehow Xavier found himself telling the old man about his father and his search for the yeti. Groping for words in Nepali, he tried to explain that he needed to find the yeti, to finish what his father had started. He tried to explain how he felt about the mountains. In a mixture of Nepali and English, he tried to describe his dreams of mountains and snow.

The old man listened intently, nodded as if he understood. Then he spoke softly, slowly, laying a hand on Xavier's hand. I can help you find the yeti, he said to Xavier. Do you want to see the yeti?

Drowsy from chang, half mesmerized by the candlelight, Xavier took the old man's hand in both of his. 'I want to find the yeti,' he said in English.

The old man fumbled for something in the pouch that dangled at his belt. He displayed his findings to Xavier on the palm of a withered hand: a small brown bone etched with spidery characters. The bone was attached to a leather thong. It was made of yeti bone, the old man explained. Very powerful, very magical.

Xavier reached out and touched the small dried object. It was warm to the touch, like a small sleeping animal. The old man smiled. His dark eyes were caught in a mesh of wrinkles, like gleaming river pebbles in a bed of drying mud.

The old man nodded, as if reaching some conclusion, then looped the leather thong around Xavier's neck. Startled, Xavier protested, but the old man just smiled. When Xavier lifted the pendant, as if to remove it, the old man scolded him in Nepali.

They had more chang to celebrate, and Xavier's memories were fuzzy after that. He remembered the old man reassuring him that he would see the yeti. He remembered lying down on a bamboo mat by the fire and pulling his still damp sleeping bag over himself.

In his dreams, he fingered the bone that hung around his neck. He dreamed of studying the mark of a bare foot on the side of a snowy mountain. Suddenly, without surprise, he realized that his own feet were bare. His feet ached from the cold of the snow, and he was hungry, very hungry.

He blinked awake in the pale morning light. He could hear the hollow clanging of metal bells: a mule train was passing on the trail. The wood smoke that drifted through the hut's open door reminded him of the cold mist that filled the mountain gorges of his dreams. His head and belly ached, and he remembered drinking too much rokshi, too much chang.

The other bamboo mats were empty. The Tibetan woman crouched by the hearth, poking the fire that burned beneath the blackened teakettle. The porters were gone; the old man was gone. Confused by lingering dream images, Xavier sat up and felt the leather thong around his neck. The bone was there. He ran a fingernail over the rough surface and felt more confident. His throat was sore and his voice was hoarse when he asked the woman where his porter, Tempa, had gone.

The woman shook her head. 'Ta chaina,' she said. I don't know.

Xavier struggled from his sleeping bag and stumbled out of the hut making for the boulder-strewn slope that served as a latrine. The wind numbed his face and the gray world outside the hut seemed less substantial than his dreams. The sky was overcast; the mountains, hidden by distant haze. The ground underfoot was composed of mottled gray and brown pebbles, swept clean by the steady wind from the north. The trail, a faint track marked by the dung of pack mules and the scuff marks of hikers' boots, led northward.

Xavier stopped beside a large boulder. He noticed a large raven, perched on a distant rock, watching him with interest as he pissed. 'What do you want?' he said crossly to the bird. The bird regarded the man with bright curious eyes, shrieked once, then took flight, leaving him alone, blinking at the gray sky.

Xavier made his way back to the hut. Tempa had gone. When he asked the Tibetan woman again, she shrugged and said something about Tempa leaving very early in the morning. The porter had taken some of Xavier's possessions along with his own: Xavier's wool gloves and hat, the wool socks that had been drying by the fire and the rupee notes that Xavier kept in his jacket pocket.

Xavier contemplated the desertion with mixed feelings. He could pursue the thieving porter, but if he turned back, he would miss his chance to search for the yeti. He was seized by uncertainty. Perhaps the weather was turning bad and he should turn back. Could he find his way without a guide? Should he abandon his provisions and trust to local supplies for his food?

At the same time, he was glad at the thought of traveling on alone. The porter had seemed skeptical of Xavier's plans from the first day on the trail. Tempa had, Xavier felt, lacked the proper spirit of adventure.

In the end, it was Xavier's memory of the old man's words that decided him. 'You will see the yeti,' said the old man. How could Xavier turn his back on such a prophecy?

Taking a loss, Xavier sold most of his remaining supplies to the Tibetan woman. He added the rest to his own load. When he left, his pack was heavier by about twenty pounds. Though he knew that his shoulders would be aching by noon, he whistled as he walked, relishing the thought of being alone in the desolate reaches of the Himalayas.

North of Ghasa, past the village of Tukche, the valley broadened. No trees grew on the great gray slopes. On the lee side of large boulders grew stunted bushes and patchy grasses, tough plants with foliage as dusty as the rocky slopes. Shaggy goats, snatching a thorny lunch in one such patch, stared at Xavier as he passed, their golden eyes faintly hostile. The children who tended the herd, two ragged boys with unruly hair and snotty noses, silently watched the white man with indifferent curiosity.

Once, a flock of ravens took flight from the hillside beside him, wheeling above him to darken the sky like a flight of demons. One raven from the flock kept pace with him for a time: flying ahead to perch on a mani wall, a jumbled construction built of flat stones carved with Buddhist prayers. As Xavier approached, the bird called out in a croaking guttural voice, then flew to a boulder a few hundred yards down the trail. Each time Xavier drew near, the bird flew on a little farther, then stopped by the trail, as if waiting for the man to catch up.

The wind blew constantly, kicking up the dust and carrying along leaves and twigs. It blasted the boulders and scoured the mani stones, as if trying to wipe the carved letters away. It chapped his lips, dried his throat, and rubbed dust into his skin and hair.

The trail followed the Kali Gandaki, a chilly turbulent river with waters as gray as the rounded granite boulders that lined its bank. In the valley, the river widened, flowing in a network of channels that merged and separated like the veins and arteries of a living animal. The trail wandered beside one of the channels. Beside the water, sparse red-brown grass grew, gray soil showing between the blades.

Without his wool cap, Xavier's ears were unprotected and the rushing of the wind blended with the rushing of the river and the shrill cries of insects in the grass. As he traveled north, signs of passing travelers grew fewer: the mark of a boot in the mud; a few hoofprints; ancient horse droppings, long since dried to dust. The trail sometimes disappeared altogether, leaving Xavier to wander by the stream, searching for another sign to show him the way.

A few trees had grown there, reached maturity, then died. Their skeletons reached for the sky, twisted by the nagging wind and crippled where peasants had chopped away branches for firewood. The landscape had a dreamlike quality, as if this were a place that Xavier had imagined for himself. Dry branches rattled in the dry breeze. He was not startled when a raven flew from a twisted tree, laughing when the wind lifted it aloft. It seemed right for the raven to be there, to laugh, to fly ahead as if showing him the way.

The village of Jomsom was an unwelcome intrusion on the landscape, a cluster of low-lying stone houses inhabited by people who had been blasted into passivity by the constant wind. The streets and houses were gray and lifeless, and he passed through as quickly as he could.

A few miles beyond Jomsom, the trail forked: one branch led to Muktinath, a destination popular with trekkers. Xavier took the other branch, the ill-marked track that led to the north. A few miles down the trail he stopped by the Kali Gandaki, clambering down the steep bank to the rushing water. Though the air was still cold, hiking had warmed him. The wind had eased and the sun was out. He stripped to the waist, draping his shirt over a rock and putting his watch beside it. He splashed the river water on his face, his chest, and up over his back, gasping when the cold water struck his skin, shaking his head like a wet dog.

He was toweling dry when he heard the harsh cry of a raven. The black bird was perched on the boulder beside his shirt. Xavier saw the raven peck at something on the rock, and he shouted, waving at the bird. The raven took flight, and Xavier saw that it carried his watch in its beak. The bird circled, the watch glinting in its beak. Then the wind caught the bird and it soared away over the woods, vanishing from sight.

Xavier did not miss the watch as much as he expected to. As the day passed, he grew accustomed to a timeless existence. He stopped to eat lunch when he was hungry, rested when he was tired. He camped out that night, stopping between villages beside the Kali Gandaki and using his mountain tent for the first time. He dreamed bright crystalline dreams; he was on a steep ice slope, pursuing a dark shape that remained always just a few steps ahead. He chased the dark shape to the edge of a precipice and slipped on the ice, realizing as he fell that the fleeing darkness was his own shadow.

When he awoke, the ground was white with frost, and his breath made clouds that the wind swept away. At dusk the next day, he reached the village of Samagaon. The villagers eyed him with great suspicion: strangers were a rare sight so far from the trekking route.

With Tempa's theft, Xavier's supply of rupees had dwindled. He found only one teahouse, and the proprietor, a Gurkha soldier who had returned to his home village, scoffed at the American's traveler's checks, puffing his cheeks out and saying that the check might be no good, he couldn't tell.

Xavier considered the matter, then offered to trade some of his equipment for cash and food. The man did not want a wool sweater or worn down jacket, but he inspected the kerosene stove carefully. On the spur of the moment, Xavier decided he could do without the stove. He demonstrated it carefully, filling the fuel tank with kerosene and lighting the burner. It coughed once or twice, then roared with a steady blue flame that lit one corner of the dark smoky tea shop. In limited Nepali, Xavier praised the stove: 'Ramro cha. Dheri ramro.' It's good, very good. His voice was hoarse from days of silence.

While Xavier bargained, two ragged little girls watched from behind the skirts of the man's wife. They stared with wide round eyes, trying to absorb this curiosity, this white man far from the places that white men were found. The shopkeeper came from a long line of traders, and he drove a hard bargain. In the end, Xavier traded for rice, lentils, curry powder, and two hundred rupees cash – a fraction of the stove's value, but he could carry no more food and the shopkeeper claimed that he had no more cash. Xavier spent the night on the shopkeeper's floor, ate a hurried breakfast of corn porridge sweetened with honey, and headed north.

He sang as he walked, a tuneless melody that seemed to ebb and flow like the rushing of the river. His beard was growing in, and when he saw his reflection in a still pool, he laughed at himself, a rough-looking character with a dirty face and good crop of stubble.

Early in the morning, he could see the mountains. But as the day progressed, clouds obscured the view, forming what looked like a new uncharted range of snow-covered peaks, billowing masses of pale gray cloud mountains.

Early in what he supposed to be the afternoon, the overcast sky grew darker. He reached a river crossing: the Kahe Lungpa, a swollen stream that tumbled down from the high peaks to meet the Kali Gandaki. The bridge over the river was down. Water rushed past one shattered wooden support, causing the rotten boards to shiver in the current. Perhaps the bridge had washed out during the monsoon storms. The crossing was far from any village and no doubt the few travelers who passed this way did not have the resources or time to repair or replace the bridge, but simply forded the river.

For a moment, he stood on the bank, gazing at the roaring stream. In one book, his father told of fording snow-fed rivers barefoot, preferring, he wrote, 'the momentary discomfort of crossing barefoot to the prolonged chafing of sodden boots.' Xavier reluctantly removed his boots, shivering in the cold breeze. He tied the boots to the pack, slipped on a pair of rubber thongs, rolled up the legs of his jeans, and stepped down into the water, knowing that if he hesitated, he would turn back.

The first few steps were painful, but the cold water numbed his feet, making the pain more bearable. The river dragged at his legs, trying to shift the rounded stones beneath his feet. He took his time, making sure that each foot was planted before trusting his weight to it, taking one slow step after another. Time had no meaning: he could have been walking through the water for an hour or a minute, he would not have known the difference.

He was halfway across when the first snowflakes fell. The pain returned to his feet: a sharp hurt that seemed to extend into his bones. He tried to move more quickly, but his feet could no longer feel the rocks beneath him. He stumbled, caught himself, then slipped again and fell, twisting to one side and catching himself on his arm. The river snatched at the pack; the current yanked it to and fro. Xavier clung to the pack's straps, struggling to regain his footing and to hoist the waterlogged pack from the river. He staggered forward, floundering, gasping from the shock of the cold water, almost losing his thongs, dragging himself on to the far bank and flinging his pack beside him.

From the scraggly bushes on the riverside, a raven laughed hysterically. Xavier ignored the bird, breathing in great gasps and clutching at the damp grass that grew on the bank. After a moment, he rolled over to check his pack. Only then did he realize that the river had snatched the boots from his pack, as well as soaking his food, and drenching his sleeping bag.

For a moment, he lay on the ground, unwilling to move. His feet ached from the cold, his hands trembled. Then he felt for the carved bone pendant around his neck. The old man had said he would see the yeti. That reassurance comforted him. He forced himself to sit up and figure out how to get warm.

A pair of damp wool socks provided some protection for his feet; his wool sweater blocked some of the wind. He warmed himself with exercise, searching for driftwood in the bushes that grew along the river. When he was moving, his arms and legs did not tremble as violently.

An hour's search yielded a small stack of sticks, none bigger around than a finger, and a few damp logs, driftwood cast on shore by the river. His teeth chattering, he searched for tinder, scraps of dry material small enough to catch quickly. But the snow had dampened the leaves and grasses, leaving nothing dry.

The wind grew stronger, slicing through his wet clothing and making him shiver uncontrollably. With his pocketknife, he whittled a few thin splinters from a stick, heaping them together in the shelter of a bush. He built a small teepee of sticks over the tinder and hunched over it.

The first match went out immediately. The head of the second match – wretched Nepali matches – broke off without catching. The third match burned reluctantly. When he held the flame beside his heap of shavings, two slivers of wood smouldered for a moment, but the red glow faded as soon as the match went out.

Xavier's hands shook as he carefully arranged grass beside the wood shavings. The grass, like the wood, would not burn. Desperate for warmth, he patted his pockets, searching for a scrap of paper. In his wallet, he found his traveler's checks, bone dry and warm from his body heat. They were worthless in the woods, and he hesitated only for a moment before crumpling a fifty-dollar check. He arranged the splinters of wood over the dry paper.

The check burned well, but it was small and it burned out before the wood caught. He sacrificed two more, holding his hands out to protect the tiny flame from the wind. The checks whispered as they burned, tiny, crackling voices that spoke of distant places and hidden secrets. When he added the fourth and fifth check, the wood caught, flames moving reluctantly from stick to stick. He propped a driftwood log near the fire where it would dry; and made himself as comfortable as he could, sitting with his back in the bushes to protect it from the wind. He draped his wet sleeping bag over his lap where the fire would warm it.

The night was long. Despite the cold, he dozed off now and then, waking only to cough, a hoarse grating sound in the darkness. When he awoke he found himself clutching the bone. He dreamed of chasing the yeti through the pale gray crevices of cloud mountains. He woke to feed the fire, then returned to dreams.

After a time, the darkness and the cold no longer seemed

alien. They were threatening, but familiar. It seemed natural to wake in the darkness, struggling for warmth.

In the morning, he hiked in rubber thongs. He coughed constantly. Once, on the outskirts of a village, a little girl who was tending a herd of goats greeted him timidly. He tried to reply, but the sound that came from his mouth was only a rough croaking noise with no meaning like the clatter of rocks in a rock slide. He tried to smile, wanting to show the child that he meant no harm, but she scampered up the slope with her goats.

He hiked on for three days. Some of his food spoiled and he knew that food would be scarce further north. But somehow, for some inexplicable reason, he was happy. The wool socks grew tattered and encrusted with mud, but his feet grew used to being cold. His beard grew thicker and he washed less frequently, growing accustomed to the grime on his face and hands. He hurried through villages, avoiding people. When he was greeted, he nodded, but remained silent.

He passed through the village of Dhi in the early evening, walking quickly through the darkness. Rather than making him eager for human company, solitude left him wishing for more solitude. A dog barked wildly from inside a house, a near hysterical baying. Xavier grunted savagely and kept walking. He despised the laundry flapping from the lines and the heaps of dung beside the trail. He slipped through the village, nodding a greeting to a woman filling a metal jug at a stream. She dropped the jug and stared at him. Though she called out, he did not stop, but kept walking away into the darkness to seek the mountains.

As he hiked, he listened to the wind, to the river's voice, to the chatter of ravens. The sound seemed to flow through him, bringing him peace. Though the weather grew colder, he did not worry.

He made camp a day's walk from Dhi by the confluence of the Mustang Khola and a smaller stream that was unnamed on his map. The wind was constant here, sweeping around the boulders and scouring the rocks. In a small hollow between two house-sized boulders, he pitched his tent.

The first night, he heard the howling of wolves in the distance. At midnight, he woke when snow began to fall, a gentle flurry that drifted against the tent. In the morning, he found the tracks of wolves in the snowflakes that powdered the ground near his fire ring.

During the first few days, he explored his surroundings. He saw fat short-tailed mice, scampering among the rocks. Wild sheep, the blue Himalayan bharal, grazed by the stream. Xavier climbed upstream, following sheep trails among the boulders.

Half a day's scramble up the stream, he found a small cave, tucked among the rocks. From the look of the cave, it had once been inhabited – by a hermit, a holy man, or a sennin, a mountain lunatic. Three fire blackened rocks formed a triangular hearth; a mound of brush in the back provided a scratchy bed. Beneath the cave, the valley broadened into a small meadow: tough, red-brown grass poked through the light snow. The cave's entrance offered a view of the river valley better than any he had found elsewhere.

He moved his gear to the cave just before the second snowfall and made his bed in the brush heap in the back. He grew adept at cooking over a small fire: the smoke made his eyes itch, but he grew used to that. In the cave, his sleep schedule changed. Daylight reflecting from the snow hurt his eyes, and so he slept through the brightest part of the day, then woke at twilight to watch the wolves chase the blue sheep through the moonlit valleys. He dreamed during those long daylight sleeps. In his dreams, the old man came to him and told him that he would see the yeti.

Somehow, he was certain that his goal was near. This valley had the flavor of the fantastic; the wind muttered of secrets, the boulders watched him as he slept. Sometimes, he believed that he would soon understand the language of the raven that perched outside his cave each evening. He knew this place as a man knows the landscape of his own dreams, and he knew that the yeti was here.

He woke and slept, woke and slept, watching the valley for signs of the unusual. His hair and beard grew long and wild. He discarded his tattered wool socks and his feet grew tough and calloused. His skin chapped in the wind. In the sand by the river, he discovered the mark of a broad bare foot; on a thorny bush, he found a red-gold tuft of hair. A few signs and a feeling, nothing more, but that was enough.

His supplies ran low, but he was reluctant to leave the valley to find more. He ate wild greens and trapped short-tailed mice in an old food tin and roasted them over the fire. Once, he found a bharal that had been killed by wolves, and he used his pocketknife to hack meat from the carcass.

In his dreams, the valley was filled with moving shadows that walked on two legs, shambling like bears, shaggy and slope-browed. When he woke, his dreams did not fade, but remained as sharp and clear as the world around him. He dreamed of the raven, but somehow the bird was more than a raven. The black bird was the old man who had given him the bone. The old man wanted something in return.

Xavier never went out by day.

At last, his food ran out completely. He captured one last mouse, charred its body in the fire, and picked its bones clean. By moonlight, he walked to the village of Dhi. The trail made him nervous; it was too well-trodden. The first smell of unfamiliar woodsmoke made him stop. He heard barking dogs in the distance.

On the edge of the village, he paused to drink in a still pool. He was startled by his own reflection. His eyes were wild and rimmed with red; his face was covered with thick red-brown hair. He crouched in the field near a house, unwilling to go closer. Stacked in racks by the house were ears of corn, dried by the wind and the sun.

Hunger drove him forward, but something held him back. He did not belong here. The sky was growing light when he moved at last. He stood below the racks and reached up to pull corn free – one ear, two ears, a dozen, two dozen. He was tying them into a bundle when he heard a sound.

Ten feet away stood a ragged boy, barefoot in the chilly morning. His face was smudged with dirt and already his nose was running. His eyes were wide, and they grew wider when Xavier looked at him. '*Meh-teh*,' he whispered, backing away from Xavier, then turning to run. '*Meh-teh!*'

Xavier ran too, losing one of his thongs in the rocks by the trail, abandoning the other. The raven led him on, laughing overhead. He ran back to his cave.

He roasted an ear of corn in the fire. It was charred and tough, but he ate it with relish. He slept for a long time, dreaming of the old man and the raven, two who were one. He knew that he belonged in this place. Each night, he went to the village and stole food. When the dogs barked, people ran from their huts, carrying torches and knives and shouting '*Meh-teh! Meh-teh!*'

One day soon, he knew he would find a pot of chang in the path. The raven told him so in a dream. When he found the chang, he would drink it and fall asleep. The villagers would capture him and the old man who was the raven would take his scalp. That was the way of things.

He was happy.